Boyle's
Law

L.G.Thomson

For Doris Watt
and The Pleiades

Boyle's Law-
while pressure doubles, volume halves.

Chapter 1

3.02 am Tuesday

It started with a woman. It usually did. She had grey eyes. They could look blue or green, depending on the light. Cold or warm, depending on her mood. She was the reason. Boyle tried to keep his mind off Stella's eyes and on the job. Outwardly, he was calm. Inside, everything had coiled up tight. His mouth was dry. His food tasted like greasy cotton wool. He crushed the fast food wrappers around the remains of his meal and tossed the bundle into the back seat.

"How long?" Macallister asked through a mouthful of half-chewed meat. There were no problems with his appetite.

Boyle shifted in the passenger seat, getting as comfortable as he could. "Not long," he replied.

Macallister chewed noisily at the lukewarm burger. They'd bought the food over an hour ago in Inverness. The chips were cold but there was just enough heat left in the burger to stop the fat congealing. Not that Macallister would have minded.

Boyle stared through the windscreen at nothing in

particular and tried not to get irritated.

"Mmm, mmm, mmm, tasty, tasty." Macallister wiped his mouth on a napkin. He balled it up with his wrappers then tossed the greasy wodge into the back seat alongside the detritus from Boyle's meal. "How long now?" he asked.

"Oh for fuck's sake." Boyle pulled a phone from his pocket and checked the time. "Not fucking long, okay? We should be getting the call any time."

"You sure this guy will come through?"

"Yes I'm sure."

"Just checking."

Boyle turned his head and stared at Macallister. Macallister stared back, a big fat *what?* scrawled across his face.

"You know something?" Boyle asked.

"What? Tell me."

"You haven't changed a bit."

"Still got my boyish good looks you mean?"

"Still a pain in the arse I mean."

Macallister grinned. Despite himself Boyle shook his head and grinned back. Macallister stroked his moustache.

"Can you not leave that fucking thing alone?"

Macallister kept on grinning and stroking. "It was your idea to grow it. Could have worn a false one."

"I told you, this isn't the fucking movies. False moustaches fall off. Growing a real one is a nice easy way to change your appearance without getting over-excited about it. It's a just-in-case thing anyway. This is going to be a nice peaceful job. No dramatics. In and out nice and easy."

"I had my doubts." Macallister preened in front of the rear view mirror.

"About what?"

"The 'tache. But it's grown on me. Ha, see what I did there? I said *it's grown on me*."

"Jesus," Boyle muttered under his breath, though secretly he was glad of the distraction. He glanced at the phone. He hadn't put it back in his pocket. Didn't seem any point when it was going to ring soon. He hoped.

"Don't get too attached," he said to Macallister. "You'll be shaving it off in a couple of hours."

Macallister liked the way Boyle thought things through, but no doubt about it, he was going to miss the 'tache. Boyle hadn't taken any care of his facial hair at all. His grizzled beard sprouted at all angles. Made him look like an old jakey. Whereas Macallister, taken aback by the dark, luxuriant growth on his upper lip, had looked after his moustache. Combing, trimming, even using a little *Captain Fawcett's Moustache Wax*, though he kept that to himself. He turned his head, admiring himself from a different angle. Pity he'd have to shave it off. He ran his thumb and forefinger down its length.

"Will you leave that fucking thing alone." Boyle, scowling at him. He always had been a moody bastard.

"I like it." Macallister lifted his chin, squinted at his reflection. "It makes a statement. It says, don't mess with Macallister."

"It makes you look like a cheap fucking porn star."

Macallister considered this for a moment.

"Big Dick Macallister with the biggest pussy tickler in the business." He gave Boyle a sideways glance. Boyle looked back at him. They laughed.

"Seriously, it makes you look like a dick," Boyle still laughing as he spoke.

"That's right, Big Dick Macallister."

Boyle shook his head and stared at the police station across the square.

Macallister followed his gaze. "How long?" he asked.

Boyle looked down at the silent phone. "Not long."

Seventy miles away, three dark figures ran along the main

street of a village on the west coast. Their trainer-clad feet barely whispering as they ran. No-one heard a thing. Nobody noticed. There wasn't as much as a whimper from a dog as they kept low and tight as shadows to the hedges and fences. The village was locked up tight.

The one called Bracko took up his position facing the end house and weighed a stone in his hand. Small enough to aim properly. Heavy enough to cause damage. He pulled his arm back and threw. It smashed through an upstairs window. A woman screamed. Bracko grinned, his cheeks rubbing against the inside of his black balaclava.

The satisfying sound of splintering glass was the signal for Shug and Gaz to lob their stones through the windows of the neighbouring houses.

The three of them worked their way back along the street, smashing windows, overturning bins, setting off car alarms. House lights flicked on. Shocked faces appeared at broken windows. Dogs finally stirred, barking and yelping. A kid wailed, men shouted.

Bracko's laughter was muffled by his balaclava. This was fantastic. Better than he'd imagined.

A hefty woman with a helmet of black hair and a face that looked like an elephant had trod on it, half-ran, half-waddled, into the street in front of him, her girth pushing against her nightdress. He could see the dark hazy triangle of her pubic hair through the thin material. He stared. Fascinated because it was a real, live fanny right in front of him. Disgusted because it belonged to this fat, ugly woman. She yelled at him, a high-pitched, nasal racket. He got over his fascination and pushed her into a hedge.

He ran on, hearing the others whooping and yippee ki-yaying behind him. Getting the buzz, same as him. He could have done this all night and was disappointed when he came to their last target.

He picked up the brick he'd planted earlier and hefted

it through the shop window. It went straight through, leaving a jagged hole in the middle of the plate glass. The alarm went off. A loud *trrrrrrrrrrrrrrrr* like his old school bell.

He looked back at the street, watching as Shug and Gaz set fire to the wheelie bins they'd primed earlier. It hadn't taken much. The bins were already lined up in the street for the morning collection. All they'd had to do was open the lids, pour in the petrol and set them alight on the way back. Easy peasy lemon fucking squeezy.

Shug joined Bracko in front of the shop and stared at the broken window.

He yelled above the trilling alarm, "Too tidy dude," and gave it a boot. The promotional posters lining the window caved in along with the glass. Bracko grinned and looked along the street to see what was keeping Gaz. He gave Shug a nudge.

Gaz was busy kicking over the flaming bins. Burning rubbish spilled across the road creating impressive waves of fire. Sparks flew into the air.

"Fucking ace," Shug shouted as Gaz jogged up to them.

Bracko surveyed the street. He liked what he saw. They hadn't really done much - smashed a few windows, lit some fires, set off a couple of car alarms - but in this small village, it looked as though a riot had broken out. Out of calm they had created chaos.

People straggled from houses. Sleep-encrusted eyes staring uncomprehendingly at the blazing scene. An old guy, dressed in trackie bottoms, was trying to haul the ugly bitch out of the hedge. The loose skin on his arms and chest quivering with the effort. He was probably trying to get a squint at her floppy old snatch while he was at it.

A man and a woman attempted to douse the flames but only succeeded in spreading the fire. They snarked at each other, arguing about whose fault it was. A big bloke wearing nothing but underpants yelled at Bracko and his mates. He had muscular arms and skinny legs, and his face was all screwed up. Bracko couldn't hear what Mr Big Bloke was saying, but it was clear that he was not a happy bunny.

A short, fat, baldy dude, trussed up tight in a snazzy satin dressing gown, joined Mr Big Bloke. They exchanged a few words and pointed at Bracko.

Bracko nudged the others. "Time to go." Shug and Gaz nodded. The trio turned their backs on the entertainment and ran along the road to a waiting car. Shug and Gaz climbed into the back. Bracko, head honcho of the trio, sat in the front passenger seat. The driver sped off before they had a chance to close the doors. Bracko watched the scene of chaos they'd created grow small and then suddenly disappear from the wing mirror as the car followed the curve of the road up and out of the village.

He was buzzing with excitement, but the driver wasn't the talkative type. Nor was he the kind of guy who would appreciate a bit of banter in the car, so Bracko kept it zipped. Going by the sound of silence from the back seat, seemed like Gaz and Shug had picked up on the no-talking vibe.

Ten miles of road sped by without a word. The driver took the twists and bends with ease, hitting the floor on the few straights. Putting the pedal to metal. Bracko fancied getting himself a new set of wheels. Pictured himself driving expertly through the night.

The driver slowed the car and made a sharp left onto a single track road, following it until they came to a sign that read *Rath Forest Car Park*. A solitary car was parked there. The driver pulled up alongside it. He opened the window before killing the lights and engine. Then he took out his phone.

Bracko glanced at the lit-up screen. There was only one number listed. The driver pressed call.

It was answered on the first ring.

Macallister glanced over his shoulder at the food wrappers lying on the back seat. He thought about rooting out the chips Boyle had dumped earlier. They'd be stone cold, but what the hell. He was bored. He was hungry. Well, maybe not hungry. But he was bored. Had even lost interest in stroking his 'tache. Felt like they'd been sitting in this fucking car since the day he was born. He decided against looking for the chips. Boyle would only get tetchy if he started rummaging about.

He stared at the cop shop for a minute or two. It wasn't much to look at. Just an old building with nobody going in, nobody coming out. *Nada*. Staking out the cop shop had sounded exciting, but this was mince. Boyle wouldn't even let him put the radio on. Had told him to stay focussed. *Focussed?* He was focussing that fucking hard he was in danger of going blind.

He checked out the square for what felt like the zillionth time that night. Behind them, a big old church took up an entire side. The other three were lined with shops and a couple of tearooms. Everything all shut up tight. Even during the day it was a nothing going on kind of place, not unless you counted going out for tea and scones as something going on. Very picturesque and all that, but fuck all happening. Not until tonight anyway.

He drummed his fingers against the steering wheel. Boyle turned his big head and stared at him.

"Can you not sit at peace for two fucking minutes? You're worse than a kid."

Macallister pouted, then laughed.

"I've got it. Uncle Albert. The beard. You look like Uncle Albert from *Fools and Horses*."

Boyle shook his head again. "Jesus Christ, I give -

The phone rang. A tingle of excitement shivered through Macallister as Boyle answered.

"Yeah?"

Macallister watched as Boyle nodded at the response. He was very fucking focussed now.

"Problems?" Boyle asked. He listened, said "Good," then hung up.

"Was that him?" Macallister asked.

"No, it was your fucking mother."

"Fuck you Boyle."

"Fuck you Macallister."

The responses were automatic. Insult neither meant nor taken. A throwback to younger, more innocent times. They weren't even listening to each other. They were staring at the police station, watching. Watching and waiting.

Bracko felt calmer now. The adrenalin rush had passed, his heart rate had settled but there was a chunk of residual excitement in his system. A decent holler would have been enough to dissipate it.

No talking. No smoking. No fucking about. Those were the rules. He wasn't sure, but he guessed that the driver might class yodelling like Tarzan on a coke high as fucking about, so he swallowed it down until it sat in his stomach, slowly fizzing away to nothing.

He glanced sidewise at the driver who was sitting with his elbow resting on the window sill, staring through the windscreen. There was a full moon. Bright enough to throw a spooky edge of moonlight along the leather sleeve of the driver's jacket.

"Fuck you looking at?" the driver growled.

Inside his balaclava, Bracko's face flushed. Beads of tension-induced sweat broke out on his upper lip as the atmosphere in the car thickened. Small movements in back seat told of muscles clenching, nerves jangling. In spite of the open window, it became hard to breathe.

Bracko snapped his gaze to the front. He'd only moved his eyes. Hadn't moved his head at all. Hadn't twitched a muscle. Man could see in the dark.

Fear ballooned and popped in Bracko's gut. His head was hot and itchy inside the balaclava. He wanted to rip it off, but that wasn't allowed. Instead, he concentrated on staring straight ahead, wondering if maybe this had been a mistake. Too late for wondering now. It had all seemed so easy. Too easy. An approach in the pub. A wee job. No hassle. Money for nothing. Now he thought that maybe they shouldn't have gotten involved. That maybe they weren't-

His thoughts were shredded by the sound of a police siren screaming up the road towards them. The sound grew louder. Bracko chewed the inside of his cheek. He resisted the urge to look at the driver again. Wished he knew what the fuck was going on.

The sound of the siren faded as the police car passed the turn off for the car park, continuing north. The local bobby on his way to save the beleaguered villagers.

They sat in silence until the scream of the siren was a memory and then the driver spoke.

"Get out," he said.

They did as they were told. The driver got out and stood facing them. Bracko was taller than the other two goons, about the same height as the driver, yet the driver loomed over them, radiating menace. He reached slowly inside his jacket. Bracko thought, *fuck, he's got a gun.* Nearly shit himself. He wasn't ready to die, especially not here, in the middle of Nowheresville.

The driver withdrew his hand. He was holding a roll of notes wrapped in a thick elastic band. He tossed the roll to Bracko along with a car key.

"Nice work, boys. Now fuck off."

The three kids didn't need telling twice. Jimmy nearly pissed himself laughing as he watched them scramble into their getaway. It was a Vauxhall. He hated fucking Vauxhalls. They were sheds to drive. Good enough for them.

The kid started the engine, scattering gravel as he reversed sharply and sped out of the car park. Burn rubber, baby. Drive as fast as you want, boy racer. No need to worry about speeding. Not when the only cop for fifty miles south had just passed them on the way to that nothing little village. Not that it would be any skin off Jimmy's nose even if they did get stopped. They didn't even know his fucking name. Only thing the wee cunts did know was that they were scared shitless of him. At least they'd done a good clean job. No fucking around. He hated it when people fucked around on a job.

Jimmy got back into the car. He pulled off his balaclava and tossed it onto the passenger seat. He rubbed his hands over his face, relieved to be rid of the damn thing, then fired up the engine and headed south.

He sat back in his seat, feeling good. Feeling relaxed. Nothing but open road ahead. He liked it when a job went according to plan. He'd thought that one of the kids might get a wee bit over-excited, that he'd maybe have to exert some control. Dish out a couple of slaps. But no, they'd done the job, nice and straightforward like.

He'd been told to create a disturbance loud and showy enough to draw the cops. Well he'd done that alright. Fucked if he knew what it was all about, but his was not to reason why any bastard wanted anything done these days. It was a crazy world they were living in. No fucking doubt. Then again, he was a bit of a crazy bastard himself, so he couldn't complain.

An hour and a half steady driving and he'd be hitting Inverness. He enjoyed night driving. Having the road to himself. The feeling that he could go on and on driving forever. Bit of soothing night music wouldn't go amiss. He scanned the unfamiliar dash for the radio and turned it on. The car had been delivered to him only a few hours before. Probably hadn't even been reported stolen yet.

Jimmy cringed as he was blasted by a poxy racket.

Fucking rap. He hated fucking rap. Just a bunch of bastards talking shite.

He muttered to himself about how much he hated it as he fiddled with the tuner. He was looking for Classic FM, but if he couldn't get that then Radio Three would do. As long as it wasn't Mahler. He hated Mahler. Miserable dirgy bastard.

The glowing, flickering numbers of the radio scanning the frequencies drew his gaze. He glanced back at the road just in time to see the glimmer of eyes caught in the full beam of headlights. He watched helplessly as the stag bounded onto the road ahead of him. It leapt in slow motion, giving him plenty of time to admire its fluid movements. A fine beast. Twelve pointer. It stopped on the road. Turned its magnificent head, stared at him. Time sped up.

Jimmy swerved hard to avoid the beast. The radio tuned into a station and an explosion of heavy metal filled the car. Jimmy tensed as the sound blasted his ears. He hated heavy metal as much as he hated rap. With a flash of its white rump, the stag leapt into the night. Jimmy jerked on the steering wheel, desperately trying to straighten the car. He yanked too far, overdoing it by a country fucking mile and missed the curve of the road. The wheels left the ground and he was flying into the dark like Shitty Shitty Bang Bang.

His mind whirred. Trying to think what was at the side of the road. Where he was going to land. How big the drop was. If there was a bog or a loch at the bottom of it. Thinking he should have been paying attention instead of fucking around with the radio. That it had all gone too smoothly. That nothing ever worked out that fucking well.

The car thunked into a peat bank. The airbag exploded out of the steering wheel, forcing Jimmy hard back into his seat before shrivelling as quickly as it had ballooned, leaving behind a trace of cordite in the air.

Jolted and dazed, Jimmy sat in a state of momentary shock before realising that he was alive, that he'd flown through the night air into the dark and survived. The relief, the joy, the knowing, lasted for a fraction of a second. There wasn't even enough time for a triumphal grin to spread its way across his lips before the car rolled.

The airbags had been deployed. That was a done deal. There was nothing left to cushion Jimmy as the car rolled. His head cracked hard against the door window. It felt as though his brain had been knocked loose. The car did a complete three-sixty. His brain rattling in his skull like a marble in a tin. There was a noise he couldn't quite place as the car came to rest.

Jimmy opened his eyes. Couldn't see a fucking thing. Something didn't feel right. The unplaced noise echoed in his head, bouncing off his loose brain. Sounded like a splash. A big one. No, couldn't be. This kind of shit didn't happen to him.

But it was happening. Water quietly, darkly, slooshing, all around. Sucking the car under. He opened his mouth to call for help. A low groan emerged. Didn't matter. Wasn't anyone out there to hear it anyway. Jimmy groaned once more as the car sank into the cold waters of the loch.

Macallister snorted as a cop ran out of the station like his arse was on fire.

"Look at the bastard go," he said as the cop jumped into the patrol car and took off with a squeal of the tyres. "Thinks he's in the fucking Sweeney."

"Right," Boyle said. "We're on."

Chapter 2

They togged up in ski goggles, baseball caps and black nitrile disposable gloves before getting out of the car and opening the boot. Boyle took out two crowbars and a holdall. He handed one of the crowbars to Macallister.

"Right?" he said.

Between the cap, the bug eye goggles and the ridiculous moustache, Macallister was pleasingly unrecognisable. Dornoch wasn't heavy on CCTV but there was a camera in the shop window they were about to smash in.

"Right." Macallister replied.

Boyle nodded. This was it.

They strolled calmly across the square, crowbars held in against their legs. Bunting, put up in honour of the big golf tournament coming to the town, scratched and flapped in the light breeze.

They were approaching the point of no return but they hadn't done anything yet. They could still turn round, get in the car, drive away. Boyle glanced at Macallister. He was like an excited puppy straining on a leash. Boyle felt the same excitement in himself. He realised that he'd passed the point of no return long before tonight. There was no going back.

It had gone like a dream. Nine thousand square kilometres to cover and the cops on duty barely scraped into double figures. At full capacity the current shift would have run to one sergeant and twenty-three constables, but as Boyle knew they never ran to full capacity. Secondments, sick leave, suspensions, training courses and annual leave took their toll, leaving a grand total of one sergeant and fourteen constables to cover a dispersed population of 40,000 people.

There had been one officer on duty in Dornoch and none between him and the village on the west coast where Boyle had set up the diversion. Boyle knew what these wee villages were like. The biggest crimes that happened in them were drink drive incidents and spats of domestic violence. Tonight's events would have seemed like a full scale insurrection. Every cop for miles would have been sent to deal with it. The whole two of them.

It was all smoke and mirrors. If the local populace had any idea of how few law enforcers stood between them and the bad guys, they'd be barricading themselves in their homes and sleeping with a shotgun under the pillow. *Always vigilant* my arse.

Boyle and Macallister stepped onto the pavement like it had been choreographed. It was beautiful. Boyle glanced along the street. The abandoned police station was three doors to his left. Lights on, nobody home. He dropped the holdall and wedged the crowbar under the corner of the steel shutter. Macallister did the same on the other side. They worked quickly, without talking. Boyle felt calm. Everything had gone just the way he'd pictured it. Just the way he'd planned it. His heart was beating faster than normal but it wasn't hammering. Now that they were getting down to it, Macallister had lost his puppy dog excitement and his professionalism had kicked in.

The steel shutter peeled off easy as flaky skin. Boyle's

eyes widened. Bunting wasn't all that was on show for the upcoming golf tournament. The Classic Cup was a big deal and attracted the big names of the game. Every available bed within a twenty mile radius of the Royal Dornoch Course had been booked up months in advance and every shopkeeper in Dornoch was dancing gleefully in anticipation of the big spenders heading their way. The jewellers, an upmarket, independent store, was no exception. They had stocked up with expensive baubles, ripe for the choosing by big name golfers, wives, girlfriends, boyfriends, fans, hell anyone who was in town for the jamboree. The refrain was *spend, spend, spend*.

It was the sixtieth anniversary of the Cup and the jewellers had gone for the theme in a big way. Diamonds adorned every imaginable item of jewellery. Boyle took a moment to take it all in before raising his crowbar and smashing it into the window.

The alarm immediately sang out. High pitched, urgent. They ignored it. Macallister struck the glass with tremendous strength. It was reinforced, but by the third blow, cracks were showing. Boyle whacked it one more time. A mass of fissures appeared across the window. Macallister tapped it with his crowbar. The centre collapsed, falling in one piece to the ground where it shattered into small cubes.

They dropped the crowbars. Boyle picked up the holdall and opened it wide. Macallister immediately dropped in a handful of glittering jewellery.

They worked quickly, not talking, but Boyle sensed Macallister was sharing his excitement. They'd done it. They'd only gone and done it. Scooped the fucking jackpot. Macallister dropped the last diamond bracelet into the bag. He grinned, his teeth showing beneath his big stupid, beautiful moustache. Boyle grinned back and zipped the bag. The whole operation from prising off the shutter to closing the bag had taken less than one minute.

They strode back across the square, Boyle carrying the

bag, Macallister the crowbars. Boyle, glad to get away from the irritating shriek of the alarm, was already thinking about the route south. Back roads all the way. No cops and no cameras either-

"Hey you!"

"Who have we got here then?" Macallister murmured.

"He's nothing. Ignore him." Boyle murmured back.

They were almost at the car. The citizen was coming at them from the other side of the square. He was a gangly sort, dressed in chef's whites. He wore a chequered skull cap and was carrying a long knife. Boyle did a double take at the blade. *What the - ?* Then he caught the faint aroma of freshly baking bread dancing on the breeze and it all made sense. Baker on the night shift. Fuck.

"Stop!" There was a nervous quake in the baker's voice but it didn't stop him coming towards them.

Jesus Christ in a hole. Just what they needed. A have-a-fucking-go hero.

"What do we do?" Macallister asked.

"Ignore him. He's not going to do anything. Just get in the car."

"That's one big fucker of a knife he's got."

"He's not going to use it," Boyle said. "He's a fucking baker. A doughboy."

"Yeah, right," Macallister snorted, "Edward fucking Scissorhands more like."

"Let's go," Boyle said.

They made a dash for the car, but when the baker saw them running he ran too. Big strides with his gangly legs. He got to the car before them, stood blocking their way.

"C'mon pal, be a good boy and get out of the fucking road before someone gets hurt. And by someone I mean you," Macallister's voice low and mean. No trace of puppy dog now.

The baker shook his head. Nervous, but standing his ground. "The police will be here soon."

He glanced over Macallister's shoulder at the station, his eyebrows screwed up in puzzlement, wondering why they weren't there yet. A sheen of sweat covered his face giving him a sickly look under the yellow street lights.

Boyle realised the only reason baker boy had taken them on was because he thought the police were going to be there any second. He almost felt sorry for the lad. He shook his head. "They're not coming, so why don't you just back off nice and easy and nobody will get hurt."

"They're coming," the baker said with a faith deeply ingrained.

"The cavalry's not coming, baker boy. Now just step away from the car." Macallister, getting riled.

Boyle didn't like the situation. The baker was a young, earnest type. He was wound up tight and Macallister's hackles were rising. The baker was scared shitless, but his essential righteousness gave him courage. That and the fact that he thought the rozzers would be here any second.

The baker shook his head again. His adam's apple bobbled in his throat.

"Oh I've had fucking enough of this," Macallister said. He strode over to the car. "Out of the fucking way kid before I smack you one." He brandished the crowbars.

The kid's eyes popped, fear scragging his face. He thrust the knife out. "Stay away from me." Hand shaking, voice wavering.

Macallister sneered, refusing to see the kid as a threat but Boyle recognised him as a cornered animal, frightened and unpredictable. Macallister moved in on the kid. Boyle yelled a warning and lunged forward, intent on shoving the kid aside with the bag.

Too late.

"The fucker stabbed me," Macallister gasped, eyes wide.

He released the crowbars. They clattered on the tarmac as Macallister collapsed onto the bonnet of the car before sliding to the ground. The kid staggered back. He looked at the knife in his hand like he didn't know how it had got there. Macallister's blood, black in the yellow light, dripped from the blade, spattering his white trainers. The kid dropped the knife like it had bitten him.

"I didn't mean it, honest, it was an accident, oh Jesus, oh God."

His head bobbed on his scrawny neck like it was on a spring. Boyle wanted to rip it off and kick it to kingdom fucking come.

Macallister lay on his back beside the wheel. Boyle knelt beside him and pulled his goggles off. Macallister's eyes and mouth formed three circles of shock. Boyle pulled his jacket open. A dark stain was blooming on his shirt.

"Oh Jesus," Boyle murmured.

"Is he all right?" the kid whined.

"You stabbed him in the fucking heart you knifing little bastard, so no, he's not all right."

The kid wailed then threw up, managing to whine as he vomited. Boyle screwed his face in disgust and turned back to Macallister.

"You're going to be okay, you hear me?"

Macallister's eyes rolled before focussing on Boyle.

"Get the fuck out of here Charlie," he said. His voice raspy.

"I'm not going to leave you." Boyle could not believe this was happening.

"The bastard murdered me..."

"I'll get you into the car - it'll be alright."

"No. You fuck off... go on."

Boyle bit on his lip. Macallister was on his way out. Of that Boyle had no doubt. And he was right, there was fuck all Boyle - or anyone - could do about it. There seemed little sense in him hanging around, but to leave him lying here in the street was extremely fucking callous. Not the kind of thing you did to your best pal from school.

"Charlie..." Macallister croaked.

Boyle leaned in close enough that he could smell the burger grease lingering on Macallister's moustache.

"Remember the canal, when we were kids?" Macallister's eyes wide, willing him to remember.

"I remember," Boyle said. He squeezed Macallister's arm.

"You can let go now," Macallister said, a faint smile on his lips before his eyes rolled and glazed over.

Boyle stood up and stared at the kid. He was leaning against the back of the car, a dazed expression on his gormless face. Nothing have-a-fucking-go about him now. Just one long streak of piss.

"Get your arse over here." The kid obeyed, like a cowed dog. "Take your top off," Boyle barked.

The kid looked terrified but did as he was told. His bony torso was naked underneath. Boyle snatched the white chef's jacket and folded it up. Macallister was as good as dead, but Boyle wasn't going to leave him lying there pumping blood into the gutter.

"Get down beside him." The kid knelt beside Macallister. Boyle passed him the folded up jacket. "Press that down on the wound. You hear?"

The kid nodded, did as he was told.

"Hard, you hear? And don't let go. You understand? Maybe you can save him from dying. Save yourself from a murder charge."

Tears welled in the kid's eyes, but he nodded. Whether he was crying for himself or for what he had done, Boyle didn't know or care. He didn't think there was a chance in hell of the kid saving Macallister, but as long as he was pressing down on the wound trying to save himself from a prison sentence, he wasn't making phone calls. Boyle wanted to be across the A9 and out on the back roads before the blues and twos came screaming up from Invergordon or Alness.

He picked up the bag and chucked it into the car. He took one last look at the kid earnestly pressing down on his victim's chest. Macallister's eyes were closed. His face looked waxy. He was well on his way to dead.

Boyle got into the car and drove. Once out of the town, he kept his speed at a steady fifty. Funny thing about this part of the world. Though the population was scattered thin, there was always the chance of someone noticing the very thing you didn't want them to see. Eyes in the shadows. Poachers and keepers. Farmers up early and old women staring out of their windows because they didn't sleep so well these days. There was no point in giving them something to remember. No point in attracting attention by screaming along as if he'd just robbed a jewellery store.

Another five minutes and he'd be swapping cars.

"Shit, no." Boyle hit the side of the steering wheel with the flat of his palm.

Macallister was the wheels man. He'd done the organising and he had the keys for the other car. There was no way Boyle could go back and get them now. There was no way he could keep this car either. Sooner or later the cops would turn up and the kid, shocked or not, would be describing him and the car. Chances were he'd be too traumatised by the whole thing to give them the licence plate, but you never knew. Maybe he was one of those people who couldn't help noticing things. He'd been pretty damn quick on the scene when the alarm sounded. Maybe he'd clocked the licence plate straight off. It wasn't likely, but it wasn't impossible either.

Boyle wasn't going to take any chances. He had no choice but to dump the car as planned, only instead of being able to drive away from it, he'd be on the hoof. He slapped the steering wheel again. Bloody baker boy.

He glanced at the bag on the passenger seat and told himself to dry his eye. It wasn't all bad. Macallister was dead and gone, *may he rest in peace*, but Boyle had the diamonds. The plan, most of it at any rate, was still intact. All he had to do was stay cool and think.

The police would find Macallister's getaway car at some point. There was a remote chance they'd make the connection between it and Macallister but there was nothing at all to connect it to Boyle. So, instead of heading to where it was uselessly waiting for him, he followed the twisting back road to Bonar Bridge. There were no speed cameras along the route, no CCTV, no cops. The whole area was wide open. Still, he forced himself to keep his speed down. No point in going through all this just to take a header off the road on some hairpin bend. And no point at all in arousing the suspicions of the local populace.

All was just as it should be in Bonar Bridge at 4.56 am. Dead quiet. The only thing missing from the sleeping village was a ball of tumbleweed blowing down the street.

Even though he *knew* it was empty, Boyle's heart-rate spiked as he cruised by the police station. As expected, there were no signs of activity. Apart from himself, the closest he was to the police were the two on the west coast dealing with the aftermath of the mini-riot and the handful on the east coast who right now would have their hands full with Macallister, baker boy and an empty jewellery store.

There was nothing but scenery between him and his fellow officers. It had been a beautiful plan. Simple. Well thought through. No fuck ups anywhere until baker boy showed up and screwed everything to hell. Almost screwed everything to hell.

Boyle wished Macallister was riding along with him, talking rubbish, preening over his stupid moustache, but dead was dead there wasn't anything he could do to change that.

He hung a left at the crossroads, assessing his situation as he crossed the bridge. Point one: Macallister was dead.

No use getting teary eyed about it. Point two: Boyle was alive and he had the diamonds. Point three: He could make this work.

There was a landscaped picnic area on the other side of the river, complete with car park and toilet block. Boyle pulled in, parking the car behind the far side of the block so that he couldn't be seen from Bonar. Any early-rising, nosy bastards looking across the river would see nothing but an empty car park.

There were two backpacks in the boot. One for him. One for Macallister. Not that Macallister would be needing his now. Boyle grabbed his pack and took it and the holdall to the toilet block.

The entrance to the gents was on the Bonar side of the block. Boyle went to the Ladies and pushed open the door. He grimaced at the immediate, familiar whiff of public toilets. Top notes of stale urine shot through with bleach, and layered underneath, that indefinable human stench they never seemed able to eradicate.

He groped the wall and found the light switch. The fluorescent tube flickered for a moment before steadying. He glanced around. It didn't get more utilitarian than this. Two cubicles. Two stainless steel sinks. One small bar of cracked soap. An empty paper towel dispenser, a dubious puddle on the floor and a clapped out hand drier. Boyle had always imagined the Ladies to be a more refined affair than the Gents. Apparently not - it was just as grotty. Way to go for sexual equality.

There was nothing to block or lock the door with, but Boyle guessed that wouldn't be a problem. Stepping over the puddle, he dropped the hold all on a dry patch of floor and opened up his backpack.

He took out a pair of scissors, a can of shaving cream and a disposable razor. He'd taken off the cap and ski goggles as soon as he'd got in the car. Now it was time to lose the beard. There was a torn sticker for a domestic abuse phone line in the corner of the flaky mirror.

Someone had used a biro to score the wall beside it with the legend *Fiona Flynn is a skank.*

The lighting was piss poor but it would have to do. Scissors poised, he studied himself for a moment. There were a few streaks of grey at his temples but the beard was almost all white, making him look much older than his forty-one years. All the better for him, but even so, there was no way he looked like Uncle Albert. Macallister had always been a cheeky fucker, but at least it meant that baker boy's description of him would be all over the place. He snipped at the beard and when he'd taken off as much as he could he got to work with the shaving cream and razor.

Clean-shaven, he peeled off his black hoodie and joggers, revealing the blue jeans and white t-shirt he was wearing underneath. He pulled a grey zip-up sweater from the backpack and put it on. Beardless and dressed in a new set of clothes, he looked nothing like the grizzled geezer baker boy had clocked. His description wouldn't be worth sharpening a pencil for.

He was still wearing the nitrile gloves. They were a pain in the arse to wear but he'd be keeping them on until he dumped the car.

Boyle transferred the jewellery to the backpack then stuffed all his old gear into the hold all. He gave the sink a good sloosh out and checked that he hadn't left anything of himself behind - no tide marks, no soap scum, no hair - then he took the bags and turned the light off as he left.

The backpack containing the jewellery went into the passenger foot-well, the holdall, ski goggles and baseball cap into the boot. Sound travelled far at night, so Boyle closed the lid gently, pressing down on it until the latch clicked then got into the car. It reeked of chips and stale grease. Boyle glanced down at the backpack stuffed with diamonds and decided he could live with the smell. He held out his hands. Steady. No sign of a tremor. That pleased him.

He considered turning on the radio and listening to the news, but he was in an almost Zen-like state of calm and decided against disrupting it. He drove on automatic pilot, reacting unconsciously to the turns and twists of the narrow lanes. He didn't think about Macallister or the diamonds, nor about what he was going to do next.

It was just him and the road.

Chapter 3

Boyle was taken by surprise when he reached Alness. He glanced at the clock on the dash. He'd been driving for almost an hour and couldn't remember any of it. The sun was rising and he felt like he'd just woken up from a satisfying nap.

As he drove through the town one car passed him going the opposite way, otherwise the place was quiet. That suited him just fine. He clocked a bus stop and pulled into the kerb, got out and checked the timetable. He liked what he saw. If he shifted, he should be able to make it. If not then the fat lady should get ready to sing because the show was going to be over. He got back into the car and wove his way through the town and down to the industrial estate.

A couple of lorries went by, but nothing else was on the go. A thick plantation of trees and shrubbery had been cultivated in an effort to conceal the estate from the town. Boyle didn't blame them. Even by industrial estate standards this was one ugly bastard of a place.

He drove around the maze of squat buildings until he found an empty car park behind a scabby breeze block and metal shed. The animal feed sign on the shed was cracked and the building looked abandoned. Boyle glanced around but couldn't see any security cameras. Figuring that this was as good as it was going to get he parked up in the shadow of the building, grabbed the backpack and got out.

Released from the protective shell of the car, he felt exposed, but the feeling of security the car had lent him was false. If anything was going to give him away, it was the car. He worked quickly. Now that he had emerged from his carapace his only thought was to destroy and abandon it as soon as possible.

He tossed the backpack aside, opened the boot and took out the petrol container and matches Macallister had stowed there. The plan had always been to burn out this car. All he'd had to do was change the location and do it without another car to drive away in.

He liberally doused the boot with petrol, then gave the interior the same treatment. He picked up the backpack and slung it over his shoulder. It was a tatty old thing he'd had for years. The fact that it looked worthless amused him. He peeled off the gloves and threw them into the boot. It was a relief to get them off his sweating hands. He struck a match and tossed it into the car. The petrol caught with a soft *whoomf*. Boyle tossed the matchbox into the flames and walked away.

He walked briskly, but didn't run. People running drew attention to themselves. He was exposed now, but there wasn't anything he could do about that. The estate was still quiet, but people would soon be turning up for work. If nothing else brought them out, the plume of black smoke rising up from the car would attract them like wasps to jam.

If his luck held out, the Alness police would have been called up to Dornoch to deal with the three ring circus he'd created there, but he couldn't rely on Alness being an entirely cop-free zone. If they were still in town, they'd be down here as soon as the burning car was reported and Mr Briskly Walking Away would be their number one suspect.

He glanced at his wrist. Forgot he didn't have a watch on. Wondered if he was going to make it on time. Hoped to fuck he didn't get picked up. He'd be finished. In every way imaginable.

He glanced over his shoulder. It was a windless morning and a thick rope of smoke rose straight up from the car, standing out against the clear blue dawn sky like a big black arrow pointing straight at him.

Boyle walked faster. On the borderline of trotting. On the edge of panic. Sweat on his back where the backpack rested against him. The nearest he'd come to losing it since the kid had stabbed Macallister. He told himself to stay cool. Easier said than done. His nerve was crumbling. Then he saw it.

A set of stairs cutting up through the shrubbery. A pedestrian short-cut to the town. *You beauty.* Boyle took the stairs two at a time and jogged up the pathway to the High Street. He arrived at the bus stop a full twenty seconds ahead of the bus.

He sat at the back. No-one paid him any mind when he got on. The bus driver barely raised his eyes from the ticket machine. The other passengers were mostly dozing or reading. One skinny youth stared vacantly out of the window, music buzzing in his ears, mouth mechanically chewing gum. He wouldn't make a good witness. None of them would.

The bus rumbled along the High Street before veering down to the industrial estate. It pulled into a bus stop just as a fire engine screamed by. Someone said something and everyone peered out of the grimy windows at the smoke rising above the buildings.

The smoke no longer rose in a neat rope. It was now dense and billowing. It had a choking, toxic look about it. Boyle figured the tyres had caught fire. Four men and one woman got off the bus. No-one got on. The bus pulled away.

It was a stop-start journey to Inverness. The seat was uncomfortable, the stench of diesel fumes strong. Boyle didn't care. He'd got away. It would take several hours at least to positively connect the burnt out car with the robbery. There was nothing at all to link him with the car. With Macallister dead, there was nothing to link him to any of it.

He stared out of the filthy windows. He couldn't see much, but it was somewhere to place his gaze without chancing on catching someone's eye. He didn't want to give anyone a reason to remember him.

Leaving Macallister lying on the street like that had been a dirty thing to do. He could have dragged him into the car with him, but Macallister would still have died, and then what? He could hardly have burned the car with him in it. He could have stayed with him, got himself arrested... and Macallister would still have died. Any which way you looked at it, Macallister ended up dead.

Boyle consoled himself with the thought that things would have played out the same if it had been the other way around. Trouble was, he didn't entirely believe it. For one thing, he wouldn't have gone barging up to the kid just begging to be stabbed the way Macallister had, and for another... when they were kids Sammy Macallister used to follow him around like a puppy. He looked up to Boyle, would have done anything for him. He'd even have jumped in the canal if Boyle asked him to. He had the uncomfortable feeling that if it was him that got stabbed, Macallister would have stayed by his side, as faithful and loyal as Greyfriars fucking Bobby.

Boyle shuffled off the bus along with the rest of the passengers at the Inverness terminus. Just another face in the crowd. His stomach growled as he passed Harry's All

Nite Café. He was tempted by the thought of a cooked breakfast but the more invisible he stayed the better. His stomach would just have to growl on.

It was a five minute walk from the bus station to his flat. His body grew heavier with every step, his head groggier. He was as spent as a burnt-out match. He planned on having a hot shower before going to bed, but by the time he climbed the stairs to the second floor he was fit for crashing out.

He woke with a jolt. He'd been dreaming about Sammy Macallister in the canal. The sound of cracking ice splintering the air. He sat up, sweating, feeling grubby. He groped in the gloom for the backpack. Nothing there. Panic flared and subsided as his hand brushed against it. He hauled it onto the bed, checked that the diamonds were still there then flopped back onto the pillows and stared at the ceiling.

He'd have to do something about the backpack. Couldn't leave it lying around like that. Anyone could waltz in and help themselves. Yeah, like he had visitors queuing up the stairs to see him. Okay, truth was his life was hardly a mad social whirl but there was no point in being lax. One thing led to another in that department and before you knew it you'd gone and done something stupid. Put yourself in a situation you couldn't get out of.

Fact was, Boyle worked with people who were paid to stick their noses into other people's business and you never knew who'd take it upon themselves to come calling. He should know. He was one of them.

He put his arms behind his head and caught a whiff of his armpits. He screwed up his face in disgust. His clothes were sticking to him. He was stinking and his head was fuzzy. Maybe he'd slept too long. He glanced at the radio alarm. He'd had five and a half hours. Not too long. Maybe not long enough. Tough. He got up and stripped off, thinking it would be a good idea to dump the clothes.

He stood under the shower for a long time then, dried and dressed, he emptied the contents of the backpack onto the bed. The diamonds glittered knowingly in the low light of his bedside lamp. He stared at them, almost hypnotised, before fetching a clean towel. He shook the towel out on the bed, neatly arranged the jewellery on it then rolled it all up, tucking in the sides as he went, until it resembled a fat sausage.

In the kitchen, he pulled his unwashed laundry out of the washing machine and placed the diamond-filled sausage into the empty drum. He covered it over with his dirty laundry and clicked the door closed.

Boyle examined the machine from every conceivable angle. Mostly it looked like a washing machine. From some angles it looked like a washing machine with washing in it.

Fifteen minutes later he was sitting in front of the television with a large mug of coffee and a heap of buttered toast. He flicked through the news channels, stopping at a talking head.

Police have issued a statement confirming that two men have been taken to the Royal Highland Hospital in Inverness. Police will not confirm the condition of the men but they are thought to be linked to an audacious jewellery robbery in the golfing town of Dornoch.

They must have bundled baker boy off to the Royal Highland along with Macallister. He'd probably been a gibbering wreck when they'd found him. No doubt they'd be keeping tight-lipped about Macallister's death until they got a handle on the story.

The scene switched from the studio to footage of the smashed up frontage of the jewellery store, jaunty bunting fluttering above it, yellow crime scene tape fluttering over it. The camera panned out to reveal the proprietor who wasn't sure whether to play it outraged or devastated. He said he'd ordered the stolen items specifically for the Diamond Anniversary of the Classic Cup. He said he'd never known anything like it in their

36

peaceful town. He said it was shocking.

To look at him banging on, you wouldn't think he was insured right up to his bald, freckled head. The reporter asked him why the diamond jewellery had been left on display in the window. The jeweller looked bewildered.

We were alarmed. We had steel shutters and shatter proof glass. We're practically right next door to the police station. Things like this just don't happen here. At least, they didn't used to. It's terrible. An outrage. I don't know what the world is coming to.

The camera panned out to show the police station just three doors away from the jeweller's. It was beautifully done.

A sour-faced woman with a tight perm and a mouth like a cat's arse appeared on screen. She was identified as the owner of a local tea shop. She was in no doubt about how to play it at all. It was outrage all the way, baby. They cut from her outraged spluttering to the studio.

At the time of the robbery, local police officers were attending a vandalism incident nearly seventy miles away. The value of the stolen jewellery is estimated to be in excess of one million pounds.

Boyle nearly choked on his toast.

Chapter 4

"Hello Stella."

"Charlie..."

The woman's eyes flashed. Grey eyes. They could look green or blue, depending on the light. Cold or warm, depending on her mood. Eyes like that could hypnotise a guy, cast a spell on him. Isn't that what she'd done to him - cast a spell on him? He'd been bewitched from the second he'd looked into those eyes. That first time she'd said, *Pleased to meet you Charlie*, and briefly placed her hand, slim and cool, in his big, hot, paw. Him feeling like an oaf. Like he had no business breathing the same air as her. She had him wrong footed from the start. But that was then and this was now.

She glanced over his shoulder. Nervous. Cracks showing in the façade. He'd never seen her look nervous before. It made him want to pull her close. Protect her. She looked back at him, eyes flashing green. September sun highlighting her dark blonde hair.

"What are you doing here?"

"Aren't you going to invite me in?"

She held his gaze for a moment, before raising an eyebrow in that what-the-hell way she had. She turned and walked into the house without another word, leaving him to do as he pleased. He closed the door and trailed after her. Sometimes when he was with her he felt like a giant amongst men. Other times she made him feel like he was two feet high, but he couldn't stop himself from coming back for more.

He followed her to the living room. She was standing in front of a big bay window that overlooked the neat garden. The late roses were in bloom. Frank's roses. He took great pride in his collection of delicate blooms and thorny stems, cutting, pruning, dead heading. Stella was wearing a dress.

She almost always wore a dress. This one was storm blue, with little black flecks. It had three quarter length sleeves. The skirt skimmed her knees. It should have been demure, and maybe it would have been on someone else. But there was something about the way it fitted at the waist, following her curves above and below. He wanted to run his hands over those curves. He came up behind her, whirled her round and kissed her long and hard on the mouth.

She responded, her lips soft and yielding. He could smell her perfume. It was fresh and light. She wore it like a second skin. She was with him all the way, and then the barriers came down. She stiffened, resisting him. Pulled away.

"You shouldn't have come here," she said.

"I had to see you."

"What for?"

"You know what for."

He bent to kiss her again but she side-stepped him and crossed the room to a bureau. He wondered if her hips always swayed that way or if she was putting on a show just for him. Either way, the sight drove him crazy. She opened a drawer and took out a packet of cigarettes.

"I thought you understood," she said. "We can't see each other anymore. It's over Charlie."

"That was then, this is now. Things have changed."

She put a cigarette between her lips, looking at him with flinty cool eyes. She used a small silver lighter to spark up, inhaled then blew a stream of smoke through pursed lips without breaking her gaze.

"What things?"

He watched the smoke trail from the tip of the cigarette. "I thought you said Frank didn't like you smoking in the house."

She shrugged.

"He doesn't, but what Frank doesn't know won't kill him."

"When does he get back?"

"Soon. Next week. Maybe sooner. He keeps it vague, likes to keep me on my toes with his little games. Who knows, maybe he'll walk through that door any minute."

Despite himself, Boyle glanced at the door. Stella caught the look and laughed.

"What do you think he'd say, Charlie, if he walked through that door and saw you standing right there on his favourite rug, large as life and twice as ugly?"

"Quit messing around. You know that's not going to happen."

"Maybe not, but then you've probably got a better idea of when he'll be back than I do."

Boyle shook his head. "I've been away."

"But now you're back."

She stubbed out the cigarette in an oversized crystal ashtray. He had a vision of her washing it, airing the room. Destroying the evidence before Frank got back. His fingers curled.

"Yeah. Now I'm back."

"So what's new Charlie? What's changed? Tell me Charlie, because from where I'm standing everything looks exactly the same. I'm married to Frank and you…"

"What about me?" He knew he was laying himself wide open to her, but he did it anyway. Like any attention from her would be better than none.

"You're a guy I had some fun with."

"That's it?" The muscles in his stomach tightened. He wanted her to say more, give more.

"We both knew it was never going to end any other way. Ships that pass in the night and all that."

"I had a different ending in mind. I thought we both did."

"That was pillow talk. Like I said, as far as I can see nothing has changed. If you want to tell me anything different you can go ahead, but otherwise I think it's time for you to leave."

Boyle glanced around the room. A place for everything and everything in its own gleaming place. Everything buffed and polished and standing to attention, just the way Frank liked it. It made his skin crawl.

"Not here," he said.

"What's wrong with here? Colour scheme not to your liking?"

"You know why."

"I want to hear you say it."

"It's his place. He's all over it."

"So why did you come? Why not call me."

"You wouldn't have taken the call."

She shrugged. "Probably not."

"Besides, I had to see you."

"Okay Charlie, you've seen me. Now what?"

"Meet me."

"What's the point?"

"I told you, things have changed. Meet me and I'll tell you."

She gave him an appraising look. Weighing up her options, but he knew that if she'd set her mind against him, he'd already be out on the driveway with his head in his hands, wondering what just happened.

He closed the gap between them and pulled her into

his arms. He kissed her on the mouth. No barriers now. She tasted of cigarettes and coffee, of late nights and dark hours. She tasted in a way Frank would never experience.

Finally, she pulled her mouth away from his, but she stayed right in his arms.

"Where?"

He told her and kissed her again.

Chapter 5

Boyle sat in a winged chair, its tartan fabric subdued and frayed by years of use. He drummed his fingers on the greasy sheen of the armrest, resisting the urge to knock back the gin and tonic sitting on the table in front of him.

He was hemmed in by a chipped plaster column on one side and an overgrown potted palm on the other, but he had a clear view across the hotel lobby to the revolving door at the entrance.

The place was worn out to a point beyond faded grandeur. There were too many water stains on the wallpaper, too many worn patches on the carpet, for it to be described as shabby chic. The Highland Star had probably been something of a beauty in her hey-day, but now she catered for low-end coach holidays and cheap Highland mini-breaks. Boyle didn't know anyone who would be seen dead there, which made it perfect for his purpose.

From the start she'd refused to go to his place. Didn't want to be seen coming or going. Didn't want to be noted. Commented on. And she was, Boyle considered, the kind of woman who would be noted and commented on. So they'd been discreet to the point of paranoia.

Used anonymous chain hotels on the periphery of the city. Never going to the same place twice. It hadn't been a problem considering they'd only met on a handful of occasions.

A handful of occasions... how many times exactly? He totted it up in his head as he waited. One Travelodge, a couple of Premier Inns and two glorious days in a decent hotel in Edinburgh where they'd been able to behave like a proper couple. Someone came through the revolving door. It wasn't her. He wondered if she'd come. Four bedrooms.

He totted up the hours. The Travelodge had been first. She'd arrived late, left early. He'd left not long after, the orange room too depressing for him to stay in on his own. Six hours. They'd fared a little better in the Premier Inns. Fifteen hours, two purple rooms. Snatched moments with a seedy edge. Then there was the weekend in Edinburgh. She'd kept him waiting at the station, turning up at the last second. The train was already moving before they'd found their seats. The train had departed Inverness at 0855. They arrived back two days later at 1506. She left the train without a backward glance. Thirty hours eleven minutes.

Total: fifty one hours and eleven minutes. Give or take. No matter how much give and take, it didn't even amount to an entire long weekend. He gave up resisting and drained his glass. Watched the door. How many minutes had it been? He calculated. Keeping his mind busy, away from the idea that she might not come.

Three thousand and seventy one minutes and he was risking everything because of them.

He caught the eye of a disinterested waiter. Signalled for another drink.

But they'd been the best three thousand and seventy one minutes of his life. And nobody had asked him to risk anything. Least of all her. And there had been other snatched moments...

A tan coloured coach pulled up outside. Within seconds the lobby was full of excited, chattering passengers. Older types who'd made the effort, dressed smart casual. The women powdered, lip-sticked and scented, dressed mostly in beige with the odd burst of colour. A fuchsia body warmer here, a cobalt blouse there. White-haired men wearing new, bright white trainers that looked too big for their feet.

The waiter returned with a fresh gin and tonic. He rolled his eyes at the clamouring guests as he set it on the table. His look said, *see what I have to put up with?* Boyle threw an empathic look right back at him. Wouldn't hurt to keep the guy on side.

A bustling woman with a backside wrapped tight in a skirt at least one size too small, read from a clip-board and doled out room numbers and keys. The crowd slowly dispersed, and there she was.

His stomach fluttered like he was fourteen again. He stood up. She saw him. He smiled, stopped smiling, smiled again, not knowing what to do with his face. She came towards him with that smooth, gliding walk of hers. She wore a charcoal trench coat, belted at the waist and carried a black bag, square shaped, made of leather. She was buttoned up tight, giving nothing away. He'd have chewed the buttons off to get to her.

He caught a trace of her perfume as she allowed him to kiss her lightly on the cheek. She sat in the chair across from his, the table between them. She seemed too far away. He wanted to be closer to her.

The waiter hovered, stealing glances at Stella. Not so disinterested now.

"Drink?" Boyle asked her. She looked at his glass.

"Okay."

Boyle looked at the waiter. "A gin and tonic for my wife please."

The waiter nodded, grinned. *Wife? Yeah, right.*

Boyle shot him a look. *Back off buddy.*

The waiter backed off. Pronto. Boyle had that kind of face.

For all Boyle knew, this dump was a regular haunt for adulterers but as far as smart-arsed waiters were concerned, Stella was off limits.

He looked at her and the looking made him feel nervous all over again. She was still wrapped up tight in her trench coat. Still giving nothing away.

They made edgy small talk till the waiter came back with her drink. He caught the frosty atmosphere between them. Shot a look at Boyle. *Sorry pal, maybe she is your wife after all.* Boyle let it go.

Stella swirled her drink, took a sip, barely wetting her lips. Sat the glass back on the table. Looked at him.

"Wife?" Tone so icy it frosted her lips.

"A joke." He grinned.

She stared at him, not amused. Grey eyes cool, flinty.

"You don't make it easy for a guy, do you?" he asked, still grinning. Keeping it light. All screwed up on the inside, just wanting her to give a little.

"I knew this was a mistake." She made to get up. He sat forward.

"Don't go." He put his hand on her arm, squeezed gently. No grin now. "Please."

She made him wait. A beat, then two, before shaking off his hand and sitting back in the chair. Look don't touch.

"You said things had changed," she said. "Tell me how."

He relaxed a little. Knew that at least she'd hear him out now.

"Remember Edinburgh?"

"I remember. What about it?"

"What we talked about?"

"We talked about a lot of things Charlie."

"I mean about how if we had the money we could get away. Leave everything behind. Start over fresh. Go someplace warm, travel the world. You said you'd always wanted to go to South America."

"It was just talk," she said. For a second there he thought she looked sad.

"It doesn't have to be. Just talk, I mean. We could do it for real."

"Oh Charlie, don't be silly."

"I'm serious. Like I say, things have changed. I've got the money now. Or at least I will have soon. Then we can go. Anywhere you like. Just the two of us."

She eyed him. "You're not joking, are you?"

"I've never been more serious about anything. Ever." He leaned forward, urging her to trust him.

"I don't know. I'd have to think about it."
She sat back in the chair, looking detached, like she'd disconnected herself from the shabby hotel and everything and everyone in it, himself included. He had to pull her back.

"What's there to think about?" he asked. "You said it yourself, those two days in Edinburgh, they were the happiest you'd ever been."

"But they weren't real. It was a fantasy."

"It doesn't have to be a fantasy, that's what I'm trying to tell you, Stella. We can make it real. You and me - we can go anywhere, do anything."

She gazed at the lobby, watching the comings and goings. Some of the coach trippers had re-appeared. They gathered in little knots, taking over sofas and chairs. Ordering drinks. Rum and coke. Whisky and lemonade. A couple of old girls went outside for a smoke.

"Where did the money come from?" she asked.
He looked at her not looking at him. She looked fragile. Like the lines of tension around her mouth could crack wide open, break her into a thousand pieces. All he wanted to do was take her in his arms. Look after her. Make her happy. Make the tension around her mouth go away.

She turned her face to his. The chill in her eyes replaced by curiosity.

"What did you do Charlie?"

He knew she'd ask. He'd thought about what he could say to her. That he'd won the lottery. Been left an inheritance by a rich aunt. Had a big win at the bookies. Knew she wouldn't buy any of it. Decided in the end to tell the truth. It would be better if she knew from the start. He didn't want secrets between them.

So he told her about the smoke and mirrors. About how he'd set up a disturbance in a village on the west coast. About how the cops, already spread thin as Marmite across Sutherland, had gone to investigate. About how when they were taking statements from crofters and old women, the real action was happening in Dornoch, three doors down from an empty cop shop.

She stared at him as he talked, not saying a word. Her eyes widened a couple of times but there were no interruptions, no questions asked, so then he told her about the diamonds and how much they were worth. Her eyes widened a little more at that. Then he told her about the baker boy and how he'd stabbed Macallister. About how much he'd hated having to leaving his old friend behind but that there was nothing he could do about it.

They sat in silence when he'd finished. Her staring at him, like she was carved out of ice. Him staring back at her. Waiting for a response. Wanting her to say something, anything. Instead, she picked up her glass. Her eyes still on his, she took a drink. More than a sip this time. She threw half of it back. Put the glass back on the table. Finally, she spoke.

"Way to go, Charlie Boyle. When you turn, you really turn. You're a regular one-man crime wave."

He didn't care for her tone. He hadn't known what to expect, but whatever it was, it wasn't this.

"I did it for you."

"I didn't ask you to."
"I did it anyway."
"So you did."

Chapter 6

She could turn him in. But Boyle didn't think she'd do that. It would be too awkward for her, having to say where the info came from. He supposed she could phone in an anonymous tip-off to Crimestoppers, but she had nothing to gain from doing so. It was a calculated risk, but he'd come to the conclusion that it was not a serious option.

Having dismissed the chances of her turning him in, he was left with two possibilities. She could stand up and walk out of there, forgetting everything that she'd heard or that she'd ever known him. Or, she could go with him.

It was a gamble - she was more than capable of cutting him dead. But it was a gamble he'd been prepared to take.

Calculated risks and gambles...

She picked up her drink again. Took a sip, her eyes never leaving his. She held the glass, swirled the ice around for a second before sitting it back on the table. She'd lost that fragile, going to break into a thousand pieces, look. Seemed now like she was cast out of carbon steel. When he caught glimpses of her like this, he thought she was capable of anything.

"When are you leaving?" she asked.

"Whenever you're ready… So, are you in?"

"Let's just say I'm interested."

She smiled and the carbon steel dissolved. His heart soared. He grinned. It was really going to happen.

"Let's do it before Friday," she said.

"The sooner the better, but for the record, what happens Friday?"

"Frank comes home."

"Right." Boyle's fingers curled.

"I'll come with you Charlie, but it's got to happen before he gets back."

"We can go right now if you like," he said.

"No…," she hesitated. "I need to sort things out."

"Okay by me." Boyle shrugged. He'd waited this long, he could wait a few hours more. All that mattered was that she had agreed to go with him.

Boyle watched as she whirled through the door and disappeared, her final words still hanging in the air along with the memory of her perfume. He'd wait ten minutes before leaving. The waiter hovered. Boyle asked for the bill.

They were going on Thursday night. They'd agreed not to see each other before then. He'd given her a parting gift. A cheap phone, pay as you go. The only number on it was the number from his own new cheapo pay as you go. He'd use it to contact her on Thursday. No land lines. No contract phones. No ripples on the water. As far as Frank was concerned, she had gone to visit her sister. That would explain the missing suitcase and clothes. Everything else - anything that might tip him the wink - would have to be left behind. This was going to be a clean break. Frank would come home and she'd be gone. By the time he realised that she wasn't where she said she was they would have sailed into the sunset. It was a neat, simple plan. Boyle liked it.

The waiter re-appeared, sat the bill on the table. It was folded in half, on a saucer.

"Everything alright with your drinks sir?"

Solicitous as fuck with the chance of a tip.

"Fine," Boyle growled.

He hadn't meant to growl. His thoughts were elsewhere and it just happened to come out that way. The waiter gave a nervous smile and retreated. Boyle watched him go. His shirt was chewing gum grey, the collar frayed. He looked as stained and threadbare as the hotel carpet and Boyle suddenly felt sorry for the guy. He guessed coach trippers weren't big on tips. He took enough cash out of his wallet to cover the bill and added an extra ten pounds, but his mind was still on Stella. She'd smoothed her coat down when she'd stood up. She'd taken the phone from him, put it in her bag, then left him with a gift of her own.

"Your friend," she'd said, "I don't think you have to worry about him. There was something on the radio earlier. I'm sure they said he was alive."

Chapter 7

Macallister was still alive. Boyle should have felt good, but didn't. Leaving his friend lying in the street had been a grubby thing to do. It was the kind of thing that could screw a guy up for years to come. Maybe even for a lifetime to come. But Boyle had buried it fast and buried it deep. Left it to fester a while with all the other bad memories.

He flopped onto the sofa and flicked through the news channels on the tv until he found their story. Just released - CCTV footage from a camera installed inside the jewellery shop showed two blurry, hairy-faced characters, wearing bug-eye goggles and hats, helping themselves to the jewellery in what was described as an audacious robbery. *Audacious*. Boyle snorted. Macallister would have enjoyed that word being applied to his work. The tape was typically fuzzy. All that money invested in diamonds yet the tightwad, slaphead jeweller wouldn't spring for a decent CCTV system.

Onscreen, the grey blur was replaced by a photo-fit of a man the police wanted to question. Boyle stared at the image. He almost laughed. Macallister had been right - the face on the screen looked like a cross between Uncle

Albert and Captain Birdseye. And it looked nothing at all like Boyle. Then they confirmed what Stella had told him. A man injured at the scene of the crime was in hospital. Sources confirmed that the man was under suspicion but police had not yet been able to interview him. A statement issued from the hospital said that the unidentified man's condition was serious but stable.

Boyle turned off the tv and paced the small room. He looked out of the window a while. No garden, no roses, just people in the street below going about their business. A fat woman in purple leggings came out of the newsagents across the road and opened up a pack of cigarettes. He watched as she stuck one in her mouth and lit it. He'd given up ten years before. Maybe more. But the desire had never gone away. It had been a matter of pride that he'd never given in to the urge, not even when Stella sparked up in front of him. Not that she'd been trying to tempt him, not in that way - she didn't even know he used to smoke. Didn't know about his craving. He wanted one now, *needed* one. It was like an out of reach itch he was desperate to scratch. He grabbed a jacket and went out.

The girl behind the counter looked at him like he was boring her to death, like she had something better to do than sell him cigarettes. She rang up the till and held out her hand. Her sharp little eyes peered at him from beneath over-plucked eyebrows while she waited impatiently for him to hand over money.

Back at the flat, he casually tossed the carton onto the coffee table like it meant nothing to him. Smoking: he could take it or leave it. He sat down, looked at the pack, picked it up and toyed with it a while before peeling off the cellophane. He flipped open the top, pulled out the foil, breathing in the comforting tobacco perfume. He pulled out a cigarette, held it between his fingers. It felt right. Natural. Realising he didn't have anything to light it with, he went through to the kitchen and turned on one of the gas rings on the hob. He lit the cigarette and inhaled.

It made him feel light headed and nauseous. He looked at the burning tip. The smoke curled. He felt sick. Sick for giving into temptation. Sick for leaving Macallister. He ran the tap, killing the cigarette in the stream of water. Taking satisfaction from the hiss it made as he extinguished it.

You can let go now.

With five little words Macallister had given Boyle a free pass.

Don't let go.

Three words said another time. When they were kids. Macallister in the canal. Panic slapped all over his face, black water sucking at him. Boyle clinging on to his arms, not strong enough to pull him out. Just clinging on. Macallister telling him not to let go. Boyle promising he wouldn't. And he didn't. Not even when help arrived. Men with strong arms. Boyle still didn't let go. He didn't let go until Macallister was on the bank, stinking water draining from him.

It's alright. You can let go now son.

That's what the men had said to him. They told him he'd saved his friend's life, that he was a hero. They didn't know it was Boyle's fault Macallister had been in the canal in the first place. That Boyle had dared him, goaded him on, had taken cruel delight in the conflict he was putting his friend through, all the while knowing that Sammy's desire to please him would triumph over his fear of the canal.

Back then he'd been almost deliriously happy that Macallister was still alive after his dip, but he wasn't happy now. He picked up the carton of cigarettes, crushed it tightly and tossed it into the bin. All he could think about was Macallister doped up to his eyeballs, not knowing what he was saying and some bastard cop sitting beside him, notepad at the ready. Waiting to write it down when Macallister said two little words.

Charlie Boyle.

Chapter 8

The Sneck looked like it had fallen off the back of a bin lorry and been left where it landed. It was little more than a concrete bunker. Mesh grilles covered the blacked-out windows. Low-end graffiti was sprayed on the walls. The pub's interior wasn't as smart.

Several pairs of eyes swivelled in Boyle's direction when he came through the door but the bar flies didn't take long to lose interest and soon slumped back into apathy. Boyle walked up to the bar and parked himself in a space between two of the bottom feeders. A clapped-out old pro who looked like she'd blow someone for a white pudding supper raised an eyebrow at him and shoogled herself in his direction. He shot her a look. She got the message, shrugged in a can't-win-'em-all kind of way and hoisted her bony arse back onto her stool. The barman kept himself busy pushing smears around a pint glass with a stained tea-towel, but all the time he was eyeing Boyle.

Boyle took out a couple of crisp twenties, knowing that in a crumpled-fiver dump like this they would demand attention. The barman put down the glass and wandered over. Boyle ordered a pint. Told the barman to have one for himself. The barman squinted at him awhile before saying thanks, he would. He pulled the pint and sat it in front of Boyle. Boyle held on to the notes. He cocked his head. The barman leaned over. The punters' faces stayed to the front while their eyes slid to the side. Watching, pretending not to.

"I'm looking for Banjo," Boyle said. Not shouting, but not whispering either. Everyone heard.

The barman eyed the twenties.

"He'll be in later. He usually is."

"Keep the change," Boyle said, dropping the notes. They disappeared before they hit the counter.

He took his drink to a table with a view, the carpet sucking at his feet like Velcro. He picked a clean spot on the bench and sat with his back to the wall. Grubby yellow foam poked out of the cracked red vinyl on the seat on either side of him. He prised his glass from the sticky table and took a tentative sip, wondering if his tetanus jabs were up to date.

A short, fat guy with a complexion like corned beef staggered to the gents. Boyle planned on nursing his drink until Banjo showed up. Apart from wanting to stay compos mentis, he didn't want to fill his bladder and risk having to wade through the piss on the toilet floor to get to the urinal.

A minute later a greasy-haired wee gadgie in an oversized jacket slid off his stool and swaggered big-man style to the door. He made a big deal of not looking Boyle's way. Boyle watched, amused. Then he waited.

Banjo showed up a scant twenty minutes later, scanning the bar. His eyes widened when he saw Boyle. He loped over and sat close enough so that Boyle could smell the dirty denim of his unwashed skinny jeans.

"Hello, Mr Boyle, long time no see."

"Hello, Banjo."

Banjo couldn't play the banjo, or any other musical instrument come to that. He was called Banjo on account of his close resemblance to the skinny hillbilly dude who laughs while Ned Beatty is raped in Deliverance. The opening chords of Duelling Banjos played in Boyle's head every time he clapped eyes on the greasy scrote.

"I thought you-"

"You thought what, Banjo?"

"Nothing, Mr Boyle."

Banjo twitched, releasing sour notes from his filthy clothes. Boyle took a sip of his pint, giving Banjo time to twitch some more.

"I need you to get me something."

"Anything, Mr Boyle. Just say the word."

Boyle told him what he wanted. Banjo's eyes widened some more, until it looked like a good slap on the back of his head would be enough to knock them out of his skull. Boyle was tempted to try just for the hell of it, but, much though he hated to admit it, right now he needed the junkie informant's help.

Banjo swore blind he could get the goods - just the way Boyle wanted them. They agreed a price. A third slipped under the table now, to cover Banjo's costs, the rest when he came back. Banjo eased out from the table, promising to return within the hour.

Boyle's pint went flat. He didn't bother ordering another. The hour came and went. Boyle watched the door. He had faith in Banjo. Mainly because he knew that Banjo knew what Boyle would do to him if he let him down. Banjo showed up half an hour later.

He slid alongside Boyle.

"You're late."

"Sorry, Mr Boyle. Couldn't be helped. You know what it's like."

"Not really. You get it?"

Banjo produced a small package from the depths of his leather jacket and sat it on the seat beside Boyle. Boyle looked down at the zip-lock bag.

"Ready to go?"

Banjo nodded. "Exactly like you asked."

Boyle slipped the package into his inside pocket and filled the empty spot on the seat with Banjo's payment. Banjo's fingers, long, white and bony, dirt ground into the creases of his skin, slid over the notes. Before he could snaffle them away, Boyle covered Banjo's hand with his own. Banjo's eyes popped. Boyle had another urge to slap him on the back of the head. Instead he squeezed the back of Banjo's hand. Felt the bones squidging together.

"What are you doing that for?" Banjo whimpered.

Boyle squeezed harder. He shoved his face right up close to Banjo's so that his nose was almost skiting off the greasy patina of Banjo's skin. Boyle could hardly stand the junkie stench. He spoke in a low growl. Nice, simple words so that Banjo wouldn't have any difficulty understanding him.

"If you have fucked this up in any way, I will make it my personal business to hunt you down. I will find you and then I will cut off your scraggy junkie balls with a blunt Stanley knife and force them down your scrawny, junkie neck. Understand?"

Banjo nodded then shook his head.

"I haven't fucked up Mr Boyle. I've done exactly what you said. I swear it on my mother's life."

Boyle gave Banjo's hand one last crushing before letting go. He stood up and walked out of the pub, grateful to get away from Banjo's junkie stench.

On his mother's life. He had to laugh.

Banjo McLafferty would sell his mother into slavery for a fix.

Chapter 9

Macallister was in a side-room, hooked up to a bank of bleeping machines. His big black moustache looked obscenely out of place in the stark surroundings. A uniformed cop sat on a hard seat beside the bed, idly flicking through a magazine, waiting for Macallister to wake up and say something. The cop was young, blond and bored.

It was late and a hush had settled on the hospital. Visiting time would have been better. He could have blended in with the masses. But since he didn't have a choice in the matter, Boyle strode the corridors like he belonged. Places to be, things to do. Brisk, but not too brisk. People in a hurry drew attention to themselves.

He knew what he had to do. How he was going to do it was another matter. It wouldn't be the first time he'd had to wing it.

His arrival at the ward was nicely timed - there was a cluster of birthday cards sitting on the desk at the nurses' station, but no nurse. He could hear the sound of hushed laughter coming from a room further down the ward. Sounded like a small celebration was under way. Perfect.

There was a door on the other side of the ward from

Macallister's room. It had a small window set at head height. The room beyond was in darkness. Boyle tried the handle. The door opened and he slipped inside. The room contained a bed, a chair and a table. Some kind of consulting room.

Boyle closed the door and looked through the window. He had a diagonal view of Macallister's room. He could see the bottom half of the bed and the cop's legs stretched out in front of the chair, knees open, ankles crossed.

The magazine suddenly flopped onto the bed. The cop stood up and stepped forward so that Boyle had a clear view of his long, lean frame. He looked like he could handle himself. He turned and stared straight at Boyle.

Boyle's guts clenched. He stepped back into the room, immersing himself in shadow. The cop took a step towards him, a frown on his face. Boyle flexed his fingers. This was a complication he could do without. The cop rubbed his neck, yawned, stretched his arms then sat back down. Boyle exhaled.

He watched PC Blond's legs crossing and uncrossing. His discomfort made Boyle happy. The more fed-up the cop was, the sooner he'd be looking for a distraction. Blond leaned forward and snatched the magazine from the bed.

Boyle took a pair of nitrile gloves from his pocket and put them on. He didn't know when his chance would come but whether it took five minutes or three hours, he was going to be ready. He leaned against the door and settled for the wait.

Waited for the cop to go for a piss, or out for a fag, or go look for a nurse to chat up. It didn't matter to Boyle what the cause was, all he knew was that the cop was human and his chance would come.

As it happened, he didn't have to wait very long. A nurse appeared. Slim, brunette, slightly flushed, very smiley. She did some fussy stuff around Macallister then spoke to the cop. He leaned forward so that Boyle could see his face. He was all smiles right back at her. She said something. He shook his head. Still smiling. Hand gestures, more smiling, lots of flirting. The cop shook his head again, but stood up. Allowed himself to be persuaded out of the room by the pretty nurse. They disappeared in the direction of the hushed party.

Boyle was out of the room and across the ward by the time they'd turned the corner. He stood over his old friend. You couldn't have a gotten a fag paper between them when they were kids. Boyle, full of ideas. Sammy, always on his heels like a shadow. He followed Boyle everywhere until Boyle took a decision that surprised everyone, not least himself, and went somewhere Sammy couldn't follow him. He joined the police.

Macallister's face had lost its sick waxy sheen. He looked peaceful. If it wasn't for the porno moustache, he'd have looked positively cherubic, which was hysterical considering how far from being an angel Macallister was. Boyle unzipped the bag Banjo had given him, took out the syringe and put the bag back in his pocket.

He'd insisted on clean works, which was funny when you thought about it. Being infected with hepatitis or HIV was hardly going to be cause for concern. But still, Boyle didn't like the idea of sticking anything dirty into his friend, so he'd ordered a clean needle, all set up and ready to go.

A recent influx of quality heroin had been wiping junkies out across the city. It was of a purer grade than they were used to, so when they shot up, it was too much for them. They overdosed and died. A similar tale had been splashed all over the news a few years before, but this time there had been pressure from on high to keep the story out of the press. Nobody wanted to advertise the fact that the city had any kind of drugs problem, least of all heroin. It wasn't an image that sat comfortably with glossy images of Loch Ness and Urquhart Castle.

Boyle hesitated a second before putting his hand on Macallister's upper arm. The same place he'd held on to him all those years ago. He blocked the memory and squished up a chunk of pink flesh between his thumb and forefinger. He held the needle at an angle against Macallister's skin, then slowly pushed down the plunger.

Macallister's eyes fluttered open and focussed on Boyle. A grin twitched under his moustache.

"Charlie?" his voice like parchment. "I knew you'd come. You gonna get me out of here?"

The air in the hospital was thick and warm, Macallister's flesh warmer still, but a cold shiver ran the length of Boyle, prickling his skin as he pushed the plunger home.

"Sure I am Sammy. Sure I am." The lie slipped out easily enough but left a toxic after-taste.

"I didn't tell them a thing Charlie. Not a thing."

"I knew you wouldn't." Another lie. Boyle withdrew the needle. Macallister didn't seem to notice. "I've got to go now."

"But you'll be back?"

"I'll be back." Boyle's voice barely a whisper.

Macallister closed his eyes, grin still twitching, happy in the knowledge that Boyle was there for him.

Boyle dropped the needle into the hazardous waste bin. He'd given Macallister a subcutaneous injection, skin popping the junkies called it. It took longer to hit the brain than mainlining, which meant that Boyle had a few minutes to get out before Macallister's machines started bleeping the wrong way. He turned his back on his friend and walked.

Boyle stripped off the gloves without breaking his stride, dropping them into a bin on his way out along with the ziplock bag. The first heroin rush was supposed to be something else. That's what hooked the junkies in the first place - they were all chasing that first hit, trying to regain that first exhilarating rush. He wondered if Macallister would experience the rush before it killed him.

At least it would be a pain-free death. In the end, wasn't that what everyone wanted? Macallister was just getting his a bit sooner than he might have imagined. Boyle pictured his friend falling back into a big squishy marshmallow before being enveloped in black velvet. Sweet and painless. Boyle was an angel of fucking mercy.

He walked out of the overheated, cloying, hospital atmosphere into the balmy night air.

September had been unseasonably warm and in truth there was little difference in heat between inside and out. Even so, Boyle blamed the sudden change in temperature for the fact that he had to blink away tears. His eyes were watering, that was all. He wasn't crying. Definitely not crying.

He walked away from the hospital. Briskly, but not too briskly.

Chapter 10

Wednesday

"Morning Charlie, good to have you back."

Saunders, who was a year younger than Boyle, beamed at him like an uncle delighted at the prospect of spending a day with his favourite nephew. He was shamelessly enthusiastic. A *let's put the show on right here* type. One of those guys whose over-excited, four year old self, still shone out at the world. Boyle frequently felt like throttling him, or at least giving him a bop on the nose. Anything to wipe the smug smile from his face.

"Good holiday Charlie?"

This from the fuckwit hovering at Saunders' elbow. Neil Farquharson, with his big daft face, stupid haircut, wearing surfer dude bracelets and necklaces, thinking he's funky and down with the kids when in fact, they all thought he was a complete plonker. Boyle wanted to grab him by the throat and snarl into his face, *It's* Sergeant Boyle *to you Fuckerson.*

He'd considered phoning in sick, but they were expecting him back and, in the end, he'd thought it better to go in. He didn't want anyone getting suspicious or even curious about him. He didn't want anyone asking questions. He wanted to be invisible, and the best way to do that was to keep it normal.

It was another perfect September day, or at least it had been until he'd walked through the door marked Community Involvement. Warm air, blue skies, summer lingering on. He'd walked the two miles from his flat. Burned off some of the twitchiness he'd been feeling. Two miles. Two days. Tomorrow night the two of them would be gone baby gone.

He'd dreamt about her last night. And Macallister. Crazy, mixed-up dreams. Blonde hair, moist mouth. Just when it was getting good, her face morphing into Macallister's. Macallister smiling, falling into black velvet. Black velvet, black water. He generally didn't remember his dreams and he'd been glad to wake up from this one.

First thing he did on waking was go to the kitchen. He emptied out the washing machine and checked that the diamonds were still wrapped up in the towel. Not that he expected them to be anywhere else, but it was reassuring to check them anyway. They were his future after all. His and Stella's. The thought gave him a warm fuzzy feeling as he rolled up the towel and shoved it back in the machine along with his reeking laundry.

It could reek away. He didn't plan on doing another wash before leaving. His old life would be left behind, including the clothes. Not that there was much to leave. He glanced round what was laughingly called the kitchen. It was a fucking crime what they charged for rent. The best you could say about it was that it was functional and more or less clean. Like living in a flat designed by Travelodge, only not as upmarket and without the orange walls.

He showered then drank coffee and ate a stack of buttered toast while he watched himself as Uncle Albert on tv. He lived on bastarding toast these days. They were showing the same photo-fit. The police were very keen to speak to him, but had advised the public on no account to approach him. He was considered dangerous. Boyle laughed, mid-bite.

The police were bound to know who Macallister was by now, but they hadn't revealed his identity. All they said was that the man found injured at the scene of the robbery had died in hospital during the night. Boyle stopped chewing, but nothing else was said other than the fact that Baker Boy had been arrested on a charge of culpable homicide. Stupid kid should have fucked off out of it when he'd been told.

His mother appeared on the screen, crying that it wasn't right. It was the good people who got arrested these days instead of the criminals. Her boy was a good boy, everybody said so. Yeah, Boyle nodded, prisons were just heaving with innocent souls.

He changed channel. Pictures appeared of a car being dragged from a loch in the middle of nowhere. The unidentified driver had still been in the car when it was discovered by a local gamekeeper but had been declared dead at the scene. Poor bastard, Boyle thought. Maybe he'd had a heart attack at the wheel and been already dead when the car hit the water. Not great, but better than being trapped in a sinking car knowing that you were going to drown. Horrible way to go.

Boyle turned the tv off and took his dishes through to the kitchen. He put the plate and mug in the sink. He'd be glad to get out of this dump.

"Be Bright."

Boyle's eyes focussed. Saunders' round little eyes were looking at him expectantly. He'd been yapping on for several minutes but Boyle hadn't taken a word of it in. Unable to take Saunders seriously, his mind had wandered off. He'd been wondering if the rumours that Saunders dyed his hair were true. There were certainly no traces of grey in the Inspector's chestnut locks. Could be it was down to his genes. On the other hand, Boyle could all too easily picture Saunders grappling with a bottle of Grecian 2000 as he desperately tried to grasp on to the last vestiges of youth.

Now Saunders was waiting for an answer and Boyle had no idea what the question was. He took a gamble.

"Sounds great boss."

Saunders blinked at him. Boyle thought, *uh-oh, wrong call*. Then the blinking stopped and a big old smile dawned bright and sunny across Saunders' face. Boyle's gamble had paid off after all. He should take a trip to Vegas. He wondered if Stella would like the idea.

"I thought you'd like it, Charlie - it's succinct. Straight to the point, a bit like yourself, eh?"

The Inspector laughed at his own joke. If he'd been close enough, Boyle would no doubt have received a nudge the ribs courtesy of Saunders' elbow. *Get it Charlie? Do you get it?* Farquharson joined in, hee-hawing like a moron. Boyle twisted his lips into a weak grin and wondered how the hell a dipshit like Farquharson had managed to pass basic training. He must have sucked a lot of cock at Tulliallan.

The image of Farquharson down on his knees at the police training college brought a genuine smile to Boyle's lips.

"That's why I'm putting you in charge of the job," Saunders said.

Boyle's smile flickered like its battery was running low.

"We're going to target the primary schools," Saunders faffed on. "Look, wait till you see this." He turned to Farquharson. "Where's that thing?"

"Thing?"

Farquharson blinked at Saunders several times. Boyle nearly cracked up laughing. If Saunders blinked back he wouldn't be able to cope. He bit on his lip. Farquharson was either doing a splendid job of taking the piss out of the Inspector's tic, or, in an effort to insinuate himself even further up Saunders' arse than he already was, he was mirroring the Inspector's habits. Except that Farquharson wasn't smart enough for either of those scenarios. The dipshit probably didn't even know he was doing it. Just as well Boyle was getting the hell out. Another week of the place and he'd be doing the blinky thing himself.

"Yes, you know - the *snappy* thing."

"Oh *that* thing," Farquharson gave a dopey grin and went off to rummage in his desk drawer.

Saunders raised his eyebrows at Boyle and gave a small shake of his head, like Farquharson was his slow-on-the-uptake pet pupil. Except that Farquharson, for all his surfer dude fandanglery, was no kid. He was a grown man, and what's more, he wasn't a surf dude, he was a hairy-arsed Highland copper with seven years experience behind him. Scratch that. He probably didn't have a hairy arse. He probably had it waxed. What did they call it - back, crack and sack? It was desperate, it really was.

Farquharson returned, triumphantly holding a thin yellow fluorescent strip, the size and shape of a small ruler.

"Show Charlie how it works," Saunders commanded.

Farquharson slapped the strip against his arm. It snapped around his wrist like a bracelet. Farquharson jiggled his arm around, dead pleased with himself.

"It's magnetic. Good, eh?" he said, "The kids will love them."

Boyle was losing the will to live.

"The best is yet to come," Saunders smugged, "I've managed to persuade McGoldrick's Industrial Supplies-"

He paused, as an announcement was made over the building's Tannoy system.

Would Constable Ian Campbell please report to the front desk. That's Constable Ian Campbell to the front desk.

That was the second time Boyle had heard Campbell's name since he'd come into the building. He was a young cop, a bit cocky and full of himself but sharp with it. The kind who'd cut himself if he wasn't careful. He was desperate to get into the Specialist Crime Division and Boyle assumed the regular Tannoy calls were a ploy Campbell was using to raise his profile. Subliminal. Boyle grinned to himself. Fair play to Campbell if it worked.

"What was I saying?" Saunders asked.

"McGoldrick's Industrial Supplies, boss," Farquharson said.

"Yes, that's right - MIS are going to sponsor the *Be Bright* project. They're going to stump up enough cash to pay for 5,000 of the little beauties."

He beamed at Boyle like he'd just announced a cure for cancer.

"Very good," Boyle said.

Saunders' expression faltered. He looked at Farquharson, who was amusing himself by snapping the strip on and off his arm.

"What are they called?"

"Er, I dunno boss."

"Well we can't keep calling them the *snappy things*."

A frown furrowed his brow, but Saunders was not one for letting life's little irritants get to him for long, and so he turned to Boyle with a smile.

"Charlie, you can find out what they're called. Or, even better, come up with a name yourself."

With that, he turned around and all but skipped to his office, leaving Farquharson still snapping the fluorescent strip on and off his arm.

Boyle wondered if he'd died without knowing it and this was hell.

Chapter 11

"Charlie Boyle! What are you - Billy-fucking-no-mates?"

A stocky fellow wearing a sharp suit slapped his tray on the table and sat on the seat facing Boyle's.

Boyle grinned. "Fuck you Polo."

"Fuck you too Boyle. How's the lasagne?"

Boyle looked down at his half eaten food.

"Terrible." He pushed the plate aside.

"Up to the usual high standard then."

"What's that supposed to be?" Boyle looked at the grey mess on Polo's plate.

"Shepherd's pie mate."

"Fucking hell."

"I know mate, if they served this muck in the cells there'd be a fucking riot. They'd be hollering human fucking rights. Pass the condiments."

Boyle slid the salt and pepper to Polo. Polo doused his food with liberal amounts of each, squeezed a sachet of brown sauce over it, then dug his fork into the mound on his plate.

Boyle tasted his coffee and grimaced before emptying a couple of packets of sugar into it. He tasted it again then added another packet. He watched, fascinated, as

Polo hoovered up his food.

"How's the diet going Polo?"

"Fuck off Boyle. A man's got to eat."

Polo had been on a diet for as long as Boyle had known him. He'd earned his moniker by way of his mint sucking habits, reckoning they curbed his appetite.

"Nice threads." Boyle spoke without sarcasm. Polo may have been fat, but he dressed way better than the average detective. Boyle suspected that in his heart Polo still felt like the skinny, sharp-suited mod he'd once been.

Polo stopped eating for a moment and looked down at his suit. His modness had come about in his mid-teens after a late night viewing of Quadrophenia. The film had been a revelation and Polo had become the only mod in his village. Hell, he'd probably been the only mod in the entire county of Sutherland.

"Thanks mate. She's a beauty. Set me back a packet, but the clothes maketh the man, know what I mean?"

Polo got stuck into his food again, eating most of what was on his plate before shoving it aside.

"That was shit. How was the holiday?"

Boyle raised an eyebrow. "Interesting."

"Good interesting or bad interesting?"

"A bit of both."

"You're not giving much away, are you? Fucking clam man."

Boyle laughed. Cops sitting at other tables slithered glances in their direction, looking away quickly if Boyle stared back. Scared they'd get themselves contaminated with whatever it was Boyle had. He was tainted goods ever since he'd been busted down from Detective Inspector. Not that his tarnished image bothered Polo.

"How's your old dear?" Boyle asked.

"Fucking mental as ever. Did I tell you she's got highland cows now? As if sixty fucking sheep weren't bad enough. Big fucking bastards with horns on them out to here."

Polo held his arms outstretched. "What the fuck does she want with highland cows?" He shook his head.

A clatter of cops made a big noise settling at a table two along from Boyle and Polo. They battered insults back and fore, full of themselves, laughing, cocksure. Boyle glanced over and caught the eye of one of them. Sandy hair, pale blue eyes and cheekbones you could slice lemons on. Well if it wasn't Danny fucking King.

King's face blushed bright pink. He turned away from Boyle's gaze looking like he wished he'd chosen another table, another time. Boyle glowered at him. King's smirking mates clocked Boyle and nudged each other before gathering into a cosy wee huddle, whispering and sniggering. So, the rumours were true. Not that anybody had said anything to Boyle. Not directly. But he'd picked up the story nevertheless.

He looked across the table at Polo, who was busy pretending he hadn't noticed anything.

"Did you know about that cunt?" Boyle asked.

Polo gave Boyle a shrug that went all the way up to his ears. "Come on man, what's it been - four years? You couldn't expect her to stay at home wasting tears on you for the rest of her life. She's a good looking woman."

"Three years. It's been three years."

"It's long enough man. You knew it was gonna happen some day."

"Aye, but not with another cop - especially not that sleazy cunt. I mean, what the fuck does she see in him?"

Polo sipped at his tea as he gave this some consideration. "I don't know mate. There's no accounting for taste, but the fact that he doesn't look like a sack of shit might have something to do with it."

"What are you - his fucking pimp? Whose side are you on anyway?"

"I'm hurt you even have to ask. I'm on your side Charlie-boy, always have been. So c'mon, tell me what's happening over in happy-clappy land."

"Nice change of subject, Polo. Real smooth," Boyle said.

He glanced back over at King's table and thought about how nice it would be to give the fucker a slap.

"I do my best," Polo said. "So what gives?"

Boyle turned back to Polo and groaned as the horrors of the morning came back to him. "Don't even ask."

"Know who Saunders reminds me of? Ed fucking Flanders from The Simpsons."

Boyle laughed even though he'd never watched The Simpsons and he didn't know who Ed Flanders was. He had to laugh at something.

"What's the story in Dornoch?" he asked. He kept his tone casual. It wasn't an unusual question to ask, in fact with it being all over the news it would have been much stranger to avoid the subject.

Polo puffed his cheeks and blew out some air. "Fucking mental," he said. "As if we've not got enough of our own shite to deal with, we're having to help out the fucking Wick boys. It's fucking crazy Charlie boy. Fucking robberies, people drowning in cars, fucking junkies dying fucking everywhere and some old dear nearly had a heart attack on the Ness islands this morning."

"What's that got to do with the SCD?"

"She was walking her dog when she came across some skanky bastard shagging a melon. He'd cut a hole in it, the dirty bastard. He scarpered pronto, but he left the melon so we've got the perv's DNA. You never know, it might match up with that rape in Culloden the other week, but I don't think so. They usually work up to a rape. I can't see him going back to a melon after the real thing, so it looks as though we've got two fucking perverts on the prowl. The DI's spinning like a top. You hear about the baker in Dornoch?"

"Saw it on the news."

Polo slid his gaze left and right before leaning over the

table and lowering his voice. "Between you and me, I feel sorry for the little fucker. It was a case of wrong-place, wrong-time. If the thieving bastard he stabbed hadn't died, he'd have been hailed as a have-a-go hero. You know the knife he stabbed him with?"

"What about it?" Boyle asked.

"He was using it to score the bread before it went in the oven. Reckons he didn't even know it was still in his hand. Poor bastard."

"You're getting soft in your old age. What about the robbery - any leads?" Tossing the question in, nice and casual like.

"Not really, but the guy who died - Macallister - came from your neck of the woods. The Glasgow boys are well familiar with him. He was a small time operator, but it looks as though he was taking a leap into the big time. Over a million grand's-worth stolen. Fucking mental leaving that lot lying in a fucking window. Just asking for fucking trouble."

"Found out much about this Macallister?" Boyle, taking a professional interest, that was all. Never mind the pitter-pat increase in his heart rate.

"He was one of those guys with his fingers in a whole heap of pies. Knew all the big boys, managed to keep on good terms with most of them too - that's a fucking skill in itself. The DS from Glasgow I spoke to said he was a fucking pain, caused them no end of grief, but he kind of liked him all the same. Seems he was quite a funny cunt. A bit of a character."

"He's not making anybody laugh now," Boyle said.

"That's for sure. Especially not me. I've got to go down to Glasgow to try and unravel the fucking mess. Fuck knows how long that will take. Maggie is not going to be happy."

"I thought she understood about the job?"

"Aye she does. Hardly ever gives me any grief, but it's our anniversary on Friday and I promised her a big night out."

"How many years?"

"Fifteen."

"Bloody hell."

"Aye, I know, don't say it - you get less time for murder."

"She must have a thing for fat blokes."

"Fuck off Boyle. Anyway, I'm not fat. Sandy fucking Henderson - he's fat. I'm more your well-built type."

Boyle laughed. "Aye right. So you are. But maybe you'll be back in time. They'll not be wanting to spend money keeping you in a hotel down there."

Polo's face brightened.

"Aye, maybe. The boss is always banging on about his fucking budget."

Boyle stared over Polo's shoulder. A dark cloud passed over his face, fracturing his smile. His fingers curled on the table. Polo turned to see what was causing the damage.

At the other end of the canteen a tall, lean, man in uniform was laughing at something one of his companions had said. He was handsome in an old-school movie star kind of way, with thick, neatly cut, silver hair and an aquiline nose. Surrounded as he was by a phalanx of acolytes, he looked for all the world like Caesar.

Polo turned back to Boyle and rolled his eyes.

"Did you hear?" he asked, jerking his head back at the man Boyle was still staring at.

"What?" Boyle asked, wondering if Stella had packed already.

"Jammy bastard got promoted to Super. Can you believe it? What a fucking leap in the pay scale that is. There is no fucking justice in the world. That's what the arse-licking party is- fuck, was that my name?"

They listened as the Tannoy announcement was repeated.

Would DS Ernest Morrison please return to SCD immediately.

"What's that about?" Boyle asked as Polo stood up.

"Fuck knows, but I'd better go. Later, yeah?"

"Yeah, later," Boyle said.

Polo picked up his tray, then paused and turned to Boyle. "Listen mate, don't let the bastards grind you down. I mean it."

"You getting soft on me Polo?"

"Fuck off, Boyle."

"Fuck off, Polo," Boyle retorted. But his heart wasn't in it.

He watched Polo strut away with his tray and felt a pang of envy. He wasn't taken in by the pretend whinge about going down to Glasgow. Polo was loving every minute of it. The SCD room would be buzzing just now. There was nothing like a big case to pull the team together. He should be part of that team. Hell, he should be leading it, not arsing around with bloody snappy things for kids which was a criminal waste of his skills and experience. Then again, if he was still in the SCD, chances were he wouldn't have set up the robbery and Macallister would still be alive.

Boyle told himself he didn't care. It was too late for regrets. Come tomorrow he'd be walking out of his empty shell of a rented flat for the last time. *Adios amigos.*

He watched as Polo slid his tray into the trolley and walked out of the canteen, giving a brief nod as he passed by Caesar and his coterie. Probably said *Sir* at the same time. Wouldn't be doing himself any favours walking by a Superintendent without acknowledging him.

Boyle's phone vibrated in his pocket. The special phone. The one with a single number on it.

"Stella?" Voice low, hand cupped around his mouth.

"Charlie, he's back. Frank's back."

"I know," Boyle said.

"How do you know?"

Boyle stared across the canteen. "I'm looking at him."

Chapter 12

"When did he get back?"

"Last night, but I couldn't call you. He's been acting strange. He's watching me all the time and he's got a funny look in his eye. It's like he *knows* something. I'm worried, Charlie."

Boyle glanced over at Frank right when Frank was glancing over at him. Their eyes locked in a stare-down. One of Frank's hangers-on caught the look, said something to Frank. Frank's lip curled. Someone came up behind him and slapped him on the back. Frank turned away, breaking the staring competition.

"He doesn't know anything," Boyle said. "Nothing's changed."

"But everything has changed, Charlie." Stella's voice rising.

He'd never heard her like this before. She was always cool, always in control. Now she sounded frightened and vulnerable. Hearing her like this scared him and he didn't like it. He twisted round, turning his back on Frank, his cronies, and the rest of the canteen. He spoke into the phone, voice low and steady. Trying to soothe and calm her.

"Listen to me Stella. Nothing has changed. You hear me? We still leave as planned - we'll go tomorrow - during the day, while he's at work."

"I don't know Charlie."

"It's easy. All you have to do is pack an overnight bag and get a taxi to the station."

"I don't think I can do it."

"Yes you can - you can do it Stella. You don't even need the overnight bag. Just walk out of the door."

"I don't know…"

"It's simple, baby. Just walk away."

Silence on the other end of the phone. Her thinking. Him wondering. The silence dragged on. He could feel the bond between them stretching like a silk rope, the fibres snapping one by one, until there was only one thin thread holding them together.

"Stella?"

"It's Frank - you don't know what he's like… you just don't know."

She had the jitters like a spooked horse.

"All you have to do is walk away." Low and coaxing. Easy does it.

"No. I can't do it. I can't. It was a crazy idea. It's over Charlie."

He started talking then realised he was talking into empty space. He looked at his phone. It said *call ended*.

The last thread had snapped.

The rest of the day was like an out of body experience. Saunders asked him a couple of stupid questions. Boyle answered. The words coming out of his mouth sounded civil enough. Maybe it was the way he said them that caused Saunders to do his blinky thing, before smiling uncertainly and backing off. Fucking space cadet.

Saunders was like a goldfish. Everything brand new and exciting every time he swam around the bowl. Still, after that particular encounter, he didn't swim too close to Boyle for the rest of the day. Just as well. If there was ever a day Boyle would finally snap and punch him on the nose, this was that day.

Farquharson reappeared later in the afternoon. He'd been giving a talk at a local high school. He drifted over to Boyle with one of those big moronic grins plastered all over his face and babbled some shite about how he felt he had this real connection with the kids. That he *really got* what they were about. Boyle stared at him, wondering how it was possible for one man to contain so much verbal diarrhoea and for that same man to be so completely unaware of what a total wanker he was.

Farquharson, taking Boyle's silence for acquiescence, pushed a pile of paperwork aside, then perched his arse on the edge of Boyle's desk. He crammed his big stupid self into Boyle's personal space and settled himself down for a good old chin-wag-cum-bonding session.

"So what do you think?" Farquharson looked expectantly at Boyle after coming out with some pathetic statement, profound only in its inanity.

Boyle looked back at him, as if seriously considering what Farquharson had said. Then he spoke.

"Piss off Fuckerson."

Perplexity wormed and squiggled across Farquharson's brow. He did a double-take then gave an unsure smile. Thinking, hoping, Boyle was joshing with him but Boyle's world was crashing in on him and he was in no mood for levity.

"Go on," Boyle said. "Fuck off. There's a good lad." Farquharson, still unsure, fucked off.

After that everyone left Boyle alone and, somehow or other, he got through the rest of the day.

He felt hollow, like he hadn't slept or eaten in 48 hours. He tried calling Stella but her phone was switched off. He thought about phoning her on the landline, but that might freak her out even more. Worse still, Frank might answer. If there was one thing Boyle knew it was that no matter how bad things were, they could always get worse.

He left the office dead on five and walked back to the flat feeling disconnected from everything and everyone around him. Like he was operating in his own special dimension. He was unlocking the front door before he even knew how he'd got there. It was like when he'd been driving to Alness. Blink and he was there.

Inside, he pulled everything out of the washing machine and carried the towel through to the living room. He closed the blinds then unrolled the bundle. He emptied the jewellery onto the coffee table and sifted through it. The diamonds sparkled in his fingers. Necklaces, bracelets, rings, brooches, ear-rings. Beautiful objects designed to be worn by beautiful women. He let them drop through his fingers back onto the towel where they landed in a shiny heap.

He'd stolen them so that he wouldn't lose her, but now he'd lost her anyway. And he'd killed Macallister. Without her, the diamonds were no more than compressed carbon. Shiny, meaningless, stones. Over a million pound's worth of meaningless. And Macallister was still dead.

Nobody was supposed to die. It was supposed to be happy ever afters all round. Well, for everyone except Frank. With his insurance claim, even the jeweller wouldn't lose out.

Boyle thought about buying a bottle of whisky and drinking himself into oblivion. He could picture himself slowly sinking into the warm, amber embrace of the bottle. Letting the bad stuff melt into an alcoholic haze. Goodbye pain, guilt, and doubt. Hello nothingness. With any luck he would never wake up and have to deal with the stinking mess he'd created.

He wallowed in the thought for a moment before rejecting it.

There were few things Boyle despised more than self-pitying drunks. This and every other town he'd ever been to was stuffed full of them. Guys his age and older, some younger, already making a career out of it, propping up bars, jaded and disappointed with life, thinking that everyone had it in for them, that the world had let them down. That it was always someone else's fault. They'd just never been given a chance. They could have been a fucking contender.

Every last dangly-dicked, soft-cocked, self-loathing, impotent fucking one of them blaming someone else. The boss who didn't value them. The wife who didn't understand them. The mother who didn't bake fairy cakes. The father who ignored them. The uncle who touched them up when they were a kid. The teacher who embarrassed them in front of the class. The girl who turned them down. The whining, ungrateful bastards they'd spawned. All of them mocking and sneering and just never, ever giving the drunken, deluded prick a chance. He'd be fucked if he was going to become one of them.

If he was going to become a bum, he was going to do it with a little style. Do it somewhere the sun shone all year round. Warm seas, blue skies. Sand between his toes. Sounded a whole lot better than lying in your own pish in The Sneck.

The stones weren't worthless. With or without Stella, they were his ticket out of the meaningless, shitty mess he'd made of his life.

He'd wrecked his marriage, losing his daughter as well as his wife in the process. The job was fucked. It had been everything, now it was nothing. The brass hadn't been particularly fond of him before, but now that Frank was one of them he was doubly fucked.

Frank knew damn well that Boyle had been a good detective and he was equally well aware of what a mind-fuck it was for him to be stuck in Community Involvement. Which is precisely why he would make sure that Boyle spent the rest of his police career there.

No doubt he hoped that Boyle would crack and punch Saunders or Fuckerson or some other peppy prick. There was no way Boyle's career would survive assaulting another officer. Then Frank would not only get the pleasure of seeing Boyle sacked, he would have the double delight of knowing he'd lost his pension. Equally, if Boyle managed not to crack, Frank would still get the pleasure of watching him slowly rot until it was time to put him out to pasture.

Either way, it was a win-win situation for Frank Valentine.

Family gone, job gone, Stella gone. There was nothing to keep Boyle there. Even if there was, even if he did have one good reason to stay, it was too dangerous. Polo was persistent, and he wasn't stupid. Sooner or later he would unearth a connection between him and Macallister. Maybe he'd come across an old newspaper story about one boy saving another from drowning in a canal. Or maybe he'd find a school photo of Macallister's and wonder who was the familiar-looking kid sitting next to him.

Boyle had to get out, and the time to go was now.

Chapter 13

The towel was too bulky to carry, so Boyle rolled the jewellery in an old grey sweatshirt and stuffed it into his backpack. That didn't leave much space for packing, but then he didn't plan on taking much with him.

Boyle had walked out of his marital home with nothing more than a holdall and the clothes he was wearing. He'd been travelling light ever since. When Karen threw him out, he discovered that all the shit he'd used to prize so highly - his CD collection, his Bose Wave, his clothes - none of it mattered a toss anymore. Later, he heard that she'd burnt his good suits on a bonfire. He didn't blame her and, as it turned out, he didn't care about the clothes. Funnily enough though, he still cared about Karen.

In theory, he knew that what she did and who she did it with were none of his business anymore. In practice, he felt it was very much his business. At least it was when the other party was Danny King. King was a creep. A good looking creep, but a creep nevertheless. He couldn't believe Karen had fallen for his well practiced charms. Time was she'd have seen straight through a snake like him. He wondered briefly if her dalliance with King was a way at getting back at him, but almost immediately dismissed the thought. Karen had already taken her pound of flesh from Boyle and then some. He couldn't see her coming back for more. Not after all this time. Most separated or divorced guys he knew either moved straight in with the other woman or else they set about creating themselves an extreme bachelor pad. Giant flat-screen TV, gaming consoles, a fridge full of lager, and a bin full of takeaway containers.

Boyle hadn't done either of those things. Neither had he gone out clubbing in a desperate attempt to relive his youth. Instead, he crashed on a variety of sofas until his goodwill credit ran out, and then he found the flat. The rent was a rip-off, but it was in the centre of town which suited him as it meant he didn't need a car, and it came furnished, which suited him even better.

Whoever had done the furnishing for the letting agency hadn't gotten over-excited about it, but most things he needed were there. Everything else he accumulated over time. Except that Boyle accumulated less of it than most people.

He never got around to replacing his CD collection or his Bose Wave and, despite living there for over three years he hadn't hung a single picture. The blank walls suited him.

He rolled a clean pair of socks and underpants inside a t-shirt and shoved the small bundle into the backpack. He added a toothbrush, toothpaste and shaving kit. He had no intention of growing his Uncle Albert, or any other beard, again.

Satisfied that he had packed everything he needed, Boyle changed into a pair of jeans and a slate grey, long sleeved top. He put on a pair of black lace-up boots and a black funnel neck jacket which, apart from being about as anonymous as a jacket could be, had the benefit of several pockets. He pocketed his phone, passport, wallet and warrant card then inspected himself in the mirror.

Everything he had on was worn-in, nothing shiny or

new. Nothing tatty either. No holes, rips or stains. In fact, nothing about anything he wore stood out in any way. No logos, no motifs, no flashes of colour. His outfit was outstanding only in its utter blandness. He was everyman. He was no-one.

He considered a hat, but decided that his face, neither jaw-droppingly handsome nor show-stoppingly ugly, would be less memorable without rather than with. He picked up the backpack and slung it casually over one shoulder. No one looking at him would guess he was carrying a pair of pants, a pair of socks and over a million pounds worth of jewellery.

He took one last look around the flat. The phone he used to contact Stella was lying on the coffee table. He picked it up and put it in a pocket. It was the only link in the flat between him and her. The only clue that there was a relationship between them. Despite the weary disappointment he felt about her refusal to come with him, he wasn't about to drop her in it. So he took the phone. He would break it up and dump it later.

Nothing else caught his eye, so Boyle walked to the front door, set to leave for the last time. He wondered how long it would be before they came looking for him. Before they started raking over his life, looking for clues. Why had he done it? Where had he gone?

Good luck. They wouldn't find much.

He turned the Yale knob and opened the door. One of the phones vibrated in his pocket. For a second, maybe two, he considered ignoring it. But then, he would always be wondering.

He took the phone from his pocket. He didn't have to look at the screen to see who was calling. Only one person had the number.

He put it to his ear.

"Hello."

"Charlie, is that you?"

A beat of silence, maybe two, then - "It's me."

"Thank God you answered. I thought maybe..."

She let the maybe hang. Boyle let the door go. It swung to. He gave it a tap with his fingertips. The Yale lock clicked home.

"Charlie? Are you still there?"

Boyle walked through to the living room, phone pressed to his ear, listening to her breathing. She sounded nervous. Excited.

"Yes Stella. I'm still here."

Waiting for her to say it. Willing her to say it.

"I've got to see you."

Boyle dropped the backpack.

Chapter 14

The pub was designed to look olde worlde. It was all exposed beams, open fireplaces and built-in nooks and crannies. The beams were fake, the open fires were gas. But the nooks and crannies were real enough.

The artifice didn't matter to Boyle. What mattered was that the plastic pub had been built to service the patrons of the budget hotel next door, which meant that the clientele was largely of the passing-through type. What was more, thanks to the dark corners, it was the kind of place in which two people could find a quiet spot in which to have a private conversation.

So effective were the recesses, he almost missed her. She was in a booth almost hidden by a fake bookcase. It was an intimate space, big enough for four people. Assuming those four people were on familiar terms.

When she looked up at him her eyes were dark.

"Drink?" he asked. She tilted her glass, checking the contents. It was all ice.

"Yes, please." She answered.

He went to the bar, wondering how long she'd been there. Long enough to finish her drink. Not long enough for the ice to melt. The barman gave him a nod, letting Boyle know he'd be with him soon. Boyle nodded back, letting the barman know he understood. It was a wordless exchange between strangers, yet each of them understood what the other meant. It was more than he could say about himself and Stella.

She'd knocked her drink back. Maybe using it to steady her nerves. Boyle wondered why she needed to do that. She'd already told him it was over. She didn't need to tell him again. Not this time.

Maybe she'd changed her mind. She didn't need a drink to tell him that. All they had to do was leave.

So, it must be something else.

The barman finished serving a smiling woman with a spiky hair-do and chubby cheeks, and turned to Boyle.

"What can I get you?"

Boyle ordered a gin and tonic for Stella and a whisky for himself. He rarely drank whisky but thinking about it earlier had given him the notion. Besides which, something told him that once he'd heard what Stella had to say, he might need it. He added a splash of water from the jug on the bar and waited for his change. When it came, he took his time putting it in his pocket.

He could have left there and then. Just walked out of the door without looking back. She couldn't see the bar from where she was sitting. He could be five minutes gone in any direction before she'd miss him.

He could have done a lot of things. Wasn't anybody holding a gun to his head. Not when he'd robbed the jewellery store. Not when he'd injected the heroin into Macallister. And not now. It was freedom of choice all the way. Except that he knew he couldn't walk out on her. Not when there was still a chance. Not now. Not ever.

She was wearing the same charcoal trench coat she'd worn the day before. It was still buttoned up, still belted tight at the waist. She wore it like a suit of armour. The same black bag was on the seat, close beside her.

He put the drinks on the table and sat down. He felt the way he always felt around her. Like a big oaf, sucking up all the air. Like one clumsy move from him would snap her in two.

It was kind of funny, because he wasn't that big and she wasn't that small. Sure he was tall enough, just a tad under six feet, but he wasn't burly. She was around five seven, with an hour-glass figure. Not fat, not skinny. As far as Boyle was concerned she went in and out in all the right places. But every now and again, underneath all her feminine attributes, he caught that glint of carbon steel. He figured if anyone was going to be doing any breaking, it would be her breaking him. But none of that stopped him feeling like a Neanderthal beside her.

She was like an ethereal creature operating on a different plane. A goddess. There were moments he could hardly believe they breathed the same air.

He wanted to reach out to her. Touch her. Flesh on flesh. Feel her warmth. Let her feel his. But he held back and did what he usually did when he was at a disadvantage. Nothing at all.

Let the other guy sweat it out. Let the other guy try to figure out how much Boyle knew. Only in this case they weren't in an interview room and the other guy wasn't a guy. It was the same deal though. She had something to say, and sooner or later she would say it. Whether or not Boyle wanted to hear it was a different matter.

He looked at her. She picked up her drink and created a vortex with the plastic cocktail stirrer. The ice chinked against the glass. Just when he was on the verge of telling her, enough already, she took out the stirrer and lined it up on a napkin beside the one from her first drink. When she'd finished messing around, she took a sip from her glass.

Displacement activities. Putting off the moment. Boyle sat still and waited, leaving his drink alone.

Finally, she put the glass down and looked at him. He

tried to read her face, but couldn't. She was an enigma to him and he wondered if that was part of the attraction. He wanted her so badly. Longed to be close to her. But whenever he thought he was getting there, she moved out of his reach.

Those few nights they'd spent together in Edinburgh had been full of passion, the days full of laughter. They felt so right together that it couldn't possibly be wrong. And yet, even then he'd felt there was a part of herself she was keeping back. A part of her he would never reach or understand. He caught a glimpse of it from time to time. An expression ghosting her face, the way her eyes seemed to change colour with her moods, the way she sometimes tensed when he touched her.

He wondered if she'd always kept herself wrapped up so tight, or if it was the result of living with Frank all these years.

"I can't live with him any longer," she finally said.

A flutter of excitement inside Boyle. "You don't have to. We can leave - right now if you like."

"No, I can't," she shook her head, eyes wide and dark. "You don't understand."

"So, tell me - make me understand. Whatever it is, I'll take care of you, Stella. You know that."

"You don't know what he's like."

"Don't I?" Boyle's fingers curled.

"No. Nobody knows."

"Then tell me, because this is driving me nuts. I was on my way out when you called. I mean I was leaving. For good. Another five minutes and I'd have trashed and dumped the phone you called me on."

His words had the desired effect. Her eyes flashed at him, alarmed, making him feel good. She *did* care.

"You were leaving?"

"Why not?" Boyle shrugged, acting casual, feeling anything but. "You dumped me and I can't hang around forever."

"I didn't dump you."

"No? What was it you said ? *It's over Charlie*, that was it. It sounded a lot like I was being dumped."

"No. I was scared, that's all."

"Why, what did he do to you?" Boyle's eyes narrowed.

"Nothing… yet. Not really. But I'm scared of what he might do. I'm terrified of him Charlie." Just for a second her mouth quivered. Blink and you'd miss it.

"So leave him. Seriously Stella, this is driving me crazy. We could be out of the door right now instead of going round in circles like this. You've got to tell me what gives or I'm out of here. It's time to make up your mind."

Brave words. He sounded calm. In control. Like it barely mattered to him if she went with him or not. Inside his heart was hammering. She was so close he could smell the light trace of her perfume. He wanted her so badly it hurt, but he couldn't show it.

For a moment he thought that she was going to bolt. Thought maybe he'd overplayed it, that he would be walking out of there alone after all. That the only thing this assignation had achieved was to delay his solo train journey. Then she started talking.

"Frank watches me all the time. He controls everything. It was bad before, but it's worse since he came home. It's like… he *knows* something."

"He doesn't know a thing, baby."

She raised a hand to hush him, touching him lightly on the lips with her fingertips. He grasped hold of her hand, held it, relishing the feel of her flesh against his.

"You haven't seen the way he looks at me. I'm scared."

"We can go now."

"No, Frank won't let me go… not ever. What you don't understand is that appearance is everything to Frank. Divorces might be ten a penny these days, but to Frank a divorce would be an admission of failure, and

Frank doesn't fail at anything. He won't divorce me and he won't let me go. Especially not now, with his promotion. It wouldn't look right, having his wife walk out on him."

"Jesus Stella, this is the twenty-first century - you don't need Frank's permission to leave him. Just do it."

She withdrew her hand from his, shaking her head again.

"He once told me that if I ever left him he would hunt me down... and when he found me, he would hurt me. Hurt me badly, he said. And I believe him. He's capable, more than capable. I think that if I ruined his perfect life, he would kill me."

Boyle clenched his fists under the table. He felt like turning it over, like smashing the place up. What he most wanted to do was tear Frank Valentine apart.

He needed to say something to Stella. Reassure her. But his throat was too tight. Felt like there was a wire around his neck, digging in, preventing him from speaking.

Even if he could speak, what would he say to her?

He'd already told her to leave him. But she was too frozen by fear to do it.

Stella said something.

She said it quietly. She'd barely spoken above a whisper since she'd started, but this time Boyle was so caught up in his own thoughts, he missed what she was saying.

"What did you say?"

She looked right at him. Her eyes were cool and grey.

"I said, I want you to kill Frank."

Chapter 15

Boyle stared at her. Waited for her to crack a smile. Tell him it was a joke. She didn't. He decided he needed that drink now. He knocked back a slug. The whisky flared all the way down his throat.

She watched him. Anxious. Waiting for his reaction. She wasn't the only one. Before he could say anything to her, he had to figure out what he thought himself. Trouble was he was having a bit of difficulty aligning his thoughts. Whatever he'd been expecting, this wasn't it.

He could hardly blame her for wanting the bastard dead. Everyone had wished someone dead at some point. He harboured no warm feelings for Frank himself. But wishing for it to happen, and asking him to actually do it were two separate things.

"It's the only way, Charlie."

He sat the glass on the table and looked into her cool, grey eyes.

"It's cold blooded murder," he said.

"I thought you hated him."

"I loathe the man... but murder? Jesus Stella, it's a hell of an ask."

"You're shocked because you've just heard it. Think

about it for a while - you'll get used to it and see how it makes sense - that it's the only way."

He couldn't handle how calm she was. She'd flipped out at the thought of walking out on the guy, but killing him... apparently that was an altogether more Acceptable idea.

"They give you life for murder."

"Only if you get caught. Besides..." She looked away.

"Besides what?"

"You've done it before." She was looking down at her hands.

Boyle's skin prickled.

"What do you mean?"

"You killed your friend." Staring him straight in the eyes now.

The silence stretching out between them as good as an admission.

"How do you know?" he finally asked.

"His condition was stable. They expected him to pull through. The next thing, he was dead. I know it was you - I saw your face when I told you he was still alive. It didn't come as good news."

Boyle shook his head. "He could have given them my name. He wouldn't even have known he was doing it because of the drugs. But he would have destroyed everything. We'd both have ended up behind bars, and what was the use in that? At least this way, I could salvage something. You and I could still make a go of it - get away from Frank and everything else. Make a new life for ourselves. Otherwise, what was the point of any of it?"

She let him finish his justification for killing Macallister before cutting through the bullshit.

"If you killed your friend, you can kill Frank."

"Jesus Stella, that was different. It was the situation."

He took another hit of whisky.

"And this is another situation," she said.

"Yeah, you're right. It is. Frank's a police Superintendent - that's big, really big. Somebody like that gets murdered and it'll be like ten circuses and a carnival have come to town on the same day. They'll be all over it, into everything, and the first thing they'll get into in this case is you, the wife. Check out the home life. It's the first rule of detective school. They'll get under your skin and in your hair. They'll study you like a bug under glass. They'll watch everything you do, every little tic, every reaction, will be noted and dissected. If you've got a diary they'll read it, if you've got a computer they'll take it apart. They'll check phone calls, incoming, outgoing. It won't be fun and it won't be pretty, and believe you me Stella - if there's anything to find, they'll find it."

She let him rant, unfazed.

"I know that. That's why you have to do it. Nobody knows a thing about us. They won't suspect you."

"They know there's bad blood between me and Frank."

"Frank has stood on a lot of people to get where he is. You're not the only cop whose career he's ruined. If they're looking for people with grudges, they'll have to line you up with a whole heap of other guys. But that won't happen, because what we have to do is make it look random. He'll be stabbed in a mugging gone wrong. A tragic case of him being in the wrong place at the wrong time. So you see, there won't be anything to connect his death to you, or to me."

"You've given this a lot of thought."

"You've no idea."

"Jesus Stella - I don't know."

"Think about it Charlie. Once all the fuss has died down, we can go wherever we want to, do whatever we please. We can be together. Go to all those places we talked about. But the best thing is, we won't be looking over our shoulders. We'll be free. You and me truly together. It will be wonderful."

Her eyes shone as she promised Boyle the world.

A couple of hours before he was ready to board the train to Lonesome Town. Now she was telling him he could have her. He could have anything he wanted. And all he had to do to get it was kill Frank. His life for theirs together.

"Charlie?"

Her hand on his arm. Under the table, the slight pressure of her leg against his. Hardly touching at all, but still it was enough to arouse his desire. The light notes of her perfume in the air. The highlights in her dark blonde hair glistening in the low light. The promise of everything that could be. If only he agreed to do what she asked. After all, what was a little murder between friends?

Suddenly she withdrew her hand and checked her watch. Alarm flashed across her face. She stood up hastily, almost knocking her glass over.

"What is it?" he asked, circling her wrist with his hand, not willing to let her go.

"I lost track of the time. I have to go. I have to be there before he gets back."

Her cool composure evaporated. She looked flustered, a little panicky. Boyle had a flash of insight, a sudden understanding of what her life with Frank was like.

Frank ignoring his wife to tend to his roses. Her keeping the house picture perfect - just the way he liked it. Just the way he liked everything. Frank never letting her go, and all that was ahead of her were years of lonely hell. If he let her live that long.

She looked down at Boyle's fingers wrapped around her wrist. Furrows on her brow.

"I have to go."

He released his grasp.

She went.

"Stella," he called.

She turned to look at him, face creased with worry,

anxious to be gone.

"I'll do it," he said. "I'll do what you asked."

Chapter 16

Thursday

He's a good boy. He might have got into a few scrapes when he was younger, but never anything like this. My Gordon is a good boy.

Baker Boy had been released on bail. His mother was proclaiming her son's innocence on the news. Boyle muttered to himself, *there are no innocents.* He was in a sour mood, but even so, he checked himself. There were innocents in the world. His own daughter was one, and no, when it came to Jenny, he wasn't deluding himself. Maybe Baker Boy was one too, but probably not.

On screen, someone put her arm across the distraught woman's shoulders and smiled nervously at the camera. He wondered what *a few scrapes when he was younger* translated as. Despite all the evidence to the contrary, his mother had probably spent her entire life convincing herself that her son was a model citizen. Boyle had come across them time and time again. Drug selling, thieving, raping little bastards all with mothers who swore blind their boy was a good boy and why didn't the filthy polis scum go and arrest some real crooks.

Meanwhile, residents in the golfing town of Dornoch are

preparing for the first day of the Classic Cup.

Images of smiling, waving crowds, and famous golfers in silly clothes filled the screen. Boyle switched the television off. He checked the phone for the umpteenth time that morning to see if Stella had called. It was a futile gesture. For one thing, she wouldn't risk calling him until Frank had left for work, and for another, there wasn't a chance in hell of him having missed a call. The phone was right beside him and he'd been checking it every two minutes since he'd got out of bed.

Truth was, he'd been checking it all through the night. Tossing and turning, picking it up, checking for a message or the missed call symbol. But there had been nothing from her. It was just him and his conscience.

He wished that she'd just gone ahead and left with him. That it was all over. That they were already on their way to a new life instead of wallowing in the detritus of the old one. Maybe even wishing that he had left without her, then wondering what the hell the point of that would have been.

It was a waiting game now. Waiting for her to call. Waiting for a chance to meet in the cold light of day and find out if she'd meant what she'd said about killing Frank. He'd been there, seen her with his own eyes, heard her with his own ears, yet he could hardly believe it. Didn't want to believe it.

Neither could he believe that he was sitting in his scabby flat with over a million pounds worth of diamond jewellery facing yet another day in Happy Clappy Rainbow Land with Saunders and Fuckerson. *Why couldn't she just leave with him?*

When it got to the stage he couldn't put it off any longer, Boyle left the flat.

It was only twenty four hours since he'd last taken the same walk. The air was as warm and the sky as blue as it had been the day before, but the day before Boyle had been looking forward to starting a new life with Stella. Today he was thinking what it would be like to stick a knife into her husband's heart.

Despite the consequences Boyle had derived a great deal of pleasure from punching Frank on the nose. The look of surprise as he'd staggered back and fallen had been a delight. But then, as he lay on the floor looking up at Boyle, his eyes had narrowed and something loosely associated with a grin had snaked its way across his lips. That's when Boyle knew Frank had won. He'd goaded Boyle into punching him and, like a fool, Boyle had taken the bait.

After the disciplinary hearing, Boyle lost his detective status and was bumped down to sergeant. If he'd tried to defend his position by saying that Frank had provoked him, no doubt he'd have been busted all the way down to constable, so he'd kept his mouth shut and sucked it up. Taken everything they'd thrown at him, including compulsory attendance at an anger management course. Meanwhile Frank had been sent away for a spot of career development before being rewarded with a big fat promotion to Superintendent.

He wouldn't have minded landing another good one on Frank. Could easily picture punching his face to a pulp. So much for anger management. But much though he loathed the man, the thought of killing him in cold blood held no appeal. Despite, or perhaps because of what had happened with Macallister, Boyle was no murderer.

He knew all about knife wounds and the damage they could do. He'd seen the results often enough. He knew that piercing human flesh took about the same amount of force as stabbing a melon and that the results were often devastating. But then that's what Stella wanted, wasn't it? Devastating results. The black coffee he'd had for breakfast turned to acid in his stomach.

It wasn't all bad news. Turned out Saunders and

Fuckerson were going to be out of the office all day. Before he left, Saunders gave Boyle a zesty little briefing and what amounted to a pile of crap to deal with. Buoyed by the fact that he wouldn't have to put up with Tweedle Dee and Tweedle Dum all day, Boyle gave the Inspector a zipadeedoodah reassurance that he would be right on top of it, boss.

He smiled Saunders out of the office, flicked through the paperwork he'd been left with, pushed it aside and, as he had nothing better to do, took a stroll up to the canteen. He hadn't eaten anything since yesterday's lunchtime lasagne, no wonder his stomach was all acid. He ordered a bacon roll and a mug of tea. He was wiping the last of the grease from his mouth when Stella called.

They met on Culloden Battlefield, site of the last pitched battle fought on British soil. Even in the bright September sun, the moor had a bleak and desolate air, but Stella looked stunning. She wore her trench coat open over a tailored dress in dark grey herringbone, and carried her usual black leather bag. In deference to the gravel paths criss-crossing the battlefield she had eschewed heels for a pair of black suede loafers. On anyone else they may have looked frumpy, but they lent Stella a beguiling youthful air.

She wore very little make-up and her face looked young and fresh. The light wind ruffled her hair making the blonde highlights dance. Her eyes sparkled green. It was all Boyle could do to keep his eyes in his head and his tongue in his mouth.

"You look good Stella." Understatement of the year.

"I feel good." She smiled at him.

She looked like a different woman to the one he had met last night. That woman had been fraught and troubled, this new, fresh-faced Stella, looked unburdened by worries.

They strolled away from the Memorial Cairn. They'd

met here a few times before when the weather was fine. Sometimes open spaces were the best place for a secret tryst.

"About last night…" he began.

She turned to him, anxious. "You haven't changed your mind have you?"

He looked into her eyes. There was no mistake. She had meant what she'd said. Boyle felt heavy inside, but he shook his head. "No, I'll do it - if that's what you really want?"

"I thought you understood Charlie - it's the only way."

Her face began to crumple. Boyle immediately swept her into his arms.

"It's okay Stella, I was only checking that you wanted to go ahead. I'll do it. I promise." He breathed in the scent of her hair.

She looked up at him.

"Are you sure?"

"I'm sure. I'd do anything for you, Stella, you know that."

He kissed her on the lips. A warm, slow kiss. God, he wanted her. Wanted her more than anything in the world.

When their lips parted she said, "I love you, Charlie."

He looked into her eyes, sparkling green and grey and felt like he was falling into them.

"I love you too, Stella."

They kissed again, lingering over it until they were disturbed by the sound of footsteps crunching on gravel. They parted hastily as an elderly couple approached, arm in arm. Boyle and Stella stood aside to let them pass. The woman smiled at them, eyes twinkling. The man bid them a good afternoon. Boyle wondered that if instead of being an old married couple, they were lovers. He shared the thought with Stella, murmuring in her ear. She laughed.

"We'll be like that one day, and all this -" she swept her

hand through the air in an all encompassing gesture, "will be nothing but a dim and distant memory."

He swirled her around, both of them laughing.

"Okay," he said, "Let's make some dim and distant memories."

"Let's start with Frank," a smile still dancing on her lips though her eyes had turned to steel. "I'd like him to be a very dim and distant memory."

"Tell me what you want me to do," Boyle said.

Neither of them laughing now.

Chapter 17

The Crest area of Inverness sat astride the hill overlooking the city centre. Originally the site of a cattle market, it now consisted mainly of large Victorian and Edwardian stone villas. The area had slumped in the Seventies, but lately its fortunes had picked up. House prices had risen. Money returned. A few smart hotels and restaurants sprang up, thriving in the Mercat Cross area. The Crest was, once again, a very desirable neighbourhood.

The Broadstone Hotel was the Grande Dame of the Crest. Boyle had never eaten there, but he knew of its reputation for fancy food with fancy prices to match. He also happened to know that the Broadstone's manager was a personal friend of the Commander's, which was why a private dining room had been reserved that night for a select few. It was a fine dining and wining welcome-aboard do, in Frank's honour. Partners not invited. Just the "team". Boyle wondered if the Commander got mate's rates.

The Broadstone was exactly the kind of place Frank aspired to. Boyle could only too well imagine his sphincter snap-snap-snapping in excitement as he stepped through its gilded doors. His shoes shined to a mirror. Razor creases on his trousers. Not a hair out of its silvery place. Not so much as a hint of lint. Frank, cut, pressed and polished. Frank - you shall go to the ball. Only, instead of arriving by coach, or even car, Frank arrived by foot, just the way Stella had predicted he would. Boyle hoped that she would be just as right about everything else.

A brisk walk from the Valentine's house to the Broadstone took less than ten minutes. Frank wouldn't take the car because the occasion demanded that he have a drink and he would not take a chance on drink-driving. There was no question of him abstaining as he would not wish to appear stand-offish. There were two women on the "team" but for various reasons, neither of them would be there that night. This was a dressed-up beano for the boys and Frank was now most definitely one of the boys.

"What about a taxi?" Boyle asked.

Stella said no, he would walk. Taxis were an indulgence for women and fat old men. Walking would make Frank feel superior to lesser mortals. He would definitely walk.

At the very least, he'd have a gin and tonic aperitif, an appropriate glass or two of wine with his meal, and very likely a couple of large malts afterwards. He'd imbibe enough to make him feel relaxed, perhaps even slightly tipsy, but he wouldn't get drunk. Frank didn't do drunk, but that would work in their favour.

A drunk Frank would have to be piled into a taxi, whereas a relaxed Frank, even a slightly tipsy Frank, would most certainly insist on walking home. After all, it was a beautiful night, the distance was short, in an upmarket, familiar part of the city, with a low crime-rate. He was in his home territory and would be in a relaxed and unguarded frame of mind, no doubt congratulating himself on how well he'd played his hand.

Boyle, sitting in a cafe across the street, watched as Frank arrived at the Broadstone. Until this moment, Boyle had been glacier cool. So cool in fact that he'd begun to wonder if, once you'd made your mind up about it, murder really was quite a simple crime to commit. But now that he had his flesh and blood mark in sight, his heart stepped up a pace and his nerves twitched beneath his skin.

He'd been going over it ever since he'd left Stella on Culloden moor. He had to hand it to her - her plan was almost genius in its simplicity, which meant there wasn't a lot to go over. But still, it had churned around and around his mind. Now, in an effort to calm his jangling nerves, he went through it again.

Nice and relaxed, Frank would be enjoying his stroll home, his head full of his own wonderfulness, blissfully unaware of how vulnerable he was. A figure would emerge from a doorway. The figure, a male, would be dressed casually, wearing a hooded top with the hood up, but his head would be down, his presence unthreatening. Frank would note him, but be unconcerned. The casually dressed man would bump into Frank. Not barge, just bump. He would mumble an apology for his transgression, whilst simultaneously stabbing Frank.

The knife Boyle chose for the job had a five inch, razor-sharp, straight edged blade. It was designed for cutting raw meat. It would leave a scant wound on Frank's skin, but havoc would be wreaked on his insides. The knife would come from below, pointing upwards. Frank would be stabbed under the ribcage and up into the heart. Boyle would be aiming, as far as it was possible to aim, for the right ventricle. A wound in this area would most likely ensure a swift death, particularly if he acted fast and managed to inflict two wounds.

Boyle would have to stab hard to penetrate Frank's clothes, especially if he had buttoned up his jacket, but once through the layers of clothing, the blade would have a smooth passage.

The element of surprise would be on his side, but there would be no time for hesitation. He would have to deal with Frank swiftly and resolutely. *Stab in. Pull out. Stab in. Pull out.* Walk away.

There would be a lot of people around. This part of the Crest was buzzy on a Thursday night. People coming and going between bars and restaurants, warming up for the weekend, but no-one would notice. It was astounding what people didn't notice. Boyle had known a woman to be raped less than ten feet from a busy thoroughfare on a weekday afternoon with no-one hearing or seeing a thing.

There was no CCTV coverage in the Crest area. There was very little CCTV coverage in the entire city. Despite the clamour that Britain had become a society under surveillance, with every move monitored by a shady authoritarian presence, the great British public weren't watched anywhere near as much as they thought they were, especially not in Inverness. Besides, hooded males were notoriously difficult to identify.

The entire assault would take less than ten seconds. Chances were Frank would still be on his feet when Boyle walked away, aware that something terrible had happened to him but not entirely comprehending it.

Boyle pictured Frank putting a hand to the red flower blossoming on his shirt. Feeling warm, sticky blood. Looking at his hand. Eyes widening as he understood that he'd been stabbed. Opening his mouth to call for help before collapsing to the ground without uttering a sound. A crowd would gather, someone would call an ambulance, initially thinking the well dressed man had suffered a heart attack. Then they would see the blood. The ambulance would arrive, but it would be too late. Frank would already be dead.

Then there would be nothing to stop him pursuing a

new life with Stella. They would have money. Lots and lots of money. More than enough to start over. They could go anywhere, do anything. And she was right - they would never have to look over their shoulders, because Frank would be gone. It would be just be the two of them, together.

Boyle walked out of the café. He'd barely touched his coffee. Had ordered it because he'd had to order something. He wanted to call Stella, let her know Frank had arrived, that it was all on, but they'd agreed, he wasn't to call her until it was over. Until Frank was dead. Then she'd have her part to play. And when the show was over, they'd be together. And then...

And then, they'd live happily ever after. Boyle and his beautiful, brittle goddess. Blue skies above them. The warmth of the sun all around, enveloping them. No fear, no worries, no looking back.

He walked the streets, lost in his fantasy, burning up his nervous energy. Finally, inevitably, his feet took him to Frank's house. That was the way he thought of it. Not Stella's house. Frank's. A tasteful mausoleum containing the withered remains of their marriage. Stella slowly suffocating within its sterile walls.

He stood on the pavement and gazed at the stone villa like a street urchin, grimy nose pressed against a baker's window.

A brand new BMW sat in the drive. No hint of dust on its gleaming waxed bodywork. No doubt a wee present Frank had given to himself for the promotion.

The sky clung onto a soft blue haze, as if it was reluctant to give up on the day, but Stella had already drawn the curtains against the encroaching dark. Chinks of light peeped out, hinting at the warmth to be found inside. The knowledge that she was in there, alone, gnawed at Boyle. He ached for her, longed to hold her. Touch her, be with her. Taste her, breathe in her scent. His love for her, his desire - it was like a sickness.

He was half way up the drive before he stopped himself.

Christ, what was he thinking? He couldn't be seen here. Couldn't go near her. Especially not tonight. He had to take care of Frank and she had to play the grieving widow, and then they could be together. Then he could touch her, hold her, breathe her in.

He turned around. Saw Frank's white roses glowing softly in the twilight. Boyle walked by them, back to the street.

Boyle outside. Frank inside. Eating, drinking. Laughing too hard at the Local Police Commander's jokes. Unaware that he was enjoying his last meal, his last drink. His last sycophantic laugh. Time would be flying by for Frank. It dragged for Boyle. Until, finally, the gilded doors flew open. Male laughter boomed from within, rattling onto the street. Time sped up for Boyle.

Mouth suddenly dry, he walked in the direction of Frank's home. Their voices mingled and faded behind him. He'd chosen the doorway earlier. It was across the street from a trendy tapas bar. Boyle walked up two stone steps to the security door leading to a block of flats. The door was set back, allowing Boyle to position himself in the recess. He leaned, nonchalantly, against the wall, as if waiting for someone. When Frank approached, he would step out. It would look as if he was coming from the flats. Nothing unusual. Nothing for Frank to take note of. There were other people around, traffic going by. Many distractions.

Boyle peered around the corner, his heart quickening as Frank peeled away from the group outside the Broadstone. He walked towards Boyle. Every step bringing him a little closer to his death.

Boyle flexed his fingers before pulling the knife from its sheath. He was already wearing a pair of black nitrile gloves. He let his arm dangle. *Hang loose baby.* The knife held lightly in his hand. Tucked in behind his leg. Frank wouldn't see it coming.

The night must have gone well. Frank looked even more pleased with himself than usual. Walked the pavement like he owned it.

Boyle's heart *ba-boomed* in his ears. His grip tightened on the knife. Any second now, he'd be stepping onto the street. A tremor ran through his legs. Anticipation, that was all. Frank coming closer.

A rush of adrenaline coursed through Boyle's system. He took a few deep breaths. He'd be fine. He could do it. Had to do it. For Stella.

Across the street, a burble of laughter and conversation erupted as a group of women emerged from the tapas bar. Boyle gave them a quick glance. It was enough to tell him they were worth a second look. Good. With their long hair and even longer legs, they'd be a nice, glossy distracter for Frank. His eyes would be all over them, lapping them up like a thirsty dog. Boyle wouldn't register with him.

Frank was here.

Boyle stepped out of the doorway.

Chapter 18

Boyle never understood what made him look across the street again. One minute he had Frank in his sights, the next he was staring at the group of women, trying to make sense of what he was seeing. Maybe it was something he'd taken in on that first glance. Maybe it was something he'd heard, a note of laughter that soared above the sounds of the street before burying itself in his brain. Whatever made him do it, he took a second look.

At first he thought he was staring at Karen. His wife. Ex-wife. Her hair was longer. She was laughing and giggling. Enjoying herself on a girls' night out. She looked good on it too. Amazingly good. She suddenly turned and stared right at him.

It was then Boyle realised his mistake. It wasn't Karen. The smile faded from the woman's face as she recognised him. Boyle went cold. He raised his empty hand. Waving. At Jenny. His daughter.

A lorry rumbled by, spewing out diesel fumes. By the time it passed, the women, Jenny included, had moved on, gliding along the pavement in the direction of the Broadstone. They shone in the street lights, radiating girlish confidence. They seemed so young. Impossibly young.

Boyle lowered his hand and stared after them, lost in a reverie until someone came out of the door behind him. He snapped out of his trance, shuffling out of the way as he mumbled an apology whilst shielding the knife from view.

Panic flared inside him as he remembered what he was supposed to be doing.

Frank. Where was Frank?

Boyle scanned the street. His target was nowhere in sight. He must have strolled right on by without Boyle seeing him.

He shoved the knife into his hoodie pocket and hurried along the street in the direction of Frank's house. He'd have to catch up with him before he reached home. As long as he got him out on the street it would be okay. Didn't matter where as long as he could come at him from behind. A couple of stabs into the kidneys ought to do just as good a job as a stab in the heart. Or maybe Frank would hear him coming and turn around. Then Boyle could get him in the heart. It didn't matter - just as long as he got him. Two good stabs in a major organ. That's all it would take.

Boyle gripped the knife inside the pocket, his gaze intent, seeking out Frank's familiar outline. He could be anywhere. He could have gone into one of the bars on the street. But no - Boyle didn't think so. He wouldn't want to rub shoulders with the hoi polloi. Not Frank's style. He'd take a brisk walk straight home, eager to crow to Stella about how smart he was, about how he was going places.

Boyle increased his pace, resisting the urge to run. Nothing stood out on a street like a running man. He didn't want to be noticed. Didn't want to be remembered. That was important.

Frank couldn't have had much of a head start. Only a minute or so - if that. But it was only a short walk from here to Frank's house. A minute or so was all it would take and Frank would be home - unscathed, unstabbed, and utterly alive.

Boyle had to kill him before he reached the safety of home. Stella wasn't expecting him. She might get a shock, blurt something out, give the game away. She'd been calm today on the moor. Calm because Boyle was going to kill Frank. But what about the way she'd been last night? Edgy and uptight. Falling apart. Who knew what she would do if Frank came strolling through the door when he was supposed to be lying in the gutter bleeding to death.

Boyle saw him. Walking tall, silver hair glinting under the sodium lights. He was strolling on the opposite side of the street, not a care in the world. Boyle crossed the road, dodging the traffic, stomach tight, blood high. He narrowed the gap, coming up on the inside. Working out his approach. He would bump into Frank from behind. Just a light brush, nothing alarming. Frank would automatically turn towards him, exposing his torso. Boyle would stab him, just the way he'd planned it all along. Frank would collapse and Boyle would walk on by, baby. Just walk on by.

Stepping up the pace. Closing in on his target. Within spitting distance now. Boyle got ready to pull out the knife. All he had to do was slip it out of his pocket and into Frank.

Frank stopped abruptly, catching Boyle by surprise. He tried to put on the brakes, but his momentum carried him into Frank's back, the knife still in his pocket.

Frank let out a surprised *oof.* Now was his chance. Boyle fumbled at the knife, but it caught on the seam of his pocket. He yanked at it. Material gave way. Frank turned round to face Boyle just as he pulled the knife free. Boyle tensed his arm, ready to plunge the knife into Frank's soft innards, roar of blood in his ears.

"Oh, I'm terribly sorry."

Boyle stared. *What the hell?* Sweat prickled in his armpits. Mouth dry. Carotid artery pulsing. The knife suddenly heavy in his hand.

"My wife is always telling me not to stop suddenly like that. She says it irritates people coming up behind me, but I see something that interests me and I forget."

Not Frank.

NOT FRANK.

"She says I'm a pest, but it was the menu, you see." Not Frank indicated a menu displayed in the restaurant window beside them. "It caught my eye. I'm intrigued…"

Not Frank's words trailed off. He peered at Boyle. He was older than Frank. At least twenty years older, his thin face heavily lined, but he carried himself well. Like a much younger man. An easy mistake to make.

No, not an easy mistake to make. A stupid, unforgivable mistake to make.

Boyle slid the knife back into his pocket before the old guy noticed it. He'd almost slid it into this old man, just the way Baker Boy had slid his into Macallister. He'd almost killed this man for no reason. If Not Frank hadn't suddenly stopped to look at the menu in the Iranian restaurant, Boyle would have stabbed him.

He could have killed him, walking away without even knowing the man he had killed wasn't Frank.

"Do you feel alright? You don't look terribly well." Not Frank inclined his head, his face creased with concern.

Boyle stared at the man he'd nearly murdered. He didn't deserve Not Frank's sympathy.

"Sorry." The word rasped out of him.

"Can I help?" The man laid a heavily veined hand on Boyle's arm.

Boyle looked down at Not Frank's hand. He didn't want the man touching him. Didn't want his concern. His kindliness. He took a stumbling step backwards.

The concern emanating from Not Frank's kindly face scalding him.

"Sorry," Boyle repeated. He moved away from Not Frank, taking a few blundering steps before finding his feet.

Steady now, his pace picked up rapidly. He wanted to put as much distance between Not Frank and himself in the shortest possible time.

In a matter of moments, Not Frank had transfigured into the living embodiment of everything that was good and decent in human form. And Boyle had come within a gossamer wing of wiping him out. Banjo McLafferty, filthy thieving junkie scumbag though he was, existed on a higher plane than Boyle.

Bloody hell. What had he almost done? What was he thinking? He wasn't a killer. He was a cop. One of the good guys. On the side of the angels. He was supposed to protect the Not Franks of the world, not slaughter them in the street.

Boyle walked, his feet pounding his self disgust into the pavement. People, lights, bars, cars, went by in a blur of light and noise until they weren't there anymore.

It took a moment or so for their absence to register. Without noticing, he'd slipped over the hazy boundary into the residential area of the Crest. To be precise, for the second time that night, he was walking down the street where Frank lived. That house. It drew him like iron filings to a magnet. And there, up ahead of him was Frank.

He could have done something then. He could have called out Frank's name. Frank would have stopped, turned around. Boyle could still have taken care of everything, could still have carried out Stella's wishes. Her heart's desire. But whatever taste he'd had for murder was gone. Leaving nothing behind but empty bitter notes.

Ahead of him, Frank crossed the threshold from the

street to his domain. He disappeared from view. No matter. Boyle could picture him as clearly as if he was the other man's shadow. Frank walking up the drive. Gravel crunching underfoot. Going towards the front door. Light on above it. Guiding him home.

Frank taking his key from his pocket. Frank inserting the key into the lock. Frank opening the door and stepping into his house. Frank calling out to his wife.

Stella, honey, I'm home.

Chapter 19

Boyle leaned on the railing and stared into the black water of the river flowing from Loch Ness into the Beauly Firth. It was quiet along here at this time of night. Just him. A man on his own, watching the water drifting by. Solitude. Peace. Quiet. It gave a man space to think.

Who was it said that an unexamined life was a life not worth living? Plato, Socrates? One of those ancient, wise guys. How was it they knew so much back then and he knew so little now?

He'd had everything. He'd been good at his job. Had made DS by twenty-four, DI by twenty-nine. It felt like he'd found his place in life, that he'd known what he was all about. His star had been in the ascendant. He had a good home and loving family. A safe haven to return to after a day of dealing with the low-life vermin scum of the world. A refuge from the junkies and paedophiles and fraudsters. A place where he could take a hot shower and let the dirt wash right down the plug-hole.

He took the knife from his pocket and removed it from its sheath. He turned it over, studying the blade, thinking about the damage he could have inflicted with it. The damage he *would* have inflicted... if it wasn't for seeing Jenny.

He let it dangle from his fingers for a moment before flipping it into the river. It slipped into the water with a gentle *plink*.

Seeing her like that tonight had rocked him to his core.

She'd been a daddy's girl from the start. She'd adored him and he'd taken her love for granted. He hadn't thought anything could get in the way of it, but when the rows with Karen got bad, Jenny had been old enough to know what was going on. And when Karen had thrown him out, she'd been old enough to understand why. Then she'd been old enough to decide that she didn't want anything to do with him.

After the split, he'd gone through a phase of hanging around on her route home from school. Hoping for an accidentally-on-purpose encounter with his daughter. A welcoming smile. A casual conversation. But if she saw him she looked the other way. Crossed the road to avoid him.

He tried phoning Karen, tried to sort something out. *If she doesn't want to see you, I can't make her.* The words cutting him.

He took to lurking instead. Hanging about in shops or cafes she had to pass. Peering out, hoping for a glimpse of her. Acting like a right sad bastard. Maybe that's why he'd stopped, because he didn't like how pathetic it made him feel. Or maybe he didn't like to admit to himself that as well as failing as a husband, he'd failed at being a father. Anyways, he'd stopped. Locked it all away and not thought about it. Not in a long time. No thinking going on here.

She'd grown up since he'd last seen her. It had happened so fast, the change from child to woman. His little girl was gone and he'd never get those years back.

She was the spit of Karen. The same thick, glossy hair. The same heart shaped face. Probably had the same expectations of life too. That somehow or other, it was all going to work out happy ever after.

He wandered upriver towards the Ness Islands before stopping to toss the sheath into the water. It disappeared like it had never existed. Boyle shivered.

He'd had it all and lost it. Then he'd wanted something he couldn't have. He'd wanted Stella. Wanted her with a mad dog crazy yearning. She'd been like a drug he couldn't get enough of. He'd craved her, yearned for her. Been insane with desire for her.

Had been... past tense. So was that it then? All that craziness over and done with, just like that? Could he be wild for her one minute, and the next - nothing?

No, not nothing. Something lingered. More than something. If she called, he'd go to her. But Frank had gone home so she wouldn't call.

The fact was, Boyle had let her down and she'd never call again. Maybe that was a good thing. He wasn't sure. Couldn't really tell a good thing from a bad thing anymore. Used to be simple. The good guys wore white hats, the bad wore black. He'd been one of the good guys. Now it was all shades of grey and he didn't know anything from anything anymore.

His loving Stella, it had been like a sickness. There was something unhealthy about the way she made him feel. Crazy the things she asked him to do. The things he agreed to do for her. If they stayed together they'd destroy each other.

Boyle was glad he'd failed her. Glad he hadn't killed Frank. The man might be a king-size prick and a mean bastard to boot, but that didn't mean he deserved to die. Not like that.

Of course he hadn't killed Frank. He'd never have been able to kill a man in cold blood. He wasn't a murderer. Frank was alive and even though Boyle hated him, he was glad about that.

He wandered along the riverside until he came to a waste bin. He peeled off the gloves and tossed them inside. All the tools of the crime he hadn't committed gone. But what of the crimes he had committed?

Macallister was dead. Forget about that. He couldn't un-dead him. And he couldn't un-steal the diamonds. Besides, the freckle-headed jeweller would already be working on his insurance claim and Boyle didn't feel inclined to complicate the paperwork. Macallister would have to stay dead and Boyle would have to keep the diamonds. But he couldn't keep on working with Saunders and Fuckerson. He'd rather turn himself in. So why keep on doing it? He could hand in his resignation next morning. Why not? It was simple.

Boyle smiled at the thought. Yeah, to hell with it. The brass would be delighted at the thought of getting shot of him so easily. Their cries of good luck and all the best would still be ringing out as the door slammed shut behind him. *Adios amigos.*

That was it then. He'd be gone by tomorrow night. He wouldn't even have to sneak off like a fugitive. No-one was looking for him. And if at some point Stella did decide to squeal, he'd already be long gone.

He could see himself living a simple life. Maybe a shack on a beach somewhere. Some place it was cheap to live. Maybe Mexico. Yeah, Mexico sounded good. Somewhere on the Pacific coast. He could drink the local brew, eat what the locals ate. Fresh fish, burritos, tacos, whatever. He pictured a whitewashed adobe house. Paint peeling, but in a picturesque kind of way. Simply furnished, a lethargic ceiling fan shifting the warm air around.

Just thinking about it, he could almost feel the sand between his toes.

Once he'd sorted himself out he could get to work on his redemption. His salvation lay with Jenny. He saw that now. He would send her the money from the diamonds. He'd keep a little, just enough to get by on and keep himself out of bother, but she'd get the rest.

He'd be able to fund her through university and beyond. Maybe some good would come out of the mess after all. Who knew, in time he might even be able to contact her.

Most likely, she wouldn't want to know, but maybe curiosity would get the better of her. Maybe she'd want to get to know him again. Could be she'd get to a stage in her life where she realised that it wasn't all black and white. That her father wasn't all bad. That everyone did things they regretted. Time heals all wounds. That's what they said.

They said a lot of things, but even so, as he thought it through, a curious sense of peace settled on Boyle. He turned around and walked back towards the city centre. There was a definite lift in his step. A lightness of spirit. Everything he did from now on he was doing it for Jenny.

He'd wear his suit for his last day at work - the only one he owned now. He'd smarten up. Put on a well-pressed show. Then, when he was free, when the door had closed on him for the last time - he'd bin it. Who the hell needed a suit in Mexico?

Out with the old, in with the new. Goodbye Scottish drizzle, hello Mexican sun. That made him laugh. It hadn't rained here in weeks. It was mental. There had been wildfires on the moors, but all this dry weather in Scotland was unnatural. It would have a different feel in Mexico. Hot and dry was normal there. He'd have sand between his toes and Jenny wouldn't have to worry about student loans or debts. It would all be taken care of.

He was below the Castle when the phone rang. He took it out of his pocket, holding it like it was a viper ready to dig its fangs in. No need to look at the screen. Only one person had that number. He thought about tossing it in the river, the same way he'd thought about walking out of the bar. But he hadn't walked out of the bar, and he didn't throw away the phone. It was all scripted and there was no way out.

Stella called. He answered.

"Charlie? Something's happened... something terrible. You've got to come to the house. Now - you've got to come now."

Chapter 20

The light over the front door was off, the windows dark. No light seeped through the chinks in the curtains. No hint of warmth from within. The front of the house was lit only by the glow of the streetlights.

Treading softly, Boyle passed Frank's BMW and walked round to the back door. He tried the handle. Locked. He tapped lightly on the door, reluctant to disturb the peace of the night.

He peered through frosted glass, looking for a hint of life within. Wondering what he was doing there. Maybe hoping there would be no answer. That Frank and Stella were tucked up all cosy for the night. That the crisis, whatever it had been, was over.

But no, a shaft of light appeared followed by Stella's voice through the door.

"Who is it?"

"It's me, open up."

His voice as hushed and urgent as hers. An increase in his heart rate. The realisation that the crisis was not over. That whatever it was, he was involved.

Smart snap of the door being unlocked. It opened a crack. Stella peeked out. Her face in shadow, eyes glinting.

"Thank God you're here. I didn't know what to do."

She ushered him in. Locked the door behind him. They were in a utility room bigger than the kitchen in his flat. A shaft of light from the kitchen revealed washing machine, tumble drier, sink unit, all lined up like soldiers along one wall. Even the brush and mop stood to attention.

"What's going on?" Still talking in hushed tones, wondering what the-

"Through here-"

She led him through the door into the light. Brown satin dressing gown swirling like bitter chocolate around her form.

He followed her into the kitchen, the halogen lights dazzling after the gloom. They'd been well thought out those lights. Lit up every square centimetre of every polished surface. No shadows thrown. Everything defined.

Boyle took it all in.

There was a lot of white. White marble worktops, white floor tiles, white blinds, tightly closed. Hints of polished steel - kettle, toaster, knife block. One empty slot.

Splashes of colour stopped it from being overly clinical. An artfully placed stack of brightly coloured tea towels. An abstract print on the wall. A vase of spiky gladioli, the showy blossoms beginning to open. And on the floor there was red. Lots of red.

Frank was lying face down beside an island unit. An overturned bar stool beside him. Stainless steel handle of a kitchen knife sticking out of his neck. The pool of blood spreading out from the wound was already congealing at the edges, the thick, metallic smell of it heavy in the air.

Boyle immediately made a move towards Frank, intent on checking his pulse. It didn't look good but his instinct was to check anyway. But before he could do anything Stella grabbed him by the arm, her nails digging through the fabric of his hoodie into his flesh. His head swivelled towards her. She was coiled up tight. Dark stains matted the sheen of her dressing gown.

"What happened? Did you phone an ambulance?"

Direct questions. All business. No messing.

"There's no point... he's dead." Her face crumpled, but she didn't release her grip. Boyle glanced at Frank. If he wasn't dead he was doing a fine impersonation of it.

Stella had two hands on him now, pulling him away from the body. She looked close to hysteria, was maybe going into shock. He turned towards her and she threw herself into him, her face against his shoulder, her words coming in frantic little bursts.

Oh Charlie... it was awful... I didn't know what else to do... thank God you're here.

Plenty of emotion on display, a whole heap of words to go with it, but when you got right down to it she wasn't giving anything away.

Boyle encircled her with his arms without touching her. Holding them at an awkward angle. He didn't know what had happened here and he didn't want to know. His instinct was to run, to get the hell out. But it was too late for running when you were already in the quicksand. Any running he had to do should have been done a long time ago. Like it or not, he was involved in this and he'd been sucked in right up to his neck, with trouble still rising.

He reluctantly rested his arms against her, felt her relax into him, her hands lying flat against his chest, like she'd been holding her breath, waiting for this moment. She looked up at him. Her face was all puckered up but there were no tears.

"This is bad, Stella."

Talk about stating the obvious. Knowing it was a stupid thing to say even as the words formed. Feeling he had to say something.

"I know," her voice weak, barely a whisper. Her eyes closed and he thought she was about to faint, but then they fluttered open again. He'd never seen her eyes look so dark. She quivered in his arms like an injured bird.

"You have to help me Charlie. You will help… won't you?" Her voice breathless, panicky. Her fingers digging into his chest like she was trying to claw her way inside him.

His throat tightened. He didn't trust himself to speak so he nodded.

"I didn't know what to do… all I could think of was to phone you." An almost imperceptible quiver rippled over her face making Boyle wonder what the hell was going on beneath the surface.

"It's okay," he said, the words hollow in his ears but they seemed to satisfy Stella.

She collapsed into him again, her face against his chest, the scent of her hair mingling with the iron tang of Frank's blood. He looked down at Frank, then up at the ceiling, rolled things around in his head for a while. Knowing she wouldn't like what he came up with.

"You've got to phone the police."

She pulled back from him, shaking her head, making her hair dance.

"No."

"Stella, you've got a dead body in your kitchen - you can't not phone them."

"Absolutely not." Her expression hardened as she glared at him, the wobble gone from her voice.

"I know it looks bad, but you can explain. Tell them what he was like. Domestic violence is taken seriously these days. They'll listen."

"Are you listening to yourself? He was the golden boy. He was one of them. They'll crucify me."

"Not if you tell the truth." Even as they left his lips, his words sounded pathetic. Since when did the truth matter?

She stared at him, mouth open, letting a silence, as thick and oppressive as the smell of Frank's blood, grow between them before ripping it open with a vitriolic outburst.

"I cannot believe you are serious." She shook her head in disbelief. "What version of the truth do you expect me to tell? It'll be my word against his dead body. I don't have any bruises to show them. Frank specialised in mental torture. There are no broken bones. No trace or record of what he was like. There has to be another way."

Her voice rose, becoming more strident, more demanding. She stared at Boyle, face set, eyes cold. He knew what she was getting at but he didn't want to hear it.

"There is another way, Charlie. You know there is." Testing him, challenging him.

Boyle looked at Frank. He was a big man. It was a lot of body to lose.

"If we go down that route there will be no way back - for either of us." His voice hoarse.

"Do you think I don't know that?" Her caustic tone burned into him.

"I'm… it's just not what I was expecting."

"And I wasn't expecting him to come walking through the door tonight!"

Her words, high pitched, on the edge of hysteria, ricocheted against the hard surfaces of the kitchen. Boyle didn't speak until the ringing tones of the accusation had faded to nothing and all that could be heard was the quiet tick-tock of the kitchen clock.

"I know…" he said, his voice low. "I didn't have time to warn you. But I thought maybe it was better that he came home… I mean murder… the whole thing Stella - it was a big fat mistake. I thought it was for the best… For both of us."

They looked at Frank's body lying stark against the white tiles.

"I didn't mean to..." her voice reduced to a whisper now.

Boyle watched her looking at Frank.

"What happened?" he asked.

"I don't really know..." She turned to him, a puzzled expression on her face. "It was all so fast." She frowned. "We argued... it got nasty. Very nasty. He said some horrible things... I was angry and I grabbed the knife. Then he started laughing at me. Mocking me..."

"Go on," Boyle urged her.

"He went on and on, sneering at me. I couldn't take it any more - so I stabbed him. Just like that, I stabbed him. The blade went into him so easily and he looked so shocked that I'd done it... he stared at me like he didn't believe it had happened... and I didn't believe it either."

She let out a sob and buried her face in her hands. The stained satin shimmered over her trembling frame, her stance practically begging him to take her in his arms.

Boyle hesitated. Frank's last minute reprieve followed by his sudden and violent death was hard enough to absorb. Throw in Stella's emotional swings from vulnerability to vindictiveness and back again and he was well and truly rattled. He was caught between his natural instinct to comfort her and his horror at what she had done. And behind all that he was thinking about Jenny.

Finally, he put a hand on Stella's shoulder. She wheeled around, falling into his arms once again. Trapping him with her helplessness.

"Oh Charlie, it was awful," her voice smothered against his shoulder.

He stroked her hair. "Self defence," he murmured.

She stiffened. "What do you mean?"

"You can plead self defence. Don't you see - it's the only way to get through this and come out clean."

She pushed herself away from him. "The only way for

who to come out clean? Who is it we're talking about here Charlie?"

Amazing how quickly her soft features hardened.

"Both of us. I'm talking about both of us."

"I hope so Charlie. I hear they don't treat ex-cops so well in prison."

A beat of silence.

"Are you threatening me?"

"Threatening you? Don't be stupid. We're in this together, aren't we? You stole the diamonds and killed your friend while he was lying in hospital, and all because you wanted to be with me. All that stood between us being together was Frank. Now I've taken care of that obstacle."

"Obstacle? Jesus Christ, Stella, have a heart - the guy was your husband."

"You're telling me to have a heart? What about the dark, empty chasm where Frank's heart should have been? You know what he was like. You were going to kill him yourself, so don't you dare berate me for having the strength to do it. All I'm saying is that neither one of us wants to go to prison."

"No, what you're saying is that if I don't help you cover up Frank's death, you're going to tell tales. It definitely sounds like you're threatening me, Stella. And guess what? I don't like to be threatened."

She came right back at him.

"Ha! That's rich coming from you. Two minutes ago you were trying to persuade me to throw myself on the mercy of the judicial system. You weren't trying to get me out of the way so that you could save your own skin by any chance? Maybe pack a diamond or two, and skip out on me. No? Don't tell me you were going to hang around and hold my hand in court? What's wrong, Charlie - can't take the truth?"

Direct hit.

Her eyes were steely, her chin thrust forward, all traces

of vulnerability shed as easily as a winter coat on a warm May morning.

"You know, I'm starting to feel sorry for Frank," Boyle said.

Stella opened her mouth to retaliate but was interrupted by a gargling moan. They looked down at Frank, both of them wide-eyed and open-mouthed.

"Jesus Christ, he's still alive," Boyle said. "I thought you said he was dead? Is that why you stopped me checking?"

Stella shook her head, looking genuinely bewildered. "No, I just assumed. I mean, he's got a knife through his throat and there's all that blood. A normal person would be dead, don't you think?"

Boyle knelt down beside Frank and rolled him over.

"Phone an ambulance," he said.

He bent down close to Frank's ear. "Frank, can you hear me?"

Frank's eyes remained closed but he did the gargling moan thing again. It was a hideous guttural sound. Boyle wanted to pull the knife from Frank's throat but if he did, there was a good chance he'd end up inflicting even more damage.

He looked around for Stella. She was leaning over a worktop, hand reaching towards the phone. But she didn't pick up the phone. Instead she picked up the stack of brightly coloured tea-towels and brought them over to Boyle.

"What are you messing around with those for? Get the phone."

She knelt down on the other side of Frank without answering him, satin dressing gown trailing in the sticky blood puddle.

"Stella, what are you doing?"

She spread the tea-towels over Frank's face.

"You can't be serious? No Stella, you can't do that."

Boyle's arms hung weakly at his side, backs of his

fingers resting on the cool tile floor. He shook his head as Stella pressed the layers of brightly coloured cloth down over her husband's nose and mouth, but he didn't make any move to stop her.

The truth was, if Frank lived they'd both end up in prison for a long time. Stella knew it, and he knew it too. Breathing or not, Frank was a dead man.

The dead man made a small, insignificant sound and Boyle felt himself drowning in the quicksand as Stella pressed down harder, the effort made clear on her face. Animals. They were animals. Not evolving. De-evolving. Slowly sinking back into the mud they'd dragged themselves out of all those millennia ago.

"Don't you see?" Speaking through clenched teeth as she squeezed the life out of her husband. "There isn't any other way Charlie. If he lives there's no get out of jail free card for either of us - it's him or us. Simple as that."

Even though he recognised the truth in her words, Boyle did not like hearing them spoken aloud.

Frank's body twitched, but he was mostly dead already and didn't put up much of a struggle. When it was over, Stella sat back against the island unit. There was a smear of blood on her face where she'd pushed back her hair.

"Well I'd say that's him definitely dead now."

"I'd say so." Boyle's voice was barely a whisper.

His gaze drifted from Stella to Frank. The tea towels lay crumpled on the floor beside Frank's head. They created an incongruous riot of colour beside the dead man's pale face. Fuchsia, sunshine yellow, aquamarine. And then there was the blood. Still very red in the middle, but drying to maroon on the edges. A Crayola box of visual noise.

"What's that smell?" Stella screwed up her face.

"It's Frank," Boyle said. "His bowels have opened. Happens when people die."

"Really? How awful."

Stella stood up, bitter chocolate swirling around her

legs as she swished by him and went to the other side of the kitchen. Boyle didn't know whether she was referring to the smell or the indignity of the situation. Perhaps both.

"I could murder a cigarette," she said. "Ha, murder, that's a funny one."

She said it without a hint of a smile. Boyle wasn't laughing either. He felt like something had shrivelled up inside him and died.

She rummaged in a drawer before producing a pack of cigarettes and the small silver lighter she'd used the other day.

The other day.

The other day Frank had been a fully functioning, self-promoting, Grade A, arsehole, with no idea that before the week was out he'd be on a one-way ticket to Deadsville.

The other day Macallister had been large-as-life and twice as loud, preening his ridiculous moustache.

The other day Boyle had been anticipating all his tomorrows with the woman he was crazy-mad in love with. The same woman who was standing in front of him now, smeared in the drying blood of her murdered husband, his still-warm corpse at her slippered feet.

Boyle got up and asked her for a cigarette. He didn't know what difference it made now whether he smoked or whether he didn't. His perspective had shifted since the guilty cigarette of the other day. He had much bigger things to feel bad about now. The other day was through the looking glass.

Stella sparked the lighter, held the flame out for Boyle.

"Didn't know you smoked," she said.

He sucked on the filter tip, noting that her hand was steady. She was super cool. Liquid nitrogen, baby. She lit her own cigarette and they stood quietly for a moment, blowing lungfuls of blue smoke at the kitchen ceiling.

He didn't know how it rated as a smoke for Stella. She

certainly looked as though she was enjoying it. For Boyle it was a satisfactory, almost sublime, smoking experience with no hint of light-headedness or nausea. Just a smooth nicotine hit. Couldn't figure why he'd ever given up.

"It's funny, you know?" Stella blew out a puff of smoke.

"What is?"

"Looks like one way or another Frank was going to get stabbed tonight."

Boyle flicked his ash into the small dish Stella had placed on the worktop.

"Hysterical," he said.

"No, really. Think about it. It was in the stars. He goes out not knowing that you are planning to stab him, comes home unstabbed and ends up stabbed anyway. It's ironic."

"If you say so."

Boyle was used to cops using black humour as a coping mechanism. He'd done it often enough himself - the worse the situation, the darker the humour - but coming from Stella it didn't sound like a coping mechanism. It sounded scary.

He looked at her sideways. She was standing motionless, like a mannequin, cigarette poised at her mouth, one eyebrow raised as if in amusement at the hilarious irony of the situation.

She'd been distraught when he'd arrived, but now she was in total control. She seemed capable of anything. Boyle made a mental note not to turn his back on her.

She might find the target irresistible, not to mention hilariously ironic.

Chapter 21

Boyle tugged on Stella's Marigolds. They were size small. His knuckles bulged through the yellow rubber, threatening to split it open. He wished he'd kept the nitrile gloves from earlier. But then if he had wishes at his disposal, he wouldn't be wasting them on disposable gloves.

He couldn't picture Stella cleaning out the oven or scrubbing a toilet, but judging by the sheer gleamingness of the house he guessed that's pretty much how she spent her days. Trying to keep up with Frank's impossibly high standards. Unless they had domestic help? That would be all they needed - some cleaner turning up with her nose twitching. He'd have to check that out with Stella.

He'd sent her off to get dressed, with strict instructions to bag the bloodied clothing she was wearing. She'd expected him to take charge, and so he had. Big tough Boyle, issuing orders, taking control of the situation as if disposing of corpses came naturally to him.

Maybe it did. He was plumbing new depths lately. Finding out all sorts about himself. Who knew what skills and talents lay untapped in the darkest corners of his psyche? Might be he had a predisposition for this sort of thing.

Maybe he'd been kidding himself all those years ago when he'd made a conscious decision to take a different path to the one Macallister had chosen.

They'd been kids at a crossroads and it could have gone either way for either one of them. Macallister made his choice. Took the easy route into a life of petty crime. Boyle had veered off, choosing a different road for himself. Moving away from his old stomping ground had been part of that decision. Starting afresh, reinventing himself.

Seemed he'd done a good job of it, but look at him now - wrapping up a dead body for disposal. Not any old dead body either. This body was a murder victim who happened to be a senior police officer. Who also happened to have been murdered by his wife. Who happened to be Boyle's lover. What was that expression about tangled webs and practicing to deceive?

Boyle had tried to do the right thing, but it seemed that no matter how you moulded it, it was still the same old clay you were working with. One bad decision led to another and another, and, before you knew it, his true form had emerged once more. He'd made a mess of being one of the good guys. Seemed like he was one of the bad guys after all. Well, if he was going to be a bad guy, he was going to make sure he was bloody well good at being bad. He pushed the fingers of the rubber gloves down tight, flexed his hands and got to work.

He unrolled the bin liners Stella had given him. They were heavy duty, not like the cheap crap he bought, which, given what he was going to use them for, was just as well. The last thing he needed was bits of body bursting through cheap plastic.

He counted three and ripped them from the roll. He laid them in a long thin rectangle on the floor beside Frank. He repeated the process until he had a rectangle measuring three bin liners deep by four wide. He taped them together using brown parcel tape. Hindered as he was by the Marigolds, Boyle had to use a knife to peel the start of the tape from the roll. Progress was slow but by the time Stella returned to the kitchen he was done.

She was dressed in jeans and a plain, light blue crewneck sweater. She dropped the bin bag containing her soiled clothes on the floor.

Boyle had never seen her in jeans before, or in anything so casual. She'd pulled her hair back from her face with an Alice band. The blood smear had been washed away and she had taken the time to apply a little light make-up. The natural look.

Despite the fine lines around her eyes, she looked incredibly young. Verging on fresh-faced and innocent. She looked like the opposite of a murderer, if there could be such a thing. But when she glanced down at Frank's body she could have been looking at a broken biscuit for all the emotion she showed.

"Give me a hand," Boyle said.

He grabbed a hold of Frank under the shoulders. Wincing at the smell, Stella took him by the ankles. Together they heaved him onto the bin liners. They didn't have to lift him high and they didn't have to move him far, but the strain of shifting the dead weight was evident on Stella's face. Boyle felt it too - Frank was no lightweight and disposing of his body was going to be no easy task.

"Have you got a cleaner?" Boyle asked. Stella stared at him blankly.

"You know, a woman who comes in."

"Oh, I see," she replied. "As a matter of fact, yes. You're looking at her."

"I'm serious."

"So am I. Frank had a thing for cleanliness, or didn't you notice? It's right up there beside godliness after all, and Frank was the god of all he surveyed. Not that it's done him much good."

She gave an edgy little laugh that made Boyle uncomfortable. Made him think that, steady hands or not, she wasn't as super-cool as she was making out. She was rattled. Fraying at the edges. Wouldn't do either of them any good if she came apart.

"Cut it out Stella. I just want to know if anyone is likely to turn up tomorrow."

"Turn up here? No, I don't think so. With the exception of our assignations, I lead a life of splendid isolation. Frank saw to that. He cut me off from everyone I ever knew. Didn't you Frank?" She looked down at the body. "Now why did you do that Frank?"

"Come on Stella," Boyle took her by the arm and turned her away from Frank's body. "We've got work to do."

Stella produced an extra pair of Marigolds from somewhere and slipped them onto her hands. They worked in silence. Boyle wrapping and taping Frank's body up in the bin liners, Stella cleaning the blood away.

When the floor was gleaming and Stella said she'd finished, Boyle told her to go over it all again. Not just the floor - the units, the barstools - anything that Frank's blood might have come into contact with.

He told her to wash the knife she'd stabbed him with, then put it through a cycle in the dishwasher. Wash everything, and then wash it again.

Stella opened the dishwasher. There were a few pieces of crockery and some cutlery already loaded. She placed the knife flat on the lower basket, set the programme for a heavy wash and switched it on.

When she'd done that he asked her if she had any red meat. She looked at him askance but said yes, she'd been to Frank's favourite butcher and stocked up for the weekend.

She rummaged in the fridge, a big fancy job with a built-in ice maker, and emerged with a joint of silverside.

It was to have been Frank's Sunday dinner. Boyle told her to unwrap it and drop it, packaging and all, on the floor where she'd just cleaned.

"Are you crazy?"

"Just do it."

She shrugged, unwrapped the meat and dropped it on the floor. It landed with a splat, little globules of blood skittering across the floor.

"Happy now?"

"Pick it up and do it again."

She did what she was told.

"Okay, put the meat in the bin and clean up the mess."

"What-"

Boyle looked up from wrapping Frank.

"Listen Stella - I don't know how closely they're going to look at you, but the chances are it's going to be very close. Microscopically close. At you, and at the house. And if they find one little dot of Frank's blood anywhere, they are going to ask questions. Awkward questions. Detailed questions. And they'll ask them over and over again until they are satisfied they've got the truth. If they look and if they find a trace of blood, you'll be able to truthfully say that you dropped the beef - that it's blood from the beef they've found, not Frank's blood. And if they test it and find that you've been telling the truth, it might, just might, be enough to put them off looking any closer. All we're doing is muddying the waters."

"Smoke and mirrors," she whispered.

"That's right Stella, smoke and mirrors."

Boyle got back to taping Frank up nice and tight, while Stella cleared up again. He didn't know if his idea with the beef blood would work or not but at the very least it was keeping Stella occupied.

When they'd finished, they stood back and surveyed their work. The kitchen looked spotless. The ad hoc ashtray had been disappeared along with the blood. The kitchen roll and cloths Stella had used were in the bag along with her stained clothes. If it wasn't for the body-shaped parcel lying on the gleaming floor you wouldn't know anything was amiss.

"You got any sleeping pills?" Boyle asked.

"How did you know?"

"A lucky guess. Take them often?"

"Only when I get one of my headaches."

"Well you've got one of your headaches tonight."

"I do?"

"Yeah. It came over you just after Frank went out -"

"So I took a tablet and went to bed. Clever boy. I see where this is going. I was in bed fast asleep and I didn't hear Frank come home."

"You're a quick study Stella. Sure you haven't done this kind of thing before?"

"No, but I've thought about it often enough."

The sweetness of her smile gave Boyle the chills. He was beginning to wonder how much of the story she'd spun him about the row she'd had with Frank was true. She'd given out that she'd stabbed him in the heat of the moment and he'd bought it wholesale. Maybe he'd bought it because he wanted it to be true, but the only thing he knew for sure was that Stella had wanted Frank dead, and that's exactly what she had got.

He tried smiling back at her, like this was situation normal, but the smile hesitated before dying on his lips. Her eyes, steely grey, bored into him, making him nervous. He didn't like it. He wasn't used to feeling nervous.

"Where were we? That's right - you didn't hear a thing. How are you in the morning after taking a pill?"

"It depends. Maybe a little groggy."

"Okay - so you wake up a little groggy, Frank's not there and you assume he's been a darling and let you sleep while he's toddled off to work."

"He is a darling, isn't he? What next?"

"I'm guessing that after a while they'll get to wondering

141

where he is, and if he isn't coming in, why he hasn't called? So, you'll get a call asking for him."

"And I'll say, why, he's at work."

"And they'll say, No, Mrs Valentine, the Superintendent didn't turn up for work today."

"But I don't understand…"

"That's right - you don't understand a thing, and that's just how you'll play it. You haven't seen Frank since he left to go for the meal the night before. You got one of your headaches, took a tablet-"

"-and went to sleep. And when I woke up he wasn't there and I naturally assumed that he had already left for work."

"Perfect. Stick with it. Don't embellish. Act worried, but don't overdo it."

"No I won't overdo it - after all, there's bound to be a logical explanation. Frank has a logical explanation for everything."

"That's right - but as the day goes on you get a little more worried, a little more anxious."

"Yes, I'm very worried now."

"And they're getting worried too. They'll send someone round to see you. They'll start reassuring you, telling you that they're doing everything they can to trace him. They'll be asking questions by now. So many questions that maybe you get another one of your headaches."

"Yes, I can see that perhaps I do. It comes on very suddenly, as they sometimes do, and I have to lie down in a dark room."

"That's right - you have to lie down, because you're worried now and very anxious and by this time they'll be getting worried too and asking you again if you can remember anything. But you can't - you can't remember a thing, because you were sleeping. All you were doing was sleeping. Think you can do it?"

"Yes."

"Good." He believed her. She was very convincing.

"What about you?"

"Don't worry about me. The less you know the better. You take one of your pills and get to bed."

"You mean you really want me to take one?"

"Absolutely. Number one, it means you'll get some sleep tonight, and number two, it means you'll be genuinely groggy when they phone in the morning."

"Yes, I see. It will be more convincing."

"Okay, let's get this show on the road."

"Charlie?" She touched him lightly on the arm. He turned towards her.

"You'll be okay," he said.

"Yes - I believe I will, but what about us? When will I see you again?"

"I don't know. Maybe not for a while. We'll have to play it safe - but don't worry - I'll be in the background."

"Can I at least call you?"

"If you get a chance, but make sure there aren't any ears flapping nearby if you do."

"I'll be careful… and Charlie?"

"Yeah?"

"Thank you."

She kissed him lightly on the lips. A barely-there kiss, just enough pressure to suggest a promise.

He watched, mesmerised, as she glided away with a slight sway of the hips. She stopped at the door, turning for just a second to look at him. Features smooth, completely unruffled, eyes glinting green, hint of a smile. Then the door clicked behind her and she was gone, leaving Boyle staring at the empty space she'd left behind.

A few seconds later the creak of a floorboard upstairs cut through the low hum of the dishwasher. Stella in her bedroom. Boyle opened the kitchen door and looked around the hall. There was a light on upstairs. She was up there, in the light. Staring up, thinking about her bathed in a warm glow, Boyle stepped into the hall. As if sensing his presence, the light clicked off leaving him in shadow. Her in the light, him in the dark. The delicate tread of footsteps. A door closing quietly. Shutting her in. Or him out.

Light from the kitchen fanned across the hall carpet. A semi-circular occasional table sat neatly against the wall near the front door. Boyle had clocked it when he'd visited Stella.

Mind firmly back on business, he went to it and felt inside the fancy bowl sitting on top of it. *Bingo.* Right first time. Some household keys and Frank's BMW key. Seemed like he knew Frank better than he knew himself. Frank was just the kind of guy who'd have a regular place to keep his keys. He'd drop them into the bowl every time he came home and pick them up on his way out. No lost keys for Frankie baby, not ever.

Boyle pocketed the keys and went back to the kitchen. He surveyed the room for a moment. Kitchen hardly seemed good enough a word for the gleaming catalogue picture of perfection on display here. Boyle wondered if it had given Frank satisfaction having a kitchen like this. If he'd taken pleasure from it. Then he told himself to stop fucking around and get on with the job. He opened the door leading to the utility room then grabbed Frank's wrapped-up body by the feet end and dragged it through. The plastic-wrapped body slid easily over the tiled floor.

Boyle left Frank lying in the utility room while he went back through to the kitchen. He picked up the bag containing Stella's stained nightwear, the tea towels she'd used to suffocate Frank and the cloths she'd used to clear up his blood. He tied up the bag and put it through beside Frank's body, then he went back into the kitchen to give it a final check over.

He stood in the middle of the room and closed his eyes for twenty seconds, then he opened them and looked around. The room was clean and well ordered. Every shiny surface shone. Nothing seemed out of place.

No stains, no spatters, no bad smells and no give-away chalk outline on the floor where Frank's body had been.

He switched off the lights and gave his eyes a few moments to adjust to the dark before he went through to the utility room and opened the back door. A rush of cool night air drove out the chemical scent of cleaning products. Boyle breathed it in deeply then picked up the bag of soiled material. He walked along the paved path at the side of the house to the gravel drive at the front. He cringed as the crunch of the gravel roared into the night, but he did not hesitate. He had to work quickly and boldly and absolutely as if he was going about his legitimate business. Look guilty and people will assume you are.

There was a soft thunk accompanied by a brief flash of orange as Boyle remotely unlocked Frank's car. He opened the front passenger door and placed the bag in the foot-well. He stiffened at the sound of a vehicle coming along the road. Breathed out as the taxi carried on by the end of the drive. He closed the door, gently as he could, wishing that the familiar *thunk* of a car door closing wasn't quite so distinctive or carried quite so well. Tough. He'd have to take his chances.

He walked to the back of the car and opened the boot. It was empty and the interior light showed it to be spotlessly clean. Leaving it open, he went back to the utility room. The entire night had been abundant with undertakings Boyle had no desire to undertake, but of them all, this next task was the one he had the least stomach for.

Working in the dark, he grabbed a hold of Frank's wrapped body. He attempted to manoeuvre it into an upright position against the inner door, intent on carrying it over his shoulder. Just as he had it in position, Frank's plastic bound feet slipped from under him and his body slumped to the floor.

Several times he slumped and several times Boyle

hauled him up again, sweat prickling at his brow, in his armpits, down his back. His hands were hot and slithery inside the gloves, but once more he gritted his teeth and hauled Frank up. Using his head and shoulder to jam Frank's body against the door, he worked his way down until the body sagged over his shoulder. Grabbing hold of Frank's upper legs, Boyle finally managed to raise him in a gruesome approximation of a fireman's lift. *Gotcha.*

Boyle staggered towards the open back door and Frank almost slid right off him. Boyle muttered and cursed. Frank was turning out to be a bigger pain dead than alive. He readjusted Frank's dead weight, nearly losing him again. It would have been comical if it wasn't so fucking tragic.

Clutching grimly onto his burden, Boyle precariously made his way out of the door and teetered around the side of the house to the car. He stumbled against the rear bumper and let Frank's body slide into the boot. Well, not so much slide in as hang half out.

He pushed, shoved, hauled and bent the plastic-wrapped body until he was slathered in sweat and Frank was jammed in. By the time this was over he'd be stinking worse than Banjo McLafferty.

He closed the boot and had a quick shufty around to see if he'd been clocked. Not that it made any difference. If he had been spotted it would be tough bloody shit. The load he had just stuffed into the car looked exactly like a dead body wrapped in black plastic. He doubted anyone would mistake it for a carpet. Especially not at suspicious o'clock in the morning. Best just get on with it then, Charlie boy.

He went and closed the back door of the house then got into the car. The rich scent of newness filled his nose, cloying at his throat. He turned the key in the ignition. The radio came on. It was tuned to Radio Ness so that Frank could keep abreast of local news bulletins. Boyle looked for the off switch, hesitated. They were playing *Children of the Revolution* - an old *T Rex* track. He hadn't listened to any music for a long time. He left the radio on.

He skirted around the city centre. Nightclubs were shutting down, clubbers spewing onto the streets. It was Thursday night. Okay, Friday morning if you wanted to be pedantic about it. Point was, didn't they have fucking jobs to get up for? Good in a way. The Beamer was less conspicuous than it would have been on empty streets.

He stopped at a red, indicating left to cross the river on the Castle Bridge. Marc Bolan's voice gave way to a disc jockey babbling shite. He made to turn the radio off but the disc jockey suddenly shut up and a single chord floated magically from the car speakers. Boyle shivered as Bowie sang the first line of *Life On Mars*.

A dark blue Mondeo taxi came from the opposite side of the junction and hauled a right onto the bridge. Boyle didn't notice. Bowie had built up to the storming chorus.

Boyle was in another place, another time.

Chapter 22

Jenny's skin prickled as Bowie's unmistakable voice sang out from the taxi radio. It was *Life On Mars*. One of her father's favourites. He used to play *Hunky Dory* in the car when they went anywhere together. That and one or two other favoured albums had been the soundtrack of her childhood.

She gazed at the lights reflecting on the black water of the River Ness as the taxi trundled over the bridge. There had been a brief exchange of small talk when she'd got in, but with a distinct lack of effort on her part it has soon spluttered out. The driver took no offence. Talk, don't talk, it was all the same to him. He'd merely shrugged and turned up the late night oldies show on the radio and she'd been happy to be left alone with her thoughts.

It was spooky. Years of no contact and tonight her father's presence was all around her. His music. His face. It had definitely been him she'd seen earlier.

He'd looked strange though, and that was apart from the shocked look he'd had on his face when he'd been staring at her. He'd looked different somehow, as if he'd been taken apart and not put back together properly. She could relate to that, except she'd never been put together right in the first place. She'd always felt out of time, out of place.

She'd been pretending to herself all night that it hadn't really been him whilst knowing all along that she was kidding herself. Seeing him had given her a bit of a shake but if her friends had noticed there was something wrong they hadn't said anything. Why would they? They'd just take it is another example of her general weirdness. Like the fact that she hadn't been charmed the way they so obviously had been by that guy tonight. He'd been cocky, full of himself. Coming out with the worst chat-up lines, flashing the cash, offering to buy them drinks. What had his moody friend called him - Bracko? Something like that. Gaby and Caitlin had giggled at his jokes like a pair of twelve year olds. It was embarrassing. And what kind of name was Bracko anyway?

She never got it when they giggled like that. And she could never take these guys seriously. The only reason this Bracko had been interested in her was because of the way she looked. She knew men thought she was pretty, but she didn't really get that either. They didn't care about what she was really like.

Gaby and Caitlin told her not to think about everything so much. To lighten up. They didn't get her either. Sometimes she wondered why they were even friends. Habit she supposed. Going to the same primary, then secondary schools. Years of playtimes and lunch breaks. Being friends with each other because they always had been. Like it was written in the rules.

But they had been there for her when her father left. Caitlin was an old hand when it came to divorced parents. Hers had split up when she was six. They'd both remarried soon after and both couples had been almost frantic in their efforts to keep Caitlin happy and Caitlin had worked the situation to her best advantage. First had come the sweets, then the make-up, the clothes, the phones. Whatever her heart desired.

There was no such Aladdin's Cave of guilt-trip presents for Jenny. It was just her and an increasingly bitter and brittle mum. His leaving them changed everything. The first year was the worst. The change in her mum was terrible and she hated her father for that. She wanted to ask him why he'd done it. Why they weren't enough for him. But as she'd refused to speak to him, she couldn't ask.

It wasn't just that she wanted to punish him by not speaking to him. It was also because she was scared that she still loved him too much, that she wouldn't be able to hate him the way she needed to hate him. Loving him would be like betraying her mother.

Gradually, things had improved. Her mum became less angry, her father less hated. He became this shadowy figure they never saw or spoke about. He was no more to them than a monthly deposit in the bank account.

Lately, her mum had been seeing someone. Another cop, would you believe? Jenny wasn't too keen on him. She'd caught him staring at her a couple of times with those pale blue eyes. Her mother thought his eyes were amazing. Jenny found them a teensy bit creepy. Okay, if she was being honest, you could take out the teensy bit. She thought he was creepy, *but*, and it was a big *but*, for the first time in years her mum seemed genuinely happy. The brittleness had gone. She seemed lighter, had a glow about her. It didn't matter if Jenny thought he was a creep because she'd be gone by Sunday, and there was the rub. If she had been staying would she have told her mother the truth?

She'd asked, all excited and girly, *what do you think of him?* And Jenny had replied, *as long as he makes you happy, mum, nothing else matters.* Her mother either didn't notice, or chose not to notice, her evasiveness.

The thing was, knowing that her mum had someone, that she wouldn't be lonely, was part of it too. Besides, her mum was a grown woman who made her own decisions. Jenny could leave with a clear conscience. An almost clear conscience. Maybe she should say something after all. Tell her mother her boyfriend was a creep and then leave her high and dry. Nice leaving present. Not for the first time, she wished she could be as sweetly air-headed as Gaby. And as honest too.

Truth was, Jenny lied all the time. She lied to her mother, her friends, and most of all, to herself. She lied about what she thought of creepy Danny and his pale blue eyes. She lied about her feelings for her father. She lied about not caring that she didn't get things the way Gaby and Caitlin did.

She wanted to get it, wanted to belong. She even lied about the way she'd felt about the Bracko character chatting her up. In fact, deep down she'd been flattered. A fact she'd rather shave her hair off than admit to. She'd been pleased that she had been the one he'd lavished his attention on. So why couldn't she just enjoy it, the way her friends did? Treat it as a bit of light entertainment. Why did she have to keep herself so wrapped up tight?

He was a bit of a wide boy. Full of patter, but his eyes had been sharp. Seemed to catch a glimmer of something inside her. Persisted in giving her his number, insisted on getting hers in return. Caitlin had supplied it, but Jenny hadn't stopped her. Maybe she was lightening up after all.

It would be different when she went to Glasgow. She would be starting over, would be free to reinvent herself. She resolved to leave her emotional baggage behind. She was going to work hard and she was going to enjoy herself. But why wait till she got to Glasgow? If wide-boy Bracko wanted to treat her to cocktails before she went, well, why the hell not? Although if he was going to phone, he'd better do it soon. It would be worth making a date with him just to see the looks on Gaby and

Caitlin's faces.

The taxi driver slowed down and killed the radio.

"This okay for you love?"

"Fine thanks," she said.

She paid the driver, giving him a generous tip for leaving her in peace. Walking up the path to the front door, she allowed herself a smile. Inverness or Glasgow, everything would be fine, just fine.

Chapter 23

Boyle switched the radio off. The music was making him think about things he didn't want to think about. It was reminding him about the man he used to be. Father, husband, all round good guy. He'd been indisputably one of the good guys. It made him think about his daughter who was now a stranger to him, and about his wife - ex-wife - who was fucking that pale-eyed prick, Danny King.

Karen was a good looking woman. She wasn't going to spend the rest of her life preserved in aspic. He got that she was bound to meet someone sooner or later. Boyle accepted that. He even wanted it for her. He'd ruined enough of her life without destroying the whole damned thing. But why did it have to be another cop? And if it had to be a cop - why that one?

It was a fucking cliché. Like rich, bored housewives and fit young tennis coaches, flabby old dads and luscious young nannies. Cops and A&E nurses. You'd think she'd have learned from last time, maybe found herself a doctor, or a male nurse, or even another cop. But not Danny fucking King.

Boyle tried telling himself that it wasn't his business, but he had a thing about cops like Danny King. The kind who went back after the shift had finished to knock on the door of an attractive mostly, but vulnerable always, victim or witness. Knowing she was on her own because her man was working on the rigs, or she was divorced or she'd recently split up with her boyfriend or had been beaten up by him.

Apologising for disturbing her, flashing a concerned smile, but he just wanted to check that she was okay.

Getting invited in for coffee. Maybe something stronger. Offering a shoulder to cry on. Building up to the sympathy shag.

He accepted that King had charm, the evidence was in the procession of women who fell for it time after time, but it was a charm that entirely eluded Boyle.

King wasn't the only one. There were plenty like him and Boyle despised them all. At least when he seduced a woman it was an honest seduction. Danny King was a fucking parasite but Karen's business wasn't his business. Not anymore. He had no right to interfere. A fact that didn't stop him wanting to smack that smug prick in the face and tell him to go peddle his charms someplace else. Preferably someplace nowhere near Karen or Jenny.

Boyle's knuckles whitened on the steering wheel at the thought of King being anywhere near Jenny, but if he was seeing Karen… He gritted his teeth and pulled his thoughts back to the business in hand.

The houses lining the road thinned, scattered, disappeared until Inverness was behind him and there was nothing but thick darkness all around. If he kept on this road he'd soon be driving alongside Loch Ness.

The loch was deep enough to lose Big Ben in twice over and then some, with the added advantage of peaty water, meaning limited underwater visibility. If it was vast enough to play home to a big bloody dinosaur, it could conceal a dead man without difficulty. Just weigh Frankie baby down with some rocks, row him out to the middle of the loch and plop him over the side. *See ya.*

Pity he didn't have a boat to hand. And it was no use trying to dump Frank from the loch side. It was a good ten feet offshore before the floor shelved away to the depths. As soon as dawn broke, anything dumped along the shoreline shallows would be spotted by the myriad of boats that steamed up and down every day.

Talking of dawn, it wouldn't be long coming. Time to ditch Frank and ditch him quick.

Boyle took a left and was soon driving up a steep, narrow road through remnants of the great Caledonian forest.

He followed the twisting road until he came to a clearing. It was a car park for the walkers, hikers and visitors who used the forest trails. He drove to the far end where a fence had been erected complete with a sign.

WARNING DANGEROUS CLIFF EDGE

The white lettering glowed in the car headlights. Boyle got out of the car, leaving the lights on and the engine running. He walked to the fence and peered over the edge. Nothing but darkness. There weren't any trails leading to where Frank was going.

He looked around, found a large stone, chucked it over the side and listened. A bit of rustling and rattling and then nothing. It could have plunged to the depths or landed on a heap of ferns ten feet below him. He couldn't see a bloody thing so he'd have to take a chance on his memory. Whatever else had happened in the intervening years, Boyle was pretty sure the ravine was still a ravine.

He hadn't been up here since Jenny was a kid. There hadn't been a fence then and they'd stood on the edge of the precipice, staring down into the chasm, fantasising about what could live way down there in that deep tangle of greenery. They'd started with fairies and goblins, then it was wolves and bears and dinosaurs. And now a dead man was going to join the mythical creatures and wild animals.

He got back in the car and reversed it up tight to the fence. He popped the boot and got out. He'd jammed Frank in good and tight and now he had to do a bit of tugging and hauling to get his legs out.

After another bout of huffing and puffing, he positioned the body so that its legs were sticking out of the boot with the feet resting on the fence. He had an idea that he could feed the body out until it see-sawed over the railing and tumbled down into the gulley. Except he'd parked too close to the fence and couldn't get in close enough to grab a good hold. He needed some leg room.

He got back in the car and inched it forward. Then he got back out and tried again. He squeezed into the small space between the car and the fence and manoeuvred Frank. It was easier to get a grip of him now, but it was still awkward as hell and Boyle's back was screaming in protest at the unnatural angle he was working at.

He stopped for a moment, wiping the sweat from his brow on the crook of his arm. He considered his situation then climbed into the boot and fed Frank out from there.

Easy, so easy. Out Frank went like toothpaste being slowly squeezed from a tube. *Minty fresh.* Boyle, squatting like a gargoyle, grinned. All he'd had to do was stop and think for a minute. And then Frank stopped doing what he was supposed to be doing.

His torso stopped pointing up towards the fence and started pointing down. *What the?* And then Boyle realised what had happened. Frank's plastic sheathed arse was drooping into the gulley between car and fence.

No, no, no. Boyle clambered out of the boot, squeezed into the space between car and fence and grabbed Frank's middle before he jack-knifed right into the gap. He heaved the body up, still trying to feed it over the fence.

156

In life, Frank had been lean and mean. In death he was a big galumphing weight and ten times meaner. Being awkward to spite Boyle. Boyle was starting to hate him again.

He heaved and hauled. Heard the black plastic snagging and ripping on the fence. Caught a whiff of shit. He didn't care. He was beyond caring about anything. And then suddenly the weight was gone. Frank was over the fence.

"*Yessss*," Boyle hissed.

Frank thudded onto the narrow strip of ground on the other side of the fence and stayed there. Boyle stared at him. *Oh for f-* Oh what was the point in fannying around? He clambered over the fence and used his feet to shove Frank towards the edge. Frank, dead and heavy, seemed reluctant to go. Finally, Boyle leant down and heaved him over.

Frank's body smashed through the undergrowth to a chorus of cracking and splintering. Boyle pictured him crashing, rolling, spinning, until he came to rest at the bottom of the ravine. And then Frank wasn't making any more noise. It was just the boom of Boyle's heart soon followed by the purr of Frank's car and the crunch of tyres on gravel.

He should have made sure Frank couldn't be seen from the car park. He should have checked the glove box for a torch and taken a look instead of haring out of there like he had a hound from hell on his tail. Guy like Frank was bound to have a torch in the glove box. Would be one of the first things he did when he got the car. Buy a torch. Put it in the glove box. Guy like Frank was always organised.

What if he'd become tangled in a tree half-way down, the branches holding him up, displaying him to the world? His face uncovered, the plastic ripped away by gorse and bramble. *He should have checked.*

157

He almost turned the car around. But he didn't even know if there was a torch in the glove box. And if there wasn't, he'd have to wait till daybreak to check on Frank's situation.

He didn't want to do that. He wanted to be long gone by dawn. If Frank was sitting on top of a big fuck-off bush for all the world to see there wasn't anything Boyle could do about it now. What was he going to do - climb down there and shake a branch? Don't be so fucking stupid. No, what was done was done. That was it. He'd dumped the body. *Finito*. End of. Time to move on to the next job. No looking back.

He was probably right at the bottom of the gulley anyway. No-one would be able to see him for the trees, and when the leaves fell in the next few weeks, they'd fall on Frank. Provide him with a shroud of red and gold. Insects, birds and small mammals would eat him and after the wildlife would come the snow, and with it, a shroud of white.

Frank was gone.

Now Boyle had to get rid of the bag then the car. Once he'd done that, he could take these bastarding gloves off. His hands had sweated off the flock lining. Felt like his fingers were turning to mush.

Inverness was asleep. The clubbers had gone home. Even the insomniacs tried to get some shut-eye at this hour.

Boyle pulled in at a row of low-rent shops and takeaways. They were closed for business, steel shutters clamped down, lights off. He opened up the big bin at the side of the Yum-yum Buddha Chinese takeaway and slung in the bag of bloodied clothes. It was now just one black bin bag amongst many. Then he drove to one of the city's less salubrious housing schemes. The kind they didn't show on the calendars with the highland cows, and castles and lochs.

The streets were lined with squat blocks of flats and mean looking houses with scratches of dirt out front instead of grass. Boyle drove to the skanky heart of the scheme and pulled into the kerbside. He killed the lights and engine, got out of the car and walked away, leaving the door open and the key dangling in the ignition. He peeled off the gloves as he walked, dropping them in the gutter beside an empty Buckfast bottle.

He wiped his hands dry on his hoodie and walked home.

Chapter 24

Friday

Boyle surprised himself by sleeping the sleep of an innocent man. Dream free, coma deep. He slept through the alarm. Didn't hear his phone. The black, velvet loveliness ended when he woke with a guilty start to pounding on the front door. Insistent, authoritative, unmistakably a policeman's knock.

He leapt out of bed, staggered through to the hall, still dizzy with sleep, wearing nothing but his underpants. Another tattoo on the door. Could almost see it billowing inwards, cartoon-style, under the assault.

They'd come to arrest him.

He looked around, trying to conjure up an escape route, but unless he was going to flush himself down the toilet or jump out of a second storey window, the door was it. One way in, one way out. Nowhere to run. Nowhere to hide. *Fuck.* This was it. If the game was up, it was up.

He opened the door before it was knocked in.

"You're alive then." Fuckerson strolled in without waiting to be asked, already giving the place the once over.

"Try not to sound so disappointed."

Boyle closed the door behind him. Relieved it had been Fuckerson on the other side of it. Surprised that he had so effectively mastered the copper's knock. He didn't look as though he had it in him.

He followed Fuckerson through to the living room. His gaze was crawling over the room. Taking in the blank walls, the scant furniture. The lack of anything indicating a life.

"Like what you've done with the place."

"Yeah, well, I like the pared-down look."

"Couldn't pare this place down any further. It takes minimalist to a new level."

"Farquharson, what are you doing here?"

"The boss is worried about you."

"Worried?"

"Thought you might have been kidnapped."

"Kidnapped? What are you talking about?"

"Superintendent Valentine has gone missing. His wife's in a right state and headquarters is in an uproar. The bosses are going mental. Then when you didn't turn up and you weren't answering your phone the Inspector got twitchy and sent me down to find you. I think he thought you might have been abducted. Don't know who would want to steal you. Why didn't you answer your phone anyway?"

"Didn't hear it."

"Oh." Fuckerson shrugged as if it didn't matter to him one way or the other. He wandered over to the window, fiddled with the blind and opened it. Dust motes sparkled in the influx of sunlight. Fuckerson peered through the slats.

"Handy for the town, I suppose. I'd better call him and let him know you're okay. Any chance of a coffee?"

"I'll get dressed first, if it's all the same to you."

"Be my guest."

Boyle went to the kitchen and put the kettle on. He could hear Fuckerson on the phone.

Yes sir, he's fine. Slept in is all. Yes, sir, I'm sure it is.

Boyle gave the washing machine a quick check. Nothing to be seen but dirty laundry.

I'll be sure and tell him. Yes. Yes. Back in ten. No problem. Okay, sir.

Boyle went to the bedroom. The clothes he'd been wearing the night before were balled up in the corner of the room. Little traces of Frank woven through the fabric. He'd have to get rid of them later. All he did these days was get rid of things.

He reappeared showered, shaved and wearing his suit. The shirt could do with being ironed, but it was more or less clean, which was more than could be said for every other item of clothing he owned.

Fuckerson wolf-whistled. He'd made himself comfy on the sofa and was flicking through the tv channels.

"Who's a pretty boy then?"

"Are you wanting a coffee or not?" Boyle growled.

Realising for once that he'd crossed the invisible line, Fuckerson sat up straight and blinked rapidly. "Yes please," he said meekly.

Boyle rattled about in the kitchen and emerged gripping two mugs in one hand and a plate piled high with buttered toast in the other.

"No milk. It'll have to be black." He clanked the mugs and the plate onto the coffee table.

"No problemo," Fuckerson replied. "Just the way I like it."

There being no place else to sit, bar the floor, Boyle told Fuckerson to nudge up and sat on the sofa beside him. It was a two-seater. Very cosy. The Jeremy Kyle show was on the telly. A veritable cavalcade of misfits, cranks and freaks on display without the hassle of a Sunday afternoon visit to Bedlam.

Fuckerson slurped his coffee and chewed his toast with his mouth open. Boyle scowled at him.

"Did your mother never tell you to eat with your mouth closed?"

Fuckerson swallowed the mush in his mouth and gave a crumby grin.

"Sorry. Good toast."

"Thanks."

They drank their coffee and munched their way through the rest of the toast, making occasional derogatory remarks about the guests on the show and one or two about Jeremy Kyle. It was a pleasant way to pass the time. Despite his whole getting down with the kids demeanour, Boyle was starting to think Fuckerson wasn't such a bad lad after all.

The mood broke when Fuckerson's phone rang. He checked the display and looked at Boyle like someone had just licked the jam out of his doughnut.

"It's the boss."

"Answer it."

Fuckerson was like a little kid who had to be told what to do all the time. He answered the phone.

Yes. We're on our way right now, sir. Be there in a few minutes. Yes. Yes. Okay. Right. Bye.

Boyle sat his empty mug on the table. "Suppose we'd better make a move."

"Suppose." Fuckerson agreed, looking gloomy.

"We'll just wait for the results of the DNA test."

"Okay." Fuckerson's face brightened.

They settled back, watching to find out which of the three fuckwits on parade had fathered the kid of the bucket-faced woman on the show.

They drove to HQ in the pool car Fuckerson had signed out.

"So what's the story on Valentine?" Boyle asked, like it was the last thing on his mind.

"He didn't show up for a meeting this morning. Didn't answer his mobile and when they called his home his wife said he was at work. Turns out she hadn't seen him since last night, so now nobody knows where he is. Disappeared. Vanished. Just like that. Mental, eh?"

Boyle gave a non-committal grunt.

"There have been no accidents reported and he's not turned up at any hospitals and that's all anyone knows."

Boyle stared out of the windscreen. People milling about in t-shirts, tattoos on display, muffin tops pouring over waistbands. Another bright September day. Sun blazing in the sky like it had been drawn there by a kid. Even the deepest, darkest gulleys would catch the light on a day like this. Sunbeams bursting through the trees, solid gold beams, like in an old style religious painting. God shining a light on the sins of the world.

The walkers would be out in force. Poking about. Looking at things. Wondering just what it was they were seeing lying way down there. Thinking maybe they should take a closer look or report it to the authorities.

Boyle thinking he should have taken a bit more time and care. Found himself a boat and dumped Frank in Loch Ness where nobody was ever going to find him. Frank Valentine sleeps with the fishes. At the very least he should have acquired a shovel and buried him properly instead of just pushing him into the ravine.

What had he been thinking, dumping Frank in such a public place? He'd have been as well leaving him in the middle of Tesco's car park. He slithered a glance at Fuckerson. He was watching the traffic lights, face blank, mouth hanging slightly open. Guy didn't have a clue. No-one had a clue. No-one, apart from Stella.

He wondered how she was holding up and then wondered why he was wondering. There was more chance of him cracking than her. He had to stay cool. No panicking. No paranoia. He was an officer of the law.

Nobody was going to suspect him - not unless he gave them reason.

Chapter 25

He'd barely stepped through the door when he was
hauled into Saunders' office.

"Close the door Sergeant."

Sergeant. Not Charlie. So that's the way it was. Kick
up the arse time. Not that he was surprised. The only
surprising thing about it was that it had taken so long.

Boyle closed the door and stood, waiting obediently
for further instruction while Saunders pretended to be
extremely busy pressing keys on his laptop.

Office was a grand word for a cramped room
overlooking the bins in the quadrangle. A desk, two
chairs, a filing cabinet and a coat stand looked less like
furnishings and more like they'd been dumped in there
for temporary storage. Still, Saunders had made the most
of it, putting more effort into his poxy wee office than
Boyle had put into his flat.

A cluster of framed family photographs sat proudly on
the ugly, utilitarian desk. Frizzy hair aside, Saunders' wife
wasn't bad looking in a whole-food, hand-knitted kind of
way. Three kids beamed gap-toothed smiles beside a big
lanky dog. Domestic bliss ruled.

There was a potted plant in the corner by the window.

Sitting on the floor beside it were a mini watering can made of blue plastic and a bottle of plant feed. A poster in a black plastic frame hung on the wall. A giant photograph of footsteps in the sand bore the legend -

The longest of journeys
Begins with a single step

It made Boyle feel like stabbing himself in the eye.

Finally, having established who was boss, Saunders looked up.

"Sit down, Sergeant."

Boyle sat. Saunders leaned back in his chair, put on his serious face and tented his fingers. He gave Boyle an appraising look. Boyle tried to look as though he gave a shit.

"You've been a great disappointment to me, Sergeant Boyle. I thought we would get the best out of you here in Community Involvement, but I'm afraid you've not been a team player. You've regularly turned up late, though today was a record even by your standards. On several occasions your appearance has been unkempt, bordering on slovenly and your attitude towards your colleagues has often been brusque, tending towards rude. In fact, you have displayed what can only be described as a bad attitude. Now what do you have to say for yourself?"

Boyle wondered how long Saunders had been practicing his little speech. Maybe he had it written on the laptop screen in front of him. Hauling a sergeant over the coals would be a big deal for Saunders. Didn't fit well with his chummy persona.

Given that it was such a big deal for the Inspector, Boyle tried to concentrate on what he was saying, but the song he'd heard on the radio last night was echoing down the years. He listened to it playing in his head. Bowie's lyric was a lot more interesting than anything Saunders had to say.

"Sorry Inspector. I'll try harder."

Bowie's voice soaring in his head.

"Hmmm. I see you've made an effort with your appearance today. I'm not a harsh man, Charlie…"

Back on first name terms. Cute.

"… I run a happy team. I like to think of myself as being firm - but fair. You understand?"

"Yes, sir."

Feeling like he was about to break into the chorus of *Life on Mars*.

"I appreciate you have had to go through a period of readjustment and, on the plus side…" Saunders glanced at his laptop screen, "I see you gave a good account of yourself on the Anger Management Course. That suggests to me that you are keen to make amends for past misdemeanours."

"Yes, sir."

Thinking it was a long time since he'd listened to music.

"All in all, I'm prepared to give you a second chance."

"Thank you, sir."

Too long.

"Don't thank me yet. In return, I expect you to be appropriately attired, punctual and punctilious. At all times, Boyle. At. All. Times. You understand?"

"Yes, sir. Thank you, sir."

Boyle stood up. He should do something about the music situation.

"Sit down, Sergeant. I'm not finished with you yet."

Boyle sat.

"I assume you are aware of the situation regarding Superintendent Valentine?"

The soundtrack in his head came to a sudden halt. Deep inside Boyle, something fluttered.

"Constable Fu-, er, Farquharson apprised me of the situation, sir."

Saunders had his attention now. Sitting up straight he was listening hard, like his life depended on it. Maybe it did.

"Yes, quite extraordinary. To all intents and purposes the Superintendent seems to have vanished from the face of the earth. I believe his wife is quite distraught."

"Understandable, sir."

No need to panic. Sounded like Stella was doing sterling work.

"Yes," Saunders glanced at the photograph of his own wife, "very understandable. Needless to say, we are doing all we can to reassure Mrs Valentine and to locate the Superintendent. I know you have had, er, difficulties with the Superintendent in the past, but we must put all that behind us now. We are all on the same team. We must stay positive, Charlie."

"Yes, sir."

"I'm sure our little chat has been of some benefit?"

"Yes, sir. Absolutely."

"Good. I'm glad we've cleared the air. SCD are short-handed - you will be seconded there to assist with the investigation into the Superintendent's disappearance. This is an ideal opportunity for you to prove yourself, Charlie. I look forward to receiving good reports about your performance when you return to Community Involvement."

No shit.

"Yes, sir."

Boyle kept the grin off his face until he'd left Saunders' office. Well, well, well. You just never knew how things were going to pan out. Out of Community Involvement and back into SCD where he'd be able to keep tabs on how it was going with Stella. And if things got too hot with the investigation into Frank's disappearance, he'd be around to cool them down. Couldn't be better. And Stella had said there were no Get Out of Jail Free cards.

Another office. Another Inspector. Another wee chat. This time from DI Ronson who really didn't give a fuck about being anyone's pal. Least of all Boyle's.

"Extreme circumstances require extreme measures, Boyle, otherwise there's not a chance in hell you'd be on my team. Get my drift?"

"Yes, sir."

Ronson, his mouth set in the grim line it rarely deviated from, gave Boyle a hard stare, seeking any nuance of sarcasm in the two syllables Boyle had uttered. Finding none, but still suspicious that there might have been *something* there, he carried on.

"You are here to assist the investigation in any way I see fit. Is that understood, *Sergeant* Boyle?"

"Yes, sir."

Tone pitch perfect. Not a hint of attitude. Boyle wasn't about to complicate matters by tangling with Ronson.

"Inspector Saunders assures me that you do not harbour any residual feelings of resentment towards Superintendent Valentine. Is that the case, *Sergeant?*"

"Yes, sir. I mean, no, sir."

"Bollocks. I know exactly what you mean. I'm not convinced you're a reformed character, Boyle. Not convinced at all. I don't want you screwing up this investigation because you've got a big fat chip on your demoted shoulders. Understand?"

"Yes, sir."

"I'll be keeping an eye on you, Boyle."

"Yes, sir."

Chapter 26

Frank's front door swung open and Boyle wondered to what new circle of hell he'd descended.

"Hello Charlie. Don't stand there gawping - come on in."

Lindy Ross tilted her round face at Boyle and gave him a knowing smile.

This was all he needed. She didn't step back so Boyle had to brush by her great big tits to get into the house. Same old Lindy. Same old tricks. Lindy closed the door behind him. Boyle turned to face her.

Her physical attributes of huge knockers, big arse and tiny wee waist coupled with her filthy mouth and natural aptitude for drinking hadn't done much for her career but had earned Lindy legendary status. It had been a while since Boyle had last seen her, and it had to be said, she was looking a bit rough.

Her skin, never great to begin with, had coarsened along with her features and she'd put on a bit of beef. She was now wobbling on the nebulous line between bodaciously curvy and plain old fat.

"I thought you were up in Wick?" Boyle said.

"Nice to see you too."

"You haven't changed," he lied.

"You have. You look like shit."

"Gee thanks. You always say the sweetest things."

"The way I remember it, you were the one who specialised in sweet talk."

She turned away from him before he could answer and wiggled down the hall, black uniform trousers stretched screamingly tight across her big arse, waist still small in comparison but nowhere near as improbably tiny as it once was. He had a sudden flashback of Lindy naked on a rumpled bed, giggling as he nibbled his teeth along that very same waistline. Christ, as if life wasn't complicated enough.

He shook the image from his head, glanced around the hall. Everything looked normal. The semi-circular occasional table still sat neatly against the wall near the front door. The fancy bowl still sat on top of it. The only thing missing was Frank's car key.

Lindy turned to Boyle and inclined her head towards the living room door. It was closed.

"She in there?" Boyle asked, his voice low.

Lindy rolled her eyes and nodded. "Just my luck - I'm back five minutes and I get lumbered with babysitting her ladyship."

"How is she?"

"Mental. Totally strung out one minute, cool as you like the next. I can't figure her, although to be honest," Lindy leaned into Boyle, one of her breasts flattening against his arm, and lowered her voice even further, "I get the impression that if she broke a nail it would be a major catastrophe, and this is on the same level. Know what I mean? Every little thing is a drama, so it's hard to tell how upset she actually is over the Supers' disappearance."

"You think she knows something?"

Lindy screwed up her face and the thing deep inside Boyle fluttered again.

"Hard to say. I can't see her getting her hands dirty,

but there's something not right about her. Maybe she paid a hit man to get rid of the Super."

"That's a bit far-fetched."

Too close to the truth, more like it.

Lindy shrugged. "Probably, but something's not right."

She opened the door. Boyle wished the fluttering thing inside him would shrivel up and die but the sight of Stella only served to rouse it up even more.

She was standing by the window when they walked into the living room, looking into the garden. Boyle wondered if she'd seen him arrive, had time to prepare herself for his appearance. She didn't show any sign of surprise when she turned around to face them.

"Any news?" she asked, directing the question at Lindy.

"I'm afraid not, Mrs Valentine. This is Sergeant Boyle. He's here to help."

Stella gave Boyle a cool once-over.

"I'm sure we've met, haven't we?" Her brow lightly furrowed.

"Yes, we have," Boyle's cool tone matching hers. "On more than one occasion, in fact."

"Yes, so many functions to attend." This tossed as a casual aside to Lindy by way of explanation.

Looked to Boyle like Stella was holding it together pretty well. She tilted her head, a question forming on her soft, pink lips.

"I thought you were an inspector? In fact, your name has an altogether familiar ring to it. Weren't you the one who-?"

"Yes, I assaulted your husband. I'm sorry about that Mrs Valentine."

Stella was doing more than holding it together. She was having herself a bit of fun and Boyle had no choice but to go along with it. She had him squirming like a worm on a hook and they both knew it.

"That's right. You were demoted for your efforts, weren't you? And Frank was promoted. Ironic, don't you think?" She waved a hand before he was forced to answer. He didn't know if she was showing him some mercy or whether she had grown bored of the game.

"Now what are you going to do about finding my husband?"

No, the games weren't finished yet.

Lindy offered to make coffee while Boyle outlined the procedure. He used the professional, reassuring tone he had on reserve for occasions such as this. He spoke calmly and evenly until sounds of Lindy clattering in the kitchen reached them. Then he strode to the door and closed it before wheeling on Stella. She had curled up in a corner of the sofa, innocent as a kitten.

"Jesus, Stella," he hissed. "What's with all the games? Are you out of your mind?"

"Oh relax, why don't you?" She patted the cushion beside her, fingers feeling for her cigarettes. She'd been chain smoking since he'd arrived. She offered him the pack, eyebrows raised.

"I don't smoke," he said, pacing the floor.

"You did last night."

"Jesus, Stella," he repeated, glancing at the door.

"Calm down, Charlie. She can't hear us. You know her, don't you?"

"Used to work with her."

"I see."

"What do you mean, *I see*?"

"I don't mean anything by it. She's a little on the fat side isn't she?"

"Don't be a bitch. And quit messing around. Anyway, it was a long time ago."

He could hear himself babbling. Once again, Stella had unnerved him. It had taken her all of ten seconds to figure him and Lindy out. Maybe less. A woman that sharp could cut a guy deep. Made Boyle wonder again about what had really gone on between her and Frank.

She blew a thin stream of smoke at the ceiling.

"It's a little odd they sent you here, isn't it? Given the circumstances, it could even be considered insensitive."

"Cutbacks. Don't you read the papers? There's not enough police."

"So they were desperate and sent you?"

"Something like that."

"So, Sergeant Boyle, how am I doing? Do I play the part of the concerned wife well?"

"She suspects something's not right."

"Who, your fat friend? No, she just loathed me on sight. The feeling was mutual. Besides they've got nothing to go on, have they?"

"No. Nothing at all."

He watched her smoking. Lindy had said she couldn't figure her. That was fine. Trouble was, Boyle couldn't figure her either. That wasn't so fine. Seemed like Stella could turn it on and off at will. Made him wonder how much of an act she'd put on for him, playing the victim. *I think he might kill me. I really think he might do it...*

Boyle had always known that she wasn't as fragile as she seemed, that there was a thread of carbon steel running through her. The contradiction between her external vulnerability and her core of inner strength was one of the things that had fascinated him about her. But the more carbon steel she exposed, the more uneasy he felt. All the bad, crazy, stupid things he'd done - the robbery, killing Macallister, getting rid of Frank - it had all been for her. Only, now that he was within grasping distance of his prize, he wasn't all that sure he wanted it anymore.

A ring tone sounded from the kitchen, followed by Lindy's voice. Boyle exchanged glances with Stella. He opened the door slightly and listened hard, but could only make out odd words.

"What is it?"

175

Stella staring at him, expecting him to know everything all the time. She was suddenly all tensed up, like she had an electric current running through her. Boyle had that fluttering sensation in his gut again. If this kept up he was going to end up with an ulcer.

"I don't-" He stepped back from the door and moved quickly to the middle of the room.

Lindy appeared, her gaze flicking between Boyle and Stella.

"I've got some news." She sat down beside Stella, her professional face on. "They've found your husband's car."

Stella's eyes widened. One hand fluttered to her throat.

"Please tell me, have they found my husband?"

It was a convincing display. Boyle gave her ten out of ten. Felt like applauding.

"I'm afraid not. The car was found wrecked and abandoned."

"Wrecked - you mean Frank was in a car crash?"

Lindy's gaze flickered to Boyle for a second.

"No, we don't think so. The car had been driven into a wall, possibly deliberately. It looks as though it was taken by joyriders."

"I don't understand-"

"Mrs Valentine." Boyle cut in. Time for some distraction. "Do you have any recollection of your husband coming home last night - anything at all that could help us - possibly you heard the car leaving the driveway?"

"No, as I told the officer I spoke to earlier, I had a migraine last night - a bad one. After Frank left I took a sleeping tablet and went to bed. I woke up late this morning - Frank wasn't here and the car was gone. I naturally assumed he'd gone to work already. And then this -"

Her face crumpled. Lindy mechanically passed her a

tissue from a box on the occasional table, flashing raised eyebrows at Boyle. *What do you think?* He shrugged back at her. *Seems genuine enough to me.*

"Thank you," Stella managed a small smile of gratitude.

"I'm so sorry, it's just that I don't know what to think."

"None of us do," Lindy said.

Boyle shot her a look, but her expression showed only mild concern for Mrs Valentine's plight. He knew she didn't like Stella but she was playing a part as much as anyone in the room. Boyle had the sudden urge to laugh. The whole thing was a pantomime. Stella playing the forlorn wife. Lindy playing the sympathy shoulder. As for Boyle - he was playing so many parts he'd lost sight of himself. It was hysterical, it really was. He bit the inside of his mouth and swallowed the laugh.

"How were relations between you and your husband Mrs Valentine?" Boyle getting into his policeman role. Stella stared at him and he could have sworn there were tears in her eyes. She was good.

"Excuse me?"

"I'm sorry, but I do have to ask."

"Yes. Of course you do." Brittle.

"Can you think of any reason why your husband would be driving around late at night, Mrs Valentine?"

"No. I cannot. But I can tell you this, my husband was not in the habit of drink driving. In fact it was something he absolutely deplored." Tense, upset, putting on a good show for Lindy.

"Of course. And I understand that he was drinking last night?" Boyle was starting to enjoy himself.

"He was at a function - a meal - with your Commander as a matter of fact."

"Er, yes, I am aware of that fact. The Commander has already given us a full statement."

"And so have I, Sergeant."

"We're just trying to help, Mrs Valentine."

"I don't see what is particularly helpful about sitting

around in my home asking me the same questions over and over again. You should be out there looking for my husband."

She looked agitated. Said it like she meant it. Like she actually believed Boyle should be out there looking for Frank. She shook another cigarette from the carton, glanced around for the lighter. Boyle saw it, picked it up.

"Don't worry, Mrs Valentine," Boyle said, "We'll find him."

He flicked the lighter and leaned in towards her. Their eyes locked over the flame as she accepted the light. She sat back, exhaling smoke.

"Thank you, Charlie. You don't mind if I call you Charlie, do you?"

The old desire welled up in Boyle. If it hadn't been for Lindy's presence he would have fucked Stella there and then.

Right on top of Frank's favourite rug.

Chapter 27

Lindy closed the kitchen door behind them and turned to Boyle. She'd made her excuses and pulled him to the kitchen for a conference.

"See what I mean? She's a real piece of work."

Boyle shrugged. He was still thinking about what he'd like to do with Mrs Valentine on top of Mr Valentine's rug.

"She's upset. Her husband's disappeared, she doesn't know what the hell's going on. What do you expect - tea and scones?"

"Maybe not. But you sure rattled her cage asking her about Valentine out driving at night."

"I don't suppose she liked what I was implying."

"What - that the Super's been trawling the streets looking for sex? You pretty much made him out to be a right perv. But who could blame him - I don't suppose he's been getting much at home from the Ice Queen. They've got separate bedrooms you know."

"No, I didn't know. Does it matter? Lots of couples sleep in separate bedrooms. Maybe he was a snorer."

"Maybe."

Lindy flicked the kettle on to make yet more coffee.

Boyle glanced around the kitchen. Shiny, whizzy clean. No blood. No spatter. No dead bodies.

"Some place, huh?" Lindy asked.

"It's a kitchen," Boyle replied, feigning disinterest. "So what do you think?" He tilted his head at the door, indicating he meant about Stella.

"I don't know, but her story checks out. She's got a history of migraines. There are sleeping tablets upstairs. Maybe she doesn't have anything to do with it. Maybe I just want her to be guilty because she's such a bitch. You know, I always thought Valentine was a bit of a prick, but now I'm starting to feel sorry for him. Maybe he did a Reggie Perrin. Smashed the car himself, to cover up. What do you think?"

"About Valentine? No idea. I wouldn't have thought he was the type to do a runner, but maybe he got involved with something dodgy."

"Valentine?" Lindy looked sceptical.

Boyle shrugged. "Why not? Happens all the time. For all we know he's got a gambling habit - maybe he got into debt and borrowed money from the wrong people."

"Aye, and maybe he's running an international drugs cartel, but I don't think so." Lindy scoffed.

"Okay, he had a few drinks last night - maybe he decided to take a stroll along by the river to clear his head and he fell in. Could be something as simple as that, but whatever it is, I don't think she's involved. I mean look at this place - everything is so bloody perfect. I don't think she could cope with the upset of something going wrong in her perfect world, never mind make a mess herself."

Lindy stopped spooning ground coffee into the cafetiere and waggled the coffee measure at Boyle.

"You might just have a point, Boyle. You know, there's not a jar of instant coffee anywhere - it's the real stuff or nothing for her ladyship. You should see what's in the cupboards. Not a Value tin in sight." She grinned.

"Poor Valentine - he was probably terrified in case he rumpled a cushion and she got upset. Who would have thought?"

Boyle had no problem returning Lindy's grin. He liked the way this was going. She'd never know how wrong she'd got it. He decided to give her another nudge in the wrong direction.

"Maybe that's why he was such a prick at work."

"Because she wore the trousers when he got home?"

"Exactly."

"Boyle?"

"What?"

"You asked her how *were* relations between her and Valentine, not how *are* relations between them. You put it in the past tense. And you said maybe he *was* a snorer."

"Did I?" Boyle raised his eyebrows, urging the fluttering thing inside him to be still. He couldn't believe he'd made such an amateurish slip-up. "Well he's gone, so I suppose I was thinking about how things were before he left." Back-tracking. Covering up.

Lindy stared at him. Coffee measure held between thumb and forefinger. She stared too long for Boyle's liking. Another slip-up - he'd forgotten that her brain was almost as big as her arse. It was a criminal waste that she hadn't been promoted.

"Or maybe," Boyle continued, "being in Community Involvement has fucked up my thinking process so much I don't know what the hell I'm doing anymore."
She stared at him a moment longer before waggling the scoop again. It was starting to annoy him.

"Boyle, you *never* knew what the hell you were doing." She left a beat before arching an eyebrow and adding, "Well maybe there were exceptions. I can think of one department you were particularly good in."

The threat of her dragging up the past had been coiling itself around his neck all afternoon. He didn't feel any happier now that she'd gone and done it. Some things should be left in the dark instead of being dragged out into the open but he returned her grin, hoping it didn't look as sick as it felt. He didn't want to piss her off - he could do without the aggro but he really wished she'd left it alone. He couldn't imagine the series of drunken fumbles they'd engaged in were among the finest moments in her life any more than they were his.

She'd had a thing for him back in the day but he'd only ever got down and dirty with her when he'd been too pissed to care. It wasn't even what you could call an affair. More a series of alcohol-fuelled one-night stands. They would yak about the job, get drunk, fuck and then he'd go home to his wife.

Lindy poured water into the cafetiere. At least she'd been distracted. Silver linings.

She faffed around making the coffee. Didn't seem to have any more to say on the subject. Maybe it was better she'd brought it out. Acknowledge it and move the fuck along. Ha, ha, remember when we did that crazy thing. Yeah, yeah, yeah. Get it out in the light, watch it disintegrate.

"Charlie?"

"Yeah?"

"I heard you got divorced."

Chapter 28

Lindy came back from the bar and set another pint of lager in front of Boyle.

"Cheers," he said.

"Welcome."

She sat down, pressing her leg against his. Boyle automatically shifted. She moved so that they were touching again. She said something.

"What's that?" he asked.

She leaned into him, repeating what she'd said, her lips brushing against his ear. He could smell her perfume. Sweet. Too sweet.

"You and me. Just like old times," she whispered.

He gazed into his pint, sucking in the perfume she'd doused herself in. It reminded him of sitting in the back of his dad's car when he was a kid. Windows closed tight because his mum complained of a draught when they were open. Hot sun beating through glass. His dad's brand new air freshener dangling from the rear view mirror. It was always vanilla, cloyingly sweet and artificial, because his mum didn't like the forest fresh ones.

"Yeah," he said, "Just like old times."

Christ, what did a man have to do to change things? He was divorced, estranged from his daughter. He'd stolen, killed, disposed of a body and yet here he was right back where he'd been six, seven years ago. Getting pissed with Lindy Ross. Her pressing her flubbery thighs and great big tits against him. Jesus H, they were even sitting in the same fucking pub. No doubt on the same worn chairs at the same frigging table. If there was a God, which he seriously fucking doubted, then God must be sitting on high, pissing himself very fucking almightily at the great big hamster wheel Charlie Boyle's life was on. Running and running and never getting anywhere, just waiting for the same old scenery to come around again.

"What's wrong, Charlie?" Lindy's hand, brushing accidentally-on-purpose against his. She still had the same old moves. Nothing ever changed.

"Wrong?" He gave a short laugh, staring into his pint like it held all the answers, if only he could figure how to get to them. "Nothing wrong with me. I'm just the same old Charlie Boyle, living the same old Charlie Boyle life. Now what could possibly be wrong with that?"

He'd spent the entire afternoon shut up in Stella's house breathing in Stella's second hand smoke, the windows shut tight, if only because Frank would have had them flung wide open. Stella needling him every time Lindy's back was turned. Eyes glinting, teasing him, winding him up.

Him thinking way too late that he should have had a better plan for the car. Got rid of it properly.

Nobody was telling him anything. Nobody that mattered at any rate. The only person speaking to him was Lindy, but she was even lower down the feeding chain than he was.

Fuck it. All he had to do was stay cool. The car being found like that only muddied the waters. There would be all sorts of strange DNA in it, just the way he'd planned it. They'd waste a heap of time chasing down the joy riders. They didn't know what was going on. They were looking everywhere and nowhere. All he and Stella had to do was hold their collective nerve.

"I thought I could trust you," Stella had said, eyes as cold as her tone.

"Of course you can trust me." Speaking low, looking at the door to make sure Lindy was out of earshot. "But I told you it would be like this. All you have to do is stick to your story and remember I'm with you every step of the way."

"You'd better be."

"We're in it together, baby."

Trying to put heart into the words as he spoke. Lusting after her one minute, desperate to get away from her the next. Loving her, hating her. Walking a tight-rope between the two, his head fit to burst. Trying not to show his relief when he got the call to return to HQ with Lindy. If Mrs Valentine desired, they would send a Families Liaison Officer. No, Mrs Valentine did not desire. Mrs Valentine very much desired to be left on her own.

Except that she called Boyle three times within the next hour. She wanted him on tap. Needed him around to reassure her that everything was going to be okay. Wanting to torment him, use him as a distraction. Taking her frustrations out on him.

He kept telling her to stay cool. Stick to her story. Don't add. Don't embellish. Keep it simple. His colleagues didn't have a thing. Nobody suspected her of anything. Saying the same stuff over and over, trying to keep the weariness, the anger, out of his voice. Resisting the desire to yell at her that if she couldn't handle the situation she shouldn't have stabbed her husband in the throat in the first place. And all the while thinking that no matter what they did, nothing was ever going to be okay again. They'd lied, cheated and killed and now she was in a big hurry to skip merrily towards her happy ever after. Rainbows in the sky, bluebirds on her shoulder, Boyle lurking in the shadows, on hand to take care of the dirty work.

He reverted to his default position. Thought about doing a runner. Knew he wouldn't get far before Stella got wind of it and spilt her guts about everything. There was no walking out on her. She'd turn him in just to spite him, even if it meant incriminating herself in the process. They were inextricably linked and the truth was, he didn't think either of them deserved any better.

Back at headquarters, Lindy caught him at a weak moment and press-ganged him into drinks at The Grapes, the unofficial drinking den for HQ staff. Interior design circa 1986.

Boyle agreed to go. Alcohol had its attractions.

"What's wrong, Charlie - you still peeved about being busted?" Lindy asked.

He managed a wry smile at that one. His demotion was about the last thing on his mind right now.

"I was only winding you up earlier today. You're a good cop, Charlie. All you need to do is keep your head down for a while. You'll get your chance."

Yeah, there was as much chance of that happening as of anyone believing Lindy was a virgin. He shifted his gaze from the lager to her face. She had put on a touch of make-up before leaving HQ. Was gazing at him adoringly, still clutching her torch. Nothing ever changed.

"You know what?" he said. "You're right. All I have to do is keep my head down and everything will be just fine." Lindy was peddling him the same line he'd peddled Stella. The irony of the situation puckered his lips into a half-smile.

She smiled a genuine smile, pleased to have helped. He raised his glass, chinked it against her bottle of Becks.

"Cheers."

He swigged back a mouthful of lager and checked out the bar. It had filled up since he'd been staring into his pint. He spied a few familiar faces. Guys who'd been standing in the same spot the last time he'd been here. Permanent fixtures, telling the same clapped out jokes, wheeling out the same tired war stories. Same old, same old. Except now their eyes had sunk a little further into their heads and the lines on their faces had etched a little deeper. Hair was grizzling, receding, or both. Some of them looking paunchy. Letting themselves go. Big, fat useless fuckers. Some of them looking like they'd been raiding the bottle every night. Broken veins threading their cheeks, whisky noses.

There were new faces too. Young and fresh and peachy keen. Swearing blind they wouldn't end up like the old farts, drinking too heavily and telling everyone how it was in their day. Yet here they were, already getting in the practice.

Boyle swirled the last of the lager in his glass and swallowed it over.

"Ready for another?" he asked.

Lindy tilted her bottle, squinting at the contents. Almost empty.

"Sure, why not." She put her hand on his arm, squeezed it. "Just like the old days."

"You're pissed," he said.

"So are you."

"Not yet. But I'm getting there."

Boyle got the drinks in then went to the gents. Lindy was gone when he got back. He wondered if she'd got a better prospect for the night. He didn't know what he thought about that. Relieved probably, but then he saw her jacket still slung over the back of her chair and that her drink was keeping his company on the table.

He sat down, took a swallow and looked around

without heart or soul. He caught sight of Lindy's head, bobbing through the crowd, weaving her way back towards him. She caught his eye and smiled. It was a beautiful smile, a secret smile, the kind that passed between lovers. Except they weren't. It made Boyle feel sad and bitter and very fucking lonely.

She'd applied a fresh slick of lipstick. He knew she had it in her head that he'd be going back to her place or she to his. He knew she'd had that thought when she'd persuaded him out for a drink. Maybe since she'd opened the door to him at Stella's. That was exactly why he shouldn't have come. No matter what else happened, he wasn't going home with Lindy. Not tonight. Not any night.

Maybe some things did change.

He picked up his pint and took a long swallow.

Someone's head moved, revealing a familiar face in the crowd. Sandy hair, pale blue eyes, cheekbones you could slice lemons on. Danny King. Ogling Lindy's big tits, nudging his mates, all of them taking a big, greedy look at her body.

Boyle's eyes narrowed. His fingers curled. Lindy sat down beside him and squeezed her arm through his. He caught a mouthful of choking vanilla. Sweat popped on his brow. He thought about fried onions, and sun shining through glass, and the back of his mother's head.

Lindy snuggled in to his side. He didn't want to hurt her. Neither did he want her rubbing herself against him like a cat wanting fed. Whatever had gone on between them was ancient history and, as far as Boyle was concerned, that's how it was going to stay.

"Aww, poor Charlie. You really are in the doldrums, aren't you?"

He shrugged her off, like an old habit he'd long since kicked. She pouted. He saw King sniggering. The room grew fuzzy. Funny. Didn't think he'd had that much to drink. King's sharp sneer cut through the blur. Boyle pictured the same sneer directed at Karen. Karen had been too good for Boyle, and she was definitely too good for that scumbag. What did she even see in him?

Lindy tried to drape herself over Boyle again, threatening to engulf him in heavy flesh and thick vanilla fumes. He squirmed, tried to tell her he wasn't interested, that she should find herself a guy who really cared about her. The words were in his head but his tongue was thick and they wouldn't come out right.

He said something about him caring about her but he didn't mean it in the way she took it. He was trying to let her down gently but she just looked at him, smiled, and moved in closer, hearing what she wanted to hear.

Her fingers on his arm, stroking and plucking the material of his suit jacket, until he felt like a piece of meat. King sniggering at Boyle then leering at a fake-tanned blonde in a short skirt. She was not much older than Jenny. Black dots dancing on the periphery of Boyle's vision. Visions of King sleeping with Karen, leching after Jenny. Black dots turning red, misting his vision.

Boyle lurched to his feet. Knocked the table. His glass teetered. Lindy caught it, but lager had already slurped over the side, adding fresh layers of sticky to the tabletop. Lindy's mouth a surprised, black O, grabbed at his arm, trying to force him to sit down.

He shook her off and took a few steps towards King. He was surprised at how unsteady his legs were and got the sudden idea that someone had spiked his drink. He put all his energy into focussing on King, everything else a background blur and a roar in his ears.

Fear scurried over King's face as he saw Boyle coming straight at him. Panic flared in those pale blue eyes. Then he noticed the hint of a stagger in Boyle's gait, perhaps caught the sheen of sweat on his face, and the fear subsided. King raised his eyebrows, stretching his face into a comic fright mask, mugging it up for his mates. Mocking Boyle, daring him on.

Boyle raised his fist and took a broad, clumsy swipe at King. Not so much telegraphing it in as giving full advance warning, including an estimated time of arrival. King stepped neatly back, lip curled in a sneer.

Boyle knew right away his aim was off. He missed his target by a country mile, but his momentum carried him forward. The crowd parted like the Red Sea before Moses. Boyle lunged through the gap and smacked into the floor.

He was looking at feet, wondering how he'd got down there. Noticing the fine details in the carpet. Burn marks from when people were allowed to smoke inside. Dark patches where dirt had clung to something spilled. Broken peanuts, open toed sandals, painted toenails, cracked heels, high heels, black boots, trainers, worn patches in the carpet, loafers, tufty bits. All sorts of smells, none of them good. Then whoosh, and he was wafting through the air like Dumbo the flying elephant.

Jenny had cried at that film.

Except he wasn't really flying. It only felt that way. Hands hauled him to his feet, then King's face was in his face. Up so close he could feel the heat from the other man's skin. See the flecks in his pale blue eyes. The faint acne scars on his razor cheekbones. Those eyes gave Boyle the creeps, but his words, murmured in Boyle's ear, sent chills through his bones.

She's a great fucking shag your wife. But your daughter? She's got better tits. High and tight, know what I mean?

Anger surged through Boyle like he'd never felt before. He tried to take another swing at King but ended on the floor again. There was a flash of pain in his head but he didn't know if he'd banged it or if someone had kicked him. It felt like a kick, but he didn't care. It seemed easier to stay where he is so he closed his eyes. When he opened them again, he wondered what he was doing on the floor.

Next thing, he was on his feet, words flying around his head. People talking about him like he wasn't there. He thought maybe he wasn't. Thought maybe he didn't even exist.

He was having a wee existential moment to himself. He grinned at that and the words flew by his head like smart-arse cartoon crows.

What a state to get in. Some people don't know when they've had enough. Twat. Arsehole. What a fucking wally. What's his problem anyway? You'd think he'd have learned by now. Oh, is that him? That's Charlie Boyle? No wonder they demoted him. Should have been sacked. Fucking clown. Tosser. Loser. Give the guy a break. Gimme a hand to get him out. You'll be alright mate. Just get yourself straightened out, eh? Somebody better shove him in a taxi. I'll do it. Sure you can manage? I'll take care of him. Let's get him outside. Fresh air will do him the world of good. Good night's sleep is what he wants. Aye that and a boot up the arse. Want a hand? Naw, he's alright. Aren't you Charlie? You're alright mate. He used to be able to handle himself. Look at the state of him now. I've got him. Come on.

Doors opened. There was cool fresh air, darkening sky, bright street lights. Boyle giggled. He heard himself so he must exist.

"Charlie Boyle is real," he yelled and giggled again.

The hands released him. He staggered along the street, abstract thoughts jimbly-jumbling through his head like the title sequence from The Twilight Zone *doo-doo-do-do doo-doo-do-do* $E=mc^2$. Rod Serling's voice. *Picture a man. A very drunk man.*

Boyle snickered.

The first punch came from behind.

191

Chapter 29

Boyle's head throbbed. He hadn't opened his eyes but already he was yearning to be asleep once more. His lips were gummed together. Tongue thick and furry and sticking to the roof of his mouth. Felt like it had been used as an ashtray. Maybe it had. He wished it belonged to someone else.

He felt the skin on his lips tearing apart when he opened his mouth. Air flooded in. His taste buds woke up and gave him a precise indication of the putrid state of his tongue.

Right now he desired one of two things. Either instantaneous, painless death, or a bathroom sink. He waited a moment. Death didn't arrive, but a vision of a bathroom sink arose in his mind like a mirage. Cool, white enamel. Silver taps, one of them turned on. Clear, cold water running from it. Perched on the sink was a green toothbrush. A generous squiggle of brilliant white, peppermint toothpaste snaked on its bristles. Man alive, what he'd give for that water and that toothbrush right now.

He made an attempt at opening his eyes. The left one sprang open, didn't like what it saw and snapped closed like a clam. If he'd had the strength he would have groaned. He wished he could drift back to unconsciousness, but he was in that half-life place where there was no chance of sweet darkness. All that was going to happen to him now was that stuff was going to come back to him. He'd have liked the stuff to stay where it was. He wouldn't bother it if it didn't bother him, but the stuff came back anyway.

He remembered lying on the floor of The Grapes breathing in carpet.

The memory didn't please him so he tried opening his eyes again, hoping the visuals would stop stuff seeping into his consciousness. His left eye opened.

Daylight strained through thin orange curtains into an unfamiliar room. Boyle lay very still, trying not move anything but his head as he looked around. Even his eyeball hurt.

He was lying on a sofa, the likes of which he hadn't seen since about 1976. The back and arms were coated in coffee coloured vinyl, patterned to look like leather. Something about the worn texture of it brought to mind cracked, peeling heels on dirty, bare feet.

The cushions were covered in ribbed, dark brown, nylon. Substances of a foul nature had been caught and compressed between the ribs of the one hundred percent man-made material. Watch that static electricity build. If he moved too quickly he was in danger of sparking off a fire. Not that there was much chance of that.

Boyle was feeling extremely fragile right now. The only movements he planned on making were small and careful. Nothing fast. Nothing sudden. No chance of a static spark engulfing him in flames.

A sour aroma emanated from the sofa. God knows what kind of filth and stains the dark brown masked. He'd been lying on top of it for hours, maybe even days, absorbing, becoming part of. Man and sofa united in one unholy being.

He shifted slightly, hearing a soft *slurp* as his cheek peeled from the vinyl. His suit jacket had been covering him. It slipped when he moved, slithering to the floor. He let it fall. It wasn't going anywhere.

He remembered being outside. The cool air had felt so good he'd been laughing. Then Lindy got in his face, fussing and flapping. Trying to tell him what to do, trying to control him.

He'd roared at her. What had he said? He couldn't remember, but it had been bad. It must have been bad. Her face had crumpled in response. She'd stepped back from him. He hadn't cared. He'd thought he was Archie. Archie? Who the fuck was Archie? Laughing and giggling like a fool. And why did he only have one eye open?

His fingers felt their way up his cheek to the swollen lump where his right eye should be. *Oh Jesus in a bucket, that hurt.* A sudden, painful flashback. Him lying on the pavement. A big, heavy boot heading straight for his face.

Boyle scrunched up his good eye and willed the vision away. He was in no mood for remembering, but the pictures kept on coming.

The dirty fuckers had come from behind. *Fuckers plural?* Had there been more than one? He thought so. One pair of boots doing the damage, other feet, trainer clad, shuffling about in the background. *C'mon, that'll do.* Dirty cowarding bastards had left him lying in the street. What kind of person left someone lying in the street?

Boyle didn't want to think about that.

He opened his good eye.

Bodies lay in humps around the room. He hoped they weren't all dead. Don't be stupid. What would he be doing in a room full of dead people? No, if you listened closely you could hear them breathing. Where was he anyway?

Two people huddled together under a thin, dirty

candlewick bedspread making one big hump on the floor. Another hump, rolled up in a manky blanket, was curled up in a foetal position by the wall. The last was stretched out on a ratty armchair, a leather jacket spread over its upper body and head. Long, skinny legs, clad in dirty denim, splayed out. Boyle peered at that last one the longest. The greasy jeans looked familiar. He tried to place them. He let his mind drift for a moment. When the answer came to him he sat bolt upright, setting off fireworks in his skull.

When the initial flare of pain subsided he slowly swung his legs around, put his feet on the floor and surveyed all around him. No doubting it. He was in a nest of junkies. How in the name of Davie fucking Jones had that happened?

He thought, trying to will the pictures back now. He remembered what he'd said to Lindy. He'd told her he wasn't interested, that he never had been. He didn't fancy her. Never had. It was all in her head. It was a sad fucking day when she had to get a man pissed before he'd sleep with her. He told her to get some respect for herself, then maybe she'd get a man who respected her. Then he turned and walked away. Left her standing, staring after him.

She yelled at his back. Told him and anyone within hearing distance that he was a bastard. She called that one right. Charlie Boyle was a bastard.

Maybe so, but he wasn't the only one and he certainly wasn't the biggest. Danny King was a much bigger bastard than Boyle. Well, he had always known that. But now it was in his head that he was *specifically* a bastard. But what had King done?

King sneering as Boyle hit the floor.

It came to him. The bastard had spiked Boyle's drink. How did Boyle know that? He couldn't remember the how of it, but as sure as his name was Charlie Boyle, he knew it to be the truth.

195

The bastard had spiked his drink and then Boyle had been beaten up. Danny King spiking him, him getting beat up - it didn't take Sherlock to make the connection.

After the beating... nothing. No memory of how he'd got from the street to the junkie's nest. What the hell had happened?

Boyle eyed the slumbering heaps. Fucking junkies. What if they'd injected some of their crap into him?

He rolled up his shirt sleeves and inspected his arms for needle marks. Nothing. Then he pulled up his trousers and pulled off his socks and checked his feet and ankles. All clear. He supposed they could have stabbed a needle into his arse. Come to think of it, they could have stabbed anything into his arse *squeal like a pig* and he wouldn't have known anything about it. He shuddered.

Boyle ran his hands around the sides of his hips and his buttocks. He was achey all over, but he'd taken a kicking then spent the night on a manky sofa. Maybe two nights. He had plenty of reasons for feeling sore. If they'd stuck him, they'd stuck him.

Thoughts of hepatitis and HIV ran through his head. Then he got a grip of himself. They wouldn't waste their gear on him. Greedy wee bastards, junkies. Would rob you blind. Now, there was a thought.

He lifted up his jacket and checked for his wallet. All the pockets were empty. Of course they were. Thieving junkie bastards would steal the shoes off your feet. Come to think of it, where were his shoes?

He looked around the floor. Nothing but greasy, bare floorboards as far as the eye could see. He had a tentative feel under the sofa. Didn't want to stick himself with a dirty needle.

His fingers brushed against something hard. A mug. He pulled it out. Full of mould. Christ, what a way to live. He had another sweep under the sofa, found something that felt suspiciously like a pair of shoes. He pulled them out. Not just any old shoes. His shoes.

And what do you know? His wallet and warrant card were tucked inside one, his keys and two phones in the other.

He took the wallet out and opened it up. As far as he could remember, which wasn't much, everything seemed as it should be. Credit cards, debit card, cash. He glanced at Banjo's slumbering form, reassessing his opinion of the junkie informer.

He looked at his phones. Both switched off. He left them that way and put his shoes on. He needed to take a piss.

He went out to a small, dark, rectangular hall. There were three doors to choose from. The front door was identifiable by an array of chains, bolts and locks. Boyle wondered who exactly the junkie thieving scum were trying to keep out.

The second door opened onto a small cupboard containing the electricity meter, a dirty rag covered in dubious stains, and some dust. The third led to a rancid, windowless bathroom containing a toilet, bath and sink that looked nothing like the one Boyle had fantasised about.

A toothbrush lay dead on its side on top of the cistern, its bristles brown, mangled and parched. There wasn't an orifice in Boyle's body he would have considered putting it in.

He peed into the seatless toilet, trying not to look at the matter coating the bowl. When he was done, he rinsed his hands at the grimy sink, then bathed his damaged eye with a handful of water. The coolness of it against his hot, swollen skin felt good.

He managed to open his eye a sliver. His vision was blurry, but at least he could see out of it. The world was still a fucked-up place, but knowing that he would be able to look at with two eyes made him feel a little bit better.

He scooped water into his mouth, swirled it around, spat it out then lapped some up from his hands. He wasn't going to risk putting his mouth near the tap. He took one look at a towel lying in a scabrous heap in the bath and dried his hands on his trousers.

He went back through to the room, telling himself he felt brand-new. It was true that he did feel a little better, but it would have been hard to feel any worse. He slipped his jacket on and began dispersing his belongings in his various pockets, saving his wallet for last.

He flipped it open and took out forty quid. He looked around for somewhere to put it. He wanted to make sure Banjo was the beneficiary, so in the end the only safe place he could think of was in the pocket of Banjo's jeans. Problem was, he really didn't fancy having to touch the manky sod. Then he had a vision of the skinny junkie removing his shoes and tucking him up on the sofa and felt like a bastard.

He folded the notes and used two fingers to poke them into Banjo's pocket. He had no choice but to get up close and personal. Funny how he didn't smell as bad as usual. Either Boyle was used to the odour by now or he was stinking as bad as his junkie saviour.

He'd just finished poking the money into the pocket when he became aware that Banjo was watching him.

Boyle straightened up. Banjo pulled his jacket down, revealing his pale, hollow face. He looked freakier than ever in the thin orange light. He gave Boyle a doped-up, toothless grin.

"Don't worry. I was looking out for you Mr Boyle."

Chapter 30

It really came to something when the only guy watching your back was a low-life piece of junkie scum. It was very fucking humbling.

Boyle walked towards the city centre, feeling like he was one step down from the winos who were tossed out of the homeless shelters every morning.

He took out the two phones and weighed them in his hands. His Joe Normal phone or his Stella phone? Which one to switch on first? *Eenie meenie minie mo.* He switched Joe Normal on, walking as it loaded. He was surprised to see the time. It was already well into Saturday afternoon. Could have been worse... could have been Sunday or Monday already. Cogs whirred and clicked behind the cotton wool in his head. Wasn't he supposed to be somewhere this morning?

Fourteen missed calls. Three voice mails. Boyle groaned and decided he really had to do something about the bad taste in his mouth. He spied a corner shop, went in and bought a tin of Irn Bru. The shopkeeper looked startled at Boyle's appearance but did his best not to stare. Boyle went outside and took a good long swig before listening to the first voicemail. Irn Bru didn't have the bite it used to. Or maybe it just wasn't strong enough to penetrate the coating on his tongue.

The first message was a long rant from an irate DI Ronson inquiring as to Boyle's whereabouts. It included various threats and three uses of the phrase *get my drift?*. The second message was also from Ronson, this time informing Boyle that he'd blown it, that he was out of SCD for good. Ronson didn't sound like he'd be shedding tears about it any time soon.

Boyle glugged the last of his drink, squashed the empty tin and pushed it into an overflowing rubbish bin.

The third message was from Saunders. He cleared his throat before ordering Boyle to report to Community Involvement at 0830 sharp on Monday morning. He put on a class act, managing to sound disappointed, hurt and angry by turns. It was enough to bring tears to a glass eye. If Boyle had one.

He strolled on, turning the phone over in his hand, glancing down at it every now and again. Finally, he opened it and took out the sim card and battery. He wondered if they were planning to bust him down to constable or boot him out altogether. Maybe he could help them decide.

He dropped the phone and stamped on it with his heel until it looked unsalvageable then kicked its corpse into the gutter. He tossed the back of the phone and the battery into a yellow skip with a stained mattress sticking out of it. He'd never seen a skip without one. He dropped the sim card down a drain.

Keeping on with the strolling on, he switched on his Stella phone. Eleven missed calls and another three voice mails, all from last night, each one colder and angrier than the one before. Biting words, acid tone. She hadn't tried to call him today. Freezing on him.

Saturday afternoon and the centre of town was heaving. The tall guy with the leather flying cap had set up his stall of ethnic jewellery. Someone else was selling shiny helium-filled balloons, in the shape of animals and cartoon characters. Most of which Boyle didn't recognise but there was a good one of Daffy Duck.

Boyle's appearance didn't exactly send people fleeing and screaming, but it wasn't far from the truth. People glanced nervously at him, averting their gaze as he passed. Women yanked children out of his path, like there was a chance he'd snatch one up and bite its head off. Burtons had a sale on. Boyle went in.

Inside the shop he bumped into a fraught woman trying to kit out a surly teenager. She turned round, hot, flustered and angry, but her expression quickly changed when she caught sight of him. She mumbled an apology and stepped aside, revealing the mirror behind her.

Boyle took a long, cool look at himself. There was dried blood splattered on his shirt. *His* blood, but they didn't know that. His bad eye looked like a big, overripe plum. Purple skin splitting open, sliver of red eye peering out. His hair stuck up in tufts. He needed a shave. Hell, he needed to be disinfected from head to toe. His clothes were dishevelled. There were boot prints on his trousers. He looked like a fucking maniac. The kind of guy you'd cross the street to avoid. Suited him fine. He grinned and looked ten times scarier.

He moved round the shop quickly, everyone getting out of his way like he was Frankenstein's monster. He gathered his purchases and took them to the counter. One long-sleeve charcoal t-shirt. One pair of dark blue straight leg jeans. A three-pack of black CAT socks. A three-pack of plain black trunks. One black zip-thru utility jacket. One pair of Skechers black casual lace-ups. One black duffel bag.

"The socks and jeans are buy one get one half price." The sales assistant had nervous eyes and a bright fixed smile. He was trying hard not to stare at his customer.

"No thanks." Boyle growled. He didn't mean to growl

but his throat was dry and it just came out that way.

The sales assistant's smile faltered. A tiny tsunami of stress washed across his face. He looked like he'd just peed his pants but at least he didn't argue. Boyle paid by credit card. The assistant bagged his goods in double-quick time.

Boyle left the shop and went to the nearest ATM where he withdrew the maximum amount allowed on his debit and credit cards. Total, one thousand, five hundred pounds.

Back in his flat, the air was dead.

Boyle went to his bedroom and emptied his pockets, dumping the contents on the bed. He stripped off his clothes, letting them lie where they fell.

He stood naked in front of the sink and brushed his teeth, his tongue and the insides of his cheeks for a full ten minutes, renewing the toothpaste three times. He shaved in the shower, sucking up the pain when the razor scraped over a tender spot. He washed his hair twice over, digging his fingers into his scalp, working up a big lather. Then he scrubbed himself, working over his body with a nail brush until his skin was singing.

Washed and dried, he put on a pair of the new trunks he'd bought and went through to the kitchen to fetch a roll of black bin liners. A value pack, recycled, not as sturdy as the ones Stella used, but good enough for his purposes.

He pulled six off the roll, opened them up and split the clothes he'd been wearing the night he'd disposed of Frank between them. Then he did likewise with the rest of his clothes, including his suit.

He jumbled everything up. Dirty socks, used underpants, jeans, t-shirts, trainers - the lot. A couple of the bags were getting full so he tied them up and put them beside the front door.

He took a half-empty bag to the kitchen and stuffed

the contents of the washing machine inside it. Everything except the rolled-up sweatshirt containing the jewellery. He tied up that bag and sat it beside the others.

He took the sweatshirt to the bedroom. He unrolled it on the bed, revealing the diamonds. He held a few pieces up, examining them in the light.

What was it about diamonds that made people so willing to kill and steal for them? Realising, even as he had the thought, that he had stolen and killed for them himself. But for Boyle they were a means to an end - an escape route, nothing more. He'd never desired them for themselves. It had never been about the diamonds.

He rolled them up in the sweatshirt again and stuffed the whole lot into his new duffel bag. He also packed the two remaining pairs of trunks and two pairs of the socks along with his toothbrush, toothpaste and passport. He sat the bag on the floor beside the bed then found himself a sheet of paper, a pen and an envelope.

Leaning on a copy of the Yellow Pages, still in its plastic wrapper, he wrote a letter. It didn't take long - it was short and he'd written it in his head often enough.

He signed it, folded it neatly and put it in the envelope. He addressed the envelope and sat it on top of the duffel bag then he went around the flat, clearing up the remnants of his life.

That didn't take long either.

By the time he was done it would have taken a forensic team to prove he'd ever lived there. It was as if he'd never existed.

He got dressed in his new clothes. Everything fitted, more or less. He checked himself in the mirror.

His battered face aside, he was so bland he could almost see through himself. He put on a pair of cheap sunglasses he'd found when he was clearing up. They hid his eye perfectly. He was Mr Invisible.

It took two trips to the communal bins at the back of the flats to get rid of the rubbish bags. He distributed them randomly among the bins, stuffing them deep. It wouldn't be long before they were covered in the detritus of other people's lives. Soiled nappies, onion peelings, take-away wrappers. On Monday the whole lot would be collected, crushed and dumped in a landfill site.

Back in the flat, he cut up his debit and credit cards and put the pieces in his back pocket for later disposal. He put his wallet in one zip-up pocket, his warrant card in another. He picked up the letter, put the duffel bag over his shoulder and walked out of the flat without looking back.

This time, when the door clicked behind him, it was for the last time.

Chapter 31

It had been a long time since Boyle had dialled this particular number, but he still knew it by heart. His call was answered on the third ring.

"Hello."

Boyle was momentarily rendered speechless by the sound of Karen's voice, familiar, yet strange, at the same time.

"Hello?" she repeated, this time with an implied question.

She'd only uttered four syllables, but the soft purr of her voice transported him to another time, another place. He came over all gooey inside like marshmallow melting into hot chocolate.

"Is there anyone there?"

Getting irritated now. A tone he had become well used to.

"Karen, it's me."

"Oh. What do *you* want?"

No purr now. Irritation all the way.

"How are you?"

The silence from Karen's end was filled by train station noise. A short man trundling a large suitcase. A woman in a too-tight, pink velour tracksuit yelling into a mobile phone. *Can you hear me now?* Two teenage boys trotting along the concourse, braying, and slapping each other on the head. Boyle was using the public payphone. It smelled of bad breath.

"Charlie, what do you want?"

"I just wanted to make sure you're okay."

"I'm fine. There, are you satisfied? Are we done here?"

After all this time, she still hated him.

"Karen, you're not going to like this, but hear me out. It's about King."

"You can stop right there."

"I'm serious Karen - it's not a jealousy thing - really - he's bad news."

"Oh that's terrific coming from you. Pot, kettle, black - sound familiar?"

"I know, I know - but King is different - he's a real prick."

"And you're not?"

"Karen, seriously, he's a nasty bit of work."

"Are you finished?"

"Yes. No - watch yourself with him - that's all I'm saying. And watch Jenny. Don't leave him alone with Jenny."

"For goodness sake, Charlie! You really are the limit. Okay, since you've taken the time to call, let's get some things straight here. Number one - who I see has got nothing to do with you. Got that, Charlie? Nothing! Number two - for your information, come tomorrow Jenny won't be living here any more."

"What do you mean - where will she be?"

"She's got a place at Glasgow University."

"That's brilliant."

"Yes it is, and you would have known about it already if you were any kind of a father. But since you've developed this sudden interest in your daughter, you might like to know that she's going on a date tonight."

"Who with?"

"Some guy she met in a club. She doesn't even know his real name, just his nickname. It's not like her... Apart from which, I've told her it's pointless to get involved with someone just when she's moving, but she doesn't listen to anything I say these days. She's hell bent on doing her own thing."

"Do you want me to speak to her?"

"Ha, that's a good one. What makes you think she'll listen to you?"

"I could try."

"You should have been with her when she was growing up. You should have been with both of us, but you weren't. It's too late for trying now. You've lost her. You've lost both of us."

"I -"

"Don't say anything else, Charlie. You've done too much damage. Broken too many promises."

"I'm know. I know. I'm sorry, really I am. But please Karen - watch yourself with King... Karen?"

She'd already hung up. Boyle was speaking to the dial tone. He replaced the receiver. The call had gone better than he'd expected. It was the longest conversation they'd had in years. At least she hadn't hung up on him straight away.

Karen might be worried about Jenny going on this date, but Boyle wasn't. What he'd heard had delighted him. Jenny was smart enough to do the right thing. Meet the guy in a public place. Not drink too much. And even if she wasn't doling out info to her mother, it was a sure thing her friends would know where she was. Jenny would go on her date tonight and tomorrow she'd put 170 beautiful miles between her and King.

Boyle crossed the concourse to the ticket office. He knew in his gut that it was King who'd spiked his drink in The Grapes, but knowing it was one thing, proving it was something else.

Even without the drink spiking thing, King was bad news. Not that Boyle had expected Karen to believe him. Not right off. All he could hope was that he'd planted enough of a seed in her mind. Enough to get her thinking and wondering about him. To maybe look at him from a different angle, see him in a different way.

At least Jenny would be out of harm's way. Jenny, his little girl, a student at Glasgow University. That was something.

Boyle took his place in the queue. Funny the way he'd seen her like that. It was because of her he hadn't killed Frank. In a funny kind of way she'd saved him. Saved them both. Hadn't stopped Frank being killed in the end though. Maybe it was his destiny to die that night. If you believed in things like destiny. The queue shuffled forward.

Boyle stared at the man behind the ticket counter.

"Are you serious?" he asked.

The man stared back at Boyle, face impassive, and repeated what he'd just told him.

"No sleeper service to London on Saturdays."

They stared at each other a minute longer. Boyle nonplussed. Unable to process this piece of incredible information. The man behind the counter just telling it like it was.

Finally realising that Boyle wasn't going anywhere unless he threw him something, the man behind the counter broke the silence.

"You could try the bus station."

Stella's street was drowsy for a Saturday afternoon. Few cars drove by. Seemed like the endless dry weather was bleaching people out. Lethargy had set in. Many of the gardens Boyle passed looked parched. Grass yellowing, leaves dull. Everything felt dusty, like the town needed a good hose down. He wondered how Frank's roses were doing.

He scouted out the house. No cars on the drive, or on the street outside. Windows closed, blinds drawn. Looked like siesta time. He fingered the tickets in his pocket and wandered along the street a little, gazing at gardens without seeing them. Two tickets.

He turned and walked back towards Frank's place. He paused at the entrance to the drive and looked at the house. Wondered if it was cool inside, or baking hot. The tickets were one way. Boyle had no intentions of coming back.

He stared at the blank windows. Wondered if she was even in there. He hesitated then walked on. Two tickets.

He paced the street like a caged bear then took out the phone. The Stella phone. He weighed it in his hand. It looked small and insignificant. He could switch it off and leave it off. She'd have no way of getting in contact with him then. He could trash it, the way he'd trashed the other phone. Then he'd have no way of getting in touch with her either. Two tickets. He pressed call. She answered on the second ring.

"Where have you been?"

He batted the question away with one of his own.

"Are you alone?"

"Yes - they were-"

"Expecting anyone?"

"No."

"Open the back door. I'll be right over."

Boyle put the phone in his pocket and walked to the house. Briskly, but not too briskly. He strolled down the drive like he had every right to be there. Glancing around, he saw Frank's roses. They looked all dried up. Fallen white petals curling on the ground, turning brown. Frank's body was barely cold and already his garden was withering. He'd be turning in his grave, if he had one.

Boyle headed straight around the back. She'd left the

door open for him, just like he'd asked. He slipped inside, and locked it behind him. He didn't want anyone walking in unannounced.

Two tickets. He figured he'd know how many he was going to need the minute he set eyes on her.

Chapter 32

She was in the kitchen. Turned round startled when he came in, maybe not expecting him quite so soon. Relief flooding her face when she saw it was him. She had on a dress he'd never seen before. Dark floral print on white, kind of floaty. Short sleeves, round neck, skimming her waist. She looked like the last person you'd imagine stabbing someone in the neck. If they were caught and the case went to court, he'd tell her to wear that dress.

She came straight to him. He dropped the duffel bag. Took his sunglasses off. Put them on the work-top.

"What happened to you?"

Concern scratching into her face, marring her features. Concern for him.

"I walked into a door."

She trailed her fingers gently down his cheek.

"Bad door," she murmured.

They kissed. Hot, hungry kisses. She tasted of cigarettes and coffee. Tasted in a way that Frank had never known and never would know.

Boyle shrugged off his jacket. Her hands were under his t-shirt, nails clawing at his back, trying to get inside him. Be part of him. He winced as she dug her fingers into his bruises but it was a delicious kind of pain.

"Where have you been?"

Hot breath whispered in his ear.

"No place in particular."

He held her tight, running his hands over her back. Breathing in her perfume. Fresh and light, not a hint of vanilla.

"They were here." She nibbled at his ear. He shivered, found the zip in the back of her dress.

"Who?" he asked, not really listening.

The zip slipped down smoothly, following the contour of her waist, coming to a stop at the top of her hips.

"The police. This morning. They went through Frank's things."

Boyle knew everything he needed to know about one way tickets and how many he'd need. He slipped a hand inside her dress.

"Did they find anything?"

Her skin, smooth, warm, inviting.

"There's nothing to find."

He teased the dress off her shoulders. It whispered to the floor, revealing her pure, white underwear. She tugged at his t-shirt. He pulled it over his head, tossed it aside.

Two tickets.

Afterwards, they sat in a crumpled heap on the kitchen floor, spent and breathless. The skin of her arm melting hot against his. Stella rested her head back against the cupboard door and gazed at the ceiling.

"I needed that," she said.

Boyle glanced at her sideways. "Me too."

She turned her face towards his. They gazed earnestly at each other for a moment before bursting into laughter.

"Charlie?" she asked, when the laughter faded.

"What is it, baby?"

"Can I see the diamonds?"

"Sure you can."

He tugged the bag towards him and opened it up, neatly stacking the contents as he took them out. Two pairs of trunks, two pairs of socks, toothbrush, toothpaste, passport.

"You travel light," Stella said.

"I didn't know there was any other way," Boyle replied.

He took out the sweatshirt and unrolled it on the floor between them, slowly revealing the diamond jewellery. Stella leaned over it, examining the pieces.

"Is this really worth over a million pounds? I thought there would have been more."

"It didn't come from Argos, baby."

"No need for sarcasm, Charlie." She held a pair of earrings up to the light, entranced. "Beautiful."

"If you like that kind of thing."

"Why, don't you?"

Boyle shrugged. Stella put down the earrings and picked up a necklace. She held it against her throat.

"Now that is stunning," Boyle said.

Her laughter was light and merry. "It's a pity we can't keep any of it."

"Not a chance."

"Not even this teeny, weeny, little ring?"

"Not even that. This tidy lot is our passage to a new life."

He took the solitaire from her and placed it back on the sweatshirt. She watched as he rolled it all up and packed it away.

"Let's go for a shower and cool down," she said.

Boyle left the duffel bag lying on the floor as they fled the kitchen. They stumbled upstairs, clutching their clothes against their naked bodies. Laughing and giggling the way lovers do at the start of an affair.

Boyle's second shower of the day. They gently washed each other, soap-lathered hands gliding over wet skin.

Flesh pressing against flesh. They kissed under the water and made love again. Slowly this time.

They dried themselves, and each other, with white, fluffy towels. Everything clean and fresh. Grime and dust and dirt washed away. Guilt put aside.

She led him to a bedroom. Her room, her bed, she said. Frank had the large bedroom to the front of the house, overlooking his roses.

Stella's room was furnished simply. It looked like it didn't belong to the rest of the house. The walls were painted soft, chalky white. The blind was drawn, shutting out the dry, dusty day. White, gauzy curtains hung at sides of the window, softening the angles and edges. Books were stacked on a bedside table.

He climbed into bed with her, slipping between cool sheets. They talked for a while, whispering secrets, caressing each other. He told her about the bus tickets. Said he couldn't stand it any longer. He was getting out. He wanted her to come with him.

"Won't it make them suspicious if I disappear?"

"Tell them you need to be with your family. You've got a sister, haven't you?"

"Yes, but I haven't seen her for years. She lives in a kind of commune."

"Your sister's a hippy chick?"

"Something like that. She and Frank didn't get on."

"There's a surprise," Boyle grinned. "I like her already."

"Won't they check that I'm there?"

"Yes, but by that time it won't matter. We'll be long gone."

"What about the diamonds?"

"Macallister had a contact - a guy in London - he'll buy them. Of course we won't get anything like what they're really worth, but we'll get enough. At least half a million."

"Half a million? Is that all?"

"Yeah, but that's the trade-off. It'll be fine. Half a mill's more than enough. We'll have to hang out in London until the deal's done, but we'll treat it like a holiday. We can do the sights if you like."

She snuggled up against him. "Tell me more - what will we see?"

"Big Ben."

"What about Westminster Abbey?"

"Definitely. And the Tower."

"Buckingham Palace?"

"Scotland Yard."

"Ha, ha, Very funny." She gave him a playful slap on the chest. "Tell me what happens next," she said, "After our holiday in London."

"Well, when we've had our fill of London we'll take the Eurostar to Paris, and from Paris we can go anywhere you like."

"It will be a wonderful, romantic adventure."

"Yes, it will."

Boyle stared dreamily at the ceiling, twirling her hair in his fingers. Thinking how stupid he'd been to have doubted her and the way he felt about her.

Chapter 33

Boyle stumbled and fell from the cliff edge. He was in freefall. Arms and legs wheeling. Rushing towards stony ground.

A spasm ran through his body, jolting him awake in a strange room. He sat up, heart racing. Disorientated, until he noticed Stella dozing beside him.

He breathed out, long and slow, his heart slowly settling back into its normal rhythm as recent events came back to him. But how recent was recent? Or, to put it another way - how long had he been sleeping?

He glanced around, wondering what had woken him. There was a small, gold travel clock on the beside table. Ten past five. The bus left the station at quarter past six. They'd have to get a move on. He put his hand on her shoulder to shake her awake, pausing as he heard a sound from downstairs. The same sound had woken him.

Someone knocking at the door.

"Stella," shaking her shoulder. Lips brushing her ear, his voice low, like there was a chance that whoever was standing on the outside of the front door, all the way downstairs and at the other side of the house could hear him.

Stella stirred, opened her eyes, gave him a drowsy smile.

"Hello, Charlie." Despite his rising anxiety, he registered her voice being husky and sexy as hell. Couldn't believe he'd ever thought about leaving without her.

The knock came again, pulling him back to the here and now.

Stella, still half asleep and not getting it.

"Stella, there's someone at the door."

The knock came again. Louder, more persistent. Whoever it was, they weren't in a hurry to leave. Stella sat up, clutching the duvet to her chest, suddenly wide awake.

"Who is it? Is it them?"

They both knew who she meant by *them*.

"Unless you haven't been paying the milkman, I can't think who else it could be."

"Oh God, what do they want?" Panic rising. "Do you think they know? Oh God, they must know."

She stumbled out of bed, looking around for clothes that weren't there. Boyle leaned over and grabbed her arm. She tensed, staring at him, wide-eyed.

"Listen, baby, if they knew they'd be breaking the door down instead of rat-a-tatting. They don't know a thing. Got that? Not a thing."

She nodded, tousled hair tumbling around her face. A little mascara had smudged under her eyes. The small imperfection only increased her beauty, his desire.

"You've got to pull yourself together."
He could talk. It was all he could do not to drag her back into bed.

"This is what you're going to do," he told her. "Put your dressing gown on, go downstairs, and answer the door. Tell them you took a tablet to help you sleep. Play dumb. Understand?"

She nodded. He let go of her arm. She lifted a

217

dressing gown from a hook on the back of the door. White and fluffy, like the towels. She wrapped herself up tight, cocooning herself from neck to calves. She looked so vulnerable it was heartbreaking.

He got out of bed, came up behind her, whispered in her ear.

"They don't know a thing, baby. Not a thing." He kissed her on the cheek.

"Don't worry Charlie," she said, "I've got it."

He followed her out to the hall. Another volley of heavy rapping as she started down the stairs. A squeak and a rattle as the letter box was pushed open.

"Mrs Valentine, it's the police. Are you in there? Are you alright?"

"I'm here. I'm coming. What's going on?" Her voice, weary, confused, maybe a little worried. My oh my, but she's good, thought Boyle.

He gathered up the scattered clothes and shoes they'd abandoned outside the bathroom. He retreated into the bedroom with the bundle, leaving the door open a crack. He wanted to hear what was going on.

He dressed quickly. The small sounds he made lost under the bustle of the door being unlocked downstairs and people being ushered in. Then he leaned against the door frame and listened.

There were some initial niceties. Niceties were a good sign. Not something you wasted on a murder suspect. Boyle lapped up the small talk. Sorry for disturbing you, hope we didn't alarm you, and so on.

He recognised the voices. The first was the Commander's slightly nasal monotone. The second had the sing-song lilt of the Western Isles. It belonged to the Commander's pet sergeant.

Boyle pondered the nature of the call. The Commander was one of the last people to see Frank alive. Maybe he felt some kind of responsibility and had come to offer his support. Whatever that meant. Or could be he actually had something to say. That would be a first.

Stella told them that there was no need to apologise, that she'd been tired and had gone for a lie down. She asked what she could do for them. The response was silence. There must have been something in their faces that gave them away, something in the way they looked at her.

"What's wrong?" Stella's voice rising, urgent, edgy.

"Something has happened hasn't it? What is it - have you found my husband? Have you found Frank?" Racking it up nicely.

"Maybe you should sit down first, Mrs Valentine."

"No. Whatever you've got to tell me, I want you to tell me right here, right now."

Smart cookie, letting Boyle listen in on the deal.

"Very well," came the Commander's monotone, "I'm sorry, Mrs Valentine, but yes, we've found your husband."

"Then where is he? Why isn't he here?"

A moment's pause. Then Stella again. "Oh no. You don't mean...?"

"I'm afraid so, Mrs Valentine," the gentle lilt of the Sergeant's voice, "Your husband is dead."

Stella gave a little cry. There was some muted kerfuffle, noises of sympathy, sounds of them moving through to the living room. For the next few minutes all Boyle could pick up was the hum of low voices, no words discernable, just the Commander droning on, doing his best to console the newly-created widow.

Stella's voice suddenly ringing out clearly, snapped Boyle out of the semi-trance he'd slumped into.

"No it's all right, thank you, I'll manage. I'm glad of something to do." Stella, leaving the living room, going through to the kitchen, her voice tight, slightly distracted, as if she couldn't quite take it all in.

No more chit-chat. Boyle pictured the Commander and his Sergeant sitting stiffly in their seats, looking at each other, relieved they hadn't had to deal with hysteria or breakdown. Quietly grateful for Mrs Valentine's distressed dignity.

Sounds emerged from the kitchen. Cupboard doors opening and closing. The chink of crockery. Soon the aroma of freshly brewed coffee drifted upstairs.

"Did you hear?" Stella whispered. She leaned against the door, face pale.

Boyle nodded. "I got the bit about them finding Frank, but once you moved out of the hall it was all mumbles."

"They know it's Frank, but I've got to formally identify the body. They said I could call someone, but I said no. I just wanted to get it over and done with. I've made them coffee. They're going to take me right now, as soon as I'm dressed. Did I do right?"

She spoke in a fast, nervous whisper. Words tumbling over themselves as they spilled from her lips.

"You did great, baby."

She slipped the dressing gown off and tossed it on the bed. Her skin was flawless. Luminous in the soft light filtering through the blind. She pulled drawers open, picked through underwear. Boyle took her in his arms. She stiffened. He murmured in her ear.

"Take it easy, baby. You've just had a big shock. They'll expect you to take a while to get yourself together."

She relaxed in his arms, turned round to face him.

"Oh Charlie, what if I do something wrong, what if they suspect?"

"Baby, you won't do anything wrong, and they don't suspect a thing. Nothing has changed."

"What about the tickets?" She glanced at the small, gold travel clock. "We'll miss the bus."

"Forget the tickets and the bus - we'll get another bus. You know, maybe it's better this way. You've had a big shock - you'll need to get away for a day or two. Spend time with that sister of yours. They'll get that - they'll understand it."

"But what about the funeral - I'll have to arrange Frank's funeral. I'm going to have to stand at his graveside and weep. Oh God, I can't face any of this. I don't want to see him lying there dead. What if I say something, what if I give myself away?"

"Stella baby, you've got to pull yourself together."

He took her by the wrists, pulled her against him and looked into her eyes. She had her back to the window and he couldn't tell what colour they were. Only that they were dark.

"Don't worry about the funeral - it'll be delayed until they've done all the forensic tests on Frank's body. We'll be long gone by then."

"But I'll still have to see him lying there. I thought I would never have to see him again and now I'm going to have to look at him. That man is impossible. I feel as though I'll never be free of him. He's going to haunt me all my days."

"It'll be over in a second, baby. That's all it takes."

"Promise?"

"I promise. By this time tomorrow we'll be out of here and the bad stuff will all be over."

"Do you keep your promises, Charlie?"

"Always."

"I hope so."

She pulled away from him, turning her head so that he couldn't read her expression.

"For both our sakes," she added. So softly, he wondered if he had imagined it.

He watched in silence as she put on her underwear, listening to the easy murmur of material swishing against her skin. She walked to the wardrobe, hips swaying in a way that almost drove him crazy. He wondered if she knew the effect she had on him.

She opened the wardrobe door and took a moment to consider the appropriate dress code for identifying a body. Going by his own experience of accompanying the nearest, though not necessarily dearest, to the morgue, it wasn't something that most people gave much consideration to. But then Stella wasn't most people.

He watched as she shrugged on a black jersey dress. The high round neck and long sleeves meant that she was modestly sheathed from head to knee, but the slight flare of the skirt as she moved coupled with the way it flowed over her soft contours made Boyle's eyes pop.

She smoothed the dress down, examined herself in the mirror, then padded towards him in stockinged feet.

"I'll fix my hair and face in the bathroom, but other than that, will I do?"

She gazed at him steadily, chin tilted up, one eyebrow arched. Her earlier anxiety eviscerated.

"You'll do," he said. Thinking that she knew exactly what she was doing to him. Sometimes she scared him.

She took a step towards the door, then stopped and turned to face him again.

"Charlie?"

"Yeah?"

"Why don't we stay and see this thing out?"

His skin prickled like someone was giving him tiny electrical shocks all over his body.

"I thought we'd agreed to -"

"But if we run, it's as good as admitting our guilt. Us disappearing, Frank dead. With big clues like that, how long before they start putting it all together? How long before they start hunting us down? How far will we get, Charlie? London? Paris?"

Her voice was low but urgent. She'd clearly been giving the matter some thought. But when? While they'd been making love? Or when she'd been making coffee? Perhaps she'd been pondering it while the Commander and his lackey were making good with their sincere

222

regrets.

"And even if we do get away," she went on, "how long will the money from the diamonds last? It's one thing dreaming about this beach paradise of yours, but I don't want to end up living in some cheap, dirty hovel, with flies and mosquitoes buzzing around me. I want a good life, Charlie. I deserve a good life. I didn't go through all-"

A voice called upstairs. Stella stopped mid-rant.

"Are you alright up there, Mrs Valentine?" The sergeant.

Stella and Boyle looked at each other for a bare moment before she opened the bedroom door and called back.

"Yes, I'm fine. I'll be with you in a moment."

She turned to Boyle, whispered to him again, then the door closed and she was gone.

Chapter 34

Boyle stood in the middle of the room, frozen like a player in a demented game of Statues. He could hear Stella moving around in the bathroom next door. The Commander wasn't the sharpest knife in the drawer. In fact he was a prime example of someone being promoted out of the way. But Boyle wasn't about to take a chance on overexciting him, or his Sergeant, by gifting them two sets of footsteps overhead to wonder about.

Having no other choice, Boyle stood very still, and had himself a little think.

First of all he thought about what Stella had said to him before she left.

You will be here when I get back, won't you?

That's what he thought he'd heard. A question. Her seeking reassurance from him that he'd be there for her. That he wouldn't let her down. But now he wasn't so sure. Now he was thinking that it had been more of an order. Her telling him that he *would* be there.

No, more than that - there was an implied threat in the words. An unspoken *or else*.

She took her time with her hair and face. He wondered about that as well. If she had deliberately left him to sweat it out, stranded in a minefield of creaking floorboards.

Finally, he heard the bathroom door open. Heard her traipsing downstairs. Then came the voices, muffled words. People moving around. *What the hell were they doing down there?* Not a sound could he make, not a muscle could he move. All he could do was wonder.

An hour ago he had been crazy, head-over-heels, in love with her, but she so constantly wrong-footed him he never knew where he was from one minute to the next. Loving her. Hating her. Wanting her. Loathing her.

He was like a fly being lured into a pitcher plant. Enticed in by the good looks and sweet smells, tumbling and falling into the depths. Struggling. Finally giving himself up. Drowning.

Had it been the same with Frank? Had he tumbled into Stella's depths, ending up dead because of it? Boyle wondered again how wrong he'd been about Frank. About everything. Had she been nervous about them finding his body when she came upstairs, or excited? Was the whole thing giving her a buzz?

He wondered if she was toying with him. Wondered if she needed him or if she had threatened him. What was real, what was imagined? His mind whirring. Paranoid thoughts merging with tumbling emotions.

A woman capable of stabbing her husband in the neck then cold-bloodedly suffocating him was capable of anything. But she'd acted out of fear when she'd stabbed Frank. Hadn't she? She'd been scared of him. Terrified of what he would do to her.

Then why did she suddenly want to stay - to carry on living in the house she'd shared with him? It could hardly be so that she could remember the good times.

How had she put it - *Why don't we stay and see this thing out?*

Where had that come from? Didn't she realise that they would never see it out. Frank was a senior police officer - their pursuit of his killer would be relentless. And now that they had his body, there would be no doubt in anyone's mind that he had been murdered. They'd never let it go.

Voices. People on the move. Front door opening and closing. Voices gone.

Boyle listened to the small creaks and groans of the house settling. Wondered if it really was empty, or if it was a trick. Could he hear breathing? Was there someone there, beyond the door? Maybe she'd given him up. She could have told them anything - that he'd come here and raped her, kept her prisoner. She could have told them, with a tremble in her voice, that he'd killed Frank.

No, she wouldn't do that. Would she? She was in too deep. Or was she?

It was a matter of record that Boyle had assaulted Frank. Everyone knew he loathed the man. It was Boyle who had driven the car, dumped the body. She could say anything and they'd believe her. Maybe she'd had her story prepared all along. All she'd been doing was waiting for her chance.

The jaws of paranoia had locked on Boyle and there was no shaking them off. He was second guessing everything and everyone, including himself. He clutched his head. *Enough!* It had to stop before he drove himself around the twist.

Fine. If he was going down, he was going down like a man, not a mouse. He strode to the door taking big fuck-off steps, not wee timorous beastie ones. The floorboards shrieked and moaned. He grasped the door-handle firmly, a man's grasp. He turned it and yanked the door open. *Boo!*

There was no-one there.

He strode into the hall and thundered down the stairs. He got to the bottom and tensed for the voice in his ear, the hand on his shoulder, but neither came. The only sound Boyle heard was the drumming of his own heart. And then he laughed.

His laughter sounded jaundiced and feverish. Sick laughter. It echoed through the empty house. She hadn't given him up after all. Well how wrong could a guy be?

Stay or go, that was the question. *So, Charlie, how are you feeling now? Love her or hate her? Want her or loathe her?* He eyed the clock on the wall. A few minutes to six. If he went pelters he could still make the bus. But if he ran out on her now she'd surely give him up. Would even be able to tell them what bus he was on. All they'd have to do was flag it down and find him sitting pretty with a bag of stolen jewellery.

But if he did stay, he wanted at least to have the illusion of choice. He didn't want to feel as if he'd been manipulated or threatened into it. Did he want her or not? Could he leave without her?

The clock ticked. If he waited much longer he wouldn't have a decision to make. He went into the kitchen. The bright, clean, sterile kitchen.

He looked for a black duffel bag. His black duffel bag. Black against white. It wouldn't be hard to spot. It would be just where he left it. Slumped on the floor, right beside where they'd fucked like a pair of alley cats.

Boyle stared at the empty space where the bag should be.

Chapter 35

Boyle glanced around, hoping that maybe he'd misremembered. That he'd dropped it someplace else. Knowing that he hadn't. A big, fat, parasitical maggot of fear, anger and confusion gnawed into his mind.

She'd done it. She'd taken it. But why? So that he couldn't run out on her or because she wanted it for herself?

That was it - she wanted the diamonds. She'd been hypnotised by them. He should never have let her see them. One peek at the shiny, shiny, ice was all it had taken. Or maybe stealing them was what she'd had in mind all along.

She wasn't worried about him running out on her, because she was the one doing the running. She wasn't going to come back from the morgue. She was planning on leaving and she was going to take a girl's best friend with her. Two could go far on half a million, one could go further.

You never thought of that, did you, Charlie? You never thought she'd run out on you. The running was always yours for the taking. No-one else's. You thought you were in charge, but she had you all along, Charlie boy. She had you from the second you first looked into those cool, grey eyes.

No, wait. Think, Charlie, think. She didn't take the bag to the mortuary. Stella with a duffel bag slung over her shoulder would be as incongruous as a race horse in a bikini. She didn't have time to do much with it before she left. She must have hidden it when she was making the coffee. No wonder she hadn't wanted any help. It had to be here somewhere. Somewhere close.

Boyle turned around and slowly scanned the kitchen. His glance caught the wall clock. It was after six. He'd never make it to the bus station now. Okay, the decision had been made for him. Forget the bus. This is where he was at. There would be other buses. There were always other buses. Hundreds of buses.

He turned three-sixty, felt himself relax. This was better. It was just like looking for a drug stash or a hidden weapon. Familiar territory. All he had to do was be methodical.

He started by opening cupboards and pulling out drawers. Even the ones that looked too shallow. You could never tell what was behind the façade in these fancy kitchens. He found his sunglasses. She'd swept them into a drawer. But no duffel bag.

He looked under the sink and in the fridge and in a cupboard that turned out to be the dishwasher. No duffel bag. He stood on a stool and felt along the cupboard tops. He looked in the oven and in the microwave. He even looked in the fancy Brabantia matt steel bin. Nothing but garbage.

When he'd finished in the kitchen he moved on to the utility room. The sight of the washing machine made his heart soar like a lark. He bent down - there was something in the drum. Something dark. He grinned as he unlatched the door.

His grin puckered and faded as he pulled out the contents. Nothing more than a load of damp washing.

The tumble dryer was as empty as his future looked right now. Getting desperate, he looked in the mop bucket. Not even a dribble of grey water.

He opened a tall, narrow cupboard. Frank's gardening jacket was hanging inside, bulging suspiciously. The bulge flattened to nothing when Boyle pressed his hand against it. He looked beneath the jacket anyway. Nothing but bare wall.

He turned the laundry hamper upside down and scuffed at the contents with his foot. There were items of Frank's still waiting to be washed. Things he'd never wear again.

Looking at the unwashed underpants of a dead man wasn't right. It gave Boyle the heebie-jeebies. He pushed the laundry aside. Still no duffel bag. She'd really done a number on him. He was a fool - he should have seen it coming.

He marched through to the hall, closed his eyes for a few seconds, turned around, went back into the kitchen and cast a fresh look over the room. He turned the stools over, looking underneath the seats in case she'd managed to wedge it inside one of them. No, she hadn't.

He looked everywhere he could think of. Then he looked again. Nada. Nothing. Sweet fuck all. He was beginning to get seriously pissed off. She'd taken him for a complete fool and he'd let himself be took.

There was a word to describe his situation. An ugly word, but then it was an ugly situation. Cunt-struck. He'd been totally cunt-struck. She'd led him about by the dick and he'd followed, panting after her like a dog driven crazy by a bitch in heat. Fuck. Fuck. Fuck. He cursed the day he'd ever set eyes on her.

Even when she was loving him, there was an edge of threat. She was capable of turning with the flicker of an eyelash. Just look what happened to Frank. Screwing her was like fucking a praying mantis - you just hoped to hell you got out with your head and your balls still intact. He supposed he should think himself lucky for not ending up with a knife in his throat. Stupid, stupid, bastard for ever getting involved.

"Looking for something?"

The voice came from nowhere.

Boyle spun around.

Chapter 36

She was standing in the doorway, cool as you like, one eyebrow raised, casually surveying the damage he'd wrought. Boyle cast a glance over his handiwork. The kitchen looked as though a hurricane had blown through.

"How could you tell?" he answered.

Boyle was impressed by how cool he managed to sound. In truth, she'd rattled him like a roof tile in a storm. She could have slid a knife right between his ribs and he wouldn't have known it was coming.

"All you had to do was ask."

She picked her way through the upturned stools and debris to the Brabantia bin.

"I looked in there," he said.

"Maybe you didn't look hard enough."

She removed the lid and took out a near empty bin bag. She sat it on the floor, reached back into the bin and pulled out a second bin bag. She opened it, turned it upside down and emptied the contents onto the floor. The duffel bag slithered out and landed with a thud.

Boyle stared at it. He couldn't believe he'd missed it.

She walked around a stool and rummaged in the back of a drawer that was hanging open. Her hand emerged clutching a packet of cigarettes and a cheap disposable lighter. She lit up then offered him the packet. He shook his head.

"Do you mind if I close this?" she asked.

"Be my guest." Fractured inside, but still sounding cool.

"I didn't want to spoil a work in progress," she replied, easily out-cooling him.

She slid the drawer closed and expelled a thin jet of smoke.

Boyle followed the trail, watching as it left her lips and dispersed against Frank's unblemished brilliant-white ceiling. He wondered when the decay would set in, when it would start to discolour. Slowly turning a cancerous shade of nicotine yellow.

"Tell me something, Charlie."

She leaned against a counter edge, cigarette poised between two fingers.

"Sure," he shrugged, "Anything for you, baby." The personification of casualness.

"You thought I'd taken it, didn't you?"

She looked at him through narrowed eyes. Boyle didn't answer.

Drawers and cupboard doors hung open on either side of her. She'd done this thing with her hair, twisted it and pinned it up, exposing the nape of her neck. She wore a light swipe of make-up, not too much, just enough. The black dress fitted like it had been made with her in mind. Amid the chaos, she looked devastatingly beautiful.

"Okay," she said, "We'll pass on that. Why don't we try this one on for size - if you'd found the bag, would you still have been here when I got back?"

Their gazes locked.

"I told you, Stella, we're in this together."

The lie flowed as smooth and easy over his lips as butter melting on a hot skillet. She took another drag on the cigarette and exhaled a plume of smoke. Boyle had stopped wondering when the decay would set in. He knew the answer. The rot had started long ago.

"Since you're so hooked on playing Twenty Questions, why don't you tell me something?" he said.

"Fire away," she answered. "I don't have anything to hide."

That struck Boyle as amusing, but he didn't comment. Instead he asked the question that had been gnawing at his mind.

"Was there any truth in what you told me about Frank - was he really the monster you made him out to be?"
Stella smiled.

"Now we're getting to it," she said. "You want the truth? Okay, I'll tell you the truth. Frank was a gentleman, he loved me. He was crazy about me and I despised him for it."

"What about all that talk about him hunting you down if you ever left him?"

"I lied. The truth is he told me that if I ever left him he'd kill himself."

"I feel sorry for the guy."

"Don't feel sorry for him - he got what he wanted. All his wishes came true the day he married me."

"He should have been more careful about what he wished for."

"There's a lesson in there for us all."

"You're poison Stella, pure unadulterated poison."

"You love me, so what does that make you?"

"A pathetic human being, and I'm not proud of it."

"You still love me, right now don't you, Charlie? At the very least you desire me - just like Frank did. Funny, isn't it?"

She stubbed the cigarette out in a small glass bowl, mashing it hard against the bottom.

"You didn't have to kill him."

"You didn't have to punch him."

"I thought he was treating you badly - oh Christ I've

been such a fool."

"Poor Charlie. Poor naïve Charlie."

She lit another cigarette.

"Naive? Naive doesn't begin to cover it. I must have been off my head to ever get involved with you."

"It's amazing."

"What is?"

"You profess to love me, but you are so ready and willing to believe the worst. You want the truth, Charlie? The real, honest to God truth? Frank was a monster. He deserved to die the way he did, and if I had the chance I'd do it all over again."

Boyle stared at her. She stared right back at him, chin tilted, defiant. A queer smile tugged at her lips. He didn't ask her what was funny.

Chapter 37

"So, how did it go at the morgue?"

Hardly small talk, but given the circumstances, it was the best Boyle could come up with.

They'd straightened the kitchen, silence ballooning between them. Now they drank coffee. Anyone casually glancing at them through a window would have thought it a typical domestic scene. Except the doors were locked and the blinds were shut. The only people watching were Boyle and Stella and the only people they were watching were each other. Sideways, and there was nothing casual about it.

"I said hello to Frank, how do you think it went?"

Boyle kept his mouth shut. He liked her a lot better before he knew her.

"Oh don't you look at me like I'm Hard Hearted Hannah. You're hardly Mr Innocent in all of this. It was fine. They handled me like I was made of the finest porcelain and they didn't want to risk breaking me. They were kind and solicitous and terrified that I might start sobbing and then they'd be stuck with an emotional woman. I held my head high and played my part with the dignity befitting the widow of a senior police officer.

Okay?"

"Fine. I was only asking."

"Well now you know."

Boyle's belly rumbled and he realised he hadn't eaten anything in over twenty-four hours. No wonder he couldn't think straight.

"I'm starving. Got any food in?"

"You should know - you've been through the entire kitchen."

Boyle scrunched up his face. "Do we have to do this?"

"Do what?"

"This. The snarky married thing."

She stared at him for a beat, eyes hard.

"No, I don't suppose we do. What do you want?"

"Anything, as long as it's fast."

Ten minutes later Boyle was scoffing down a pile of hot buttered toast. The more things changed, the more they stayed the same.

She stared at the crumb-laden plate when he'd finished.

"Come to think of it, I'm pretty hungry myself. There's a couple of steaks in the fridge if you fancy?"

Boyle fancied.

Plump sirloin, rare. Baby potatoes, boiled and tossed in butter. Crisp mange tout on the side. They shared a bottle of red. Boyle didn't know what kind. He didn't care. Certain phrases mouthed at his mind. Phrases like *last meal* and *condemned man*.

The edge fell away from them as they ate. By the time they'd finished he could almost pretend they were a normal couple getting over a normal spat. He swallowed a glug of wine and sat back from the table, pushing the insistent phrases aside along with his empty plate. It was the best meal he'd had in a long time.

"What did you mean about staying?"

She looked at him sharply, grey eyes glinting. He put

his hands up in mock surrender.

"Whoa. I'm not starting anything, but if we're gonna get out of this thing intact, we've got to get everything straight between us."

She took a moment to think about it.

"Okay. I know we've got the diamonds, but don't you see, we could have so much more."

"Like what?"

"This house for a start, it's got to be worth at least four hundred thousand, maybe even half a million. Put that together with the half million from the diamonds and we're millionaires. And then there's the car and Frank's life insurance."

"And what about his gold fillings and police pension while we're at it?"

"Don't be so facetious."

"Stella, baby, you're living in the land of cloud cuckoo. We'd never get away with it. The longer we hang around, the tighter the net is going to close. Even if we were innocent as new born lambs, it would still take God knows how long to sort it all out. It could be weeks before there's even a funeral. And who says he left the house to you anyway?"

"Who else would he leave it to?"

"I dunno, you tell me, but if he was the monster you made him out to be, he could have left it to the home for one-legged goldfish just to spite you."

"What do you mean, *if* he was a monster?"

"All I'm saying is, who knew what way his mind worked? It's just not worth the risk. The only chance we have is if we get away and it's got to be soon. For your sake as much as mine. As far as we know, I'm not even in the frame yet - but baby, you're in it up to your neck."

"You said they didn't have a thing."

"They don't. Not yet. But I told you, they always start by looking close to home. Before today, Frank was only missing and that was bad enough. Now he's turned up murdered. They'll go through your marriage like a dose of Epsom Salts. They already know you slept in separate bedrooms."

"I didn't tell them that."

"They know it anyway. I mean it's pretty damn obvious - all his stuff is in one room, yours is in another. C'mon baby - they're detectives."

"Lots of couples sleep in separate rooms."

"Maybe so, but anyone taking one look at you is gonna wonder what kind of man would kick you out of bed. And if it was the other way around, and you left the marital bed, they're going to want to know why."

"Maybe he was a heavy snorer."

"That's what I said."

"What do you mean, that's what you said?"

"To Lindy - that officer who was here yesterday-"

"The fat one?"

"Yeah Stella, the fat one. She commented on you having separate bedrooms and I said that maybe Frank was a snorer."

"And what did she say?"

"That maybe he was."

"See?"

"Well maybe he was and maybe they'll buy it, but maybe they won't. But I tell you one thing for sure, baby, they will be looking for cracks and chinks in your marriage and when they find them they're going to be working at them until they burst wide open. All these people do is deal with the dirty, rotten side of humanity. If a kid's abused, the first person they suspect is daddy. If a husband is bumped off, the number one suspect is the wife. And do you know why? Because mostly that's the way it is. They'll be thinking, they didn't sleep together so who was having an affair - him or her? Either would be a motive for you killing him. All they need is someone who's seen us together and before you know it they'll be joining the dots and making big, ugly pictures."

"Okay, okay, I get it. We don't hang around - we get out - but only on one condition."

"Name it."

"I need to know if you trust me, Charlie."

He stood up, pulled her up beside him, held her close, murmured in her ear.

"Of course I trust you, Stella. I told you, we're in this together, baby, all the way."

Glad she couldn't see the doubt scrawled all over his face.

"You sure?" Whispered in his ear.

"Absolutely, baby."

She squeezed him tight. He felt a stabbing pain where her fingers dug into a bruise. This time it didn't feel so good.

"Charlie?"

"What is it, baby?"

"Let's go now, Charlie, let's run away together."

He looked at her.

"You sure?"

"I am if you are."

"Okay, you'd better get packed. Pack light and change into something low key and practical."

"And here I was planning to put on a ball gown and tiara."

She smirked at him then turned and walked away. He stared after her, watching the hem of her dress swaying to the same beat as her hips.

"You're funny, Stella, really funny," he murmured as she sashayed through the door, but he wasn't laughing.

Chapter 38

Boyle paced the floor, trying not to look at the clock as the seconds crawled by. The house was a lie. Boyle couldn't wait to get out of it. It made him sick with all its pretensions of good lives well spent.

He glanced at the clock again. Less than a minute had passed since he'd last looked. It was after ten. Nearly half past.

It was only four days since he'd first crossed the threshold and it was already full of bad memories. It wasn't just the house. The whole town reeked to him of broken relationships and decay. He'd fucked up in the most spectacular fashion. It would be good to get away. Start again, reinvent himself, change his name, become the person he wanted to be instead of the one he was.

He tried to conjure up images of his new life. This place he was running to where food was cheap and life was easy, and every day he'd feel sun on his face and sand between his toes, and he'd make love to Stella with the sound of surf in the background. But when he pictured her, she had a smear of blood on her face and her eyes glittered like sun on a razor's edge.

"Charlie?"

She'd snuck up on him again. He'd have to watch that. She'd dressed in jeans and a white shirt. Her hair hung loose and silky. She looked clean and fresh in a way that made him think of big skies above a wide blue ocean.

"Yeah?"

"I can't go with you."

"I thought we'd settled all that - we're in this together, baby."

"But we're not, are we?"

"What do you mean?"

His mind crackled, trying to figure her angle but she'd wrong footed him again. Just the way she had right from the start.

"I know you don't trust me, Charlie. You think I lied about Frank, about the kind of man he was, but you're wrong. It was true - every word. He was a monster hiding behind the face of a civilised man. You've got no idea. He was a sadist. You still don't understand do you? The only chance I had to get away from him was by killing him. It was me or him."

Either she'd just given him the performance of a lifetime, or she was telling the truth. Boyle pulled her into his arms, buried his face in her hair. It smelled good.

"I believe you, Stella. I'm with you all the way."

He meant it when he said it. He felt her relax against him and he had a warm cosy feeling that everything was going to work out okay after all. She was an innocent blighted. He'd done bad things but for all the right reasons. They were just trying to survive. Together they would make it all come good. Then she pulled away from him.

"It's too late, Charlie. Maybe it was always too late for us. Everything we have together is based on lies and deceit. How can anything good ever come out of adultery, theft and murder? It's no use."

"But Stella-"

She put a finger on his lips to hush him.

"There's no future for us together, Charlie. But apart, who knows - we might be better people."

"But I did it all for you, Stella - for us."

Now that she was ending it, he realised that he'd got her all wrong. He wanted her. Needed her.

"I know you did, but it's not going to work out. It was never going to work out. You have to go. Go now."

She looked heartbreakingly sad, but it was clear she'd made up her mind. It was over.

"What about you? What will you do?" he asked.

"I'm going to do what I said and see this thing out. I'll come through it, I know I will. After that, I don't know, but I'll be alright. Don't worry, I won't say anything about you. I won't give you away, Charlie, I promise."

"Do you always keep your promises?"

"Always."

He hefted the duffel bag onto the counter.

"Here, at least take some of the diamonds."

She put a hand on his wrist, halting him.

"No, you keep the diamonds, Charlie. Make a future for yourself. A good future. And don't forget your daughter."

He looked at her, eyebrows raised. She smiled.

"You mentioned her once. She needs you, Charlie. Maybe she doesn't realise it yet, but she will, and when she does, you make sure you're there for her."

Boyle slung the bag over his shoulder.

"Don't forget your sunglasses." Stella said, dangling them from her fingers.

"Sunglasses after dark? I don't think so."

Chapter 39

The night air felt thick and heavy as treacle. Thunder rumbled in the distance. Boyle walked out to the street without looking back. The first fat plops of rain had fallen by the time he'd taken two steps towards the city centre.

The rain felt good. It would wash away the dust and grime and make the world clean again. He pulled his collar up.

There was a car parked in the street he hadn't seen before. A Mercedes C-Class. Boyle wasn't big on cars, but this one looked nice. The rain came on heavy. He thought for a moment how convenient it would be to be able to get in and go. He admired the sleek lines of the silver car as he passed. Looked like it would be a smooth ride. There was a discreet sticker in the windscreen. A hire car. He considered and almost immediately junked the idea of hiring a car for himself. He'd need to show i-d and then he'd be logged onto their system and easily traceable. Forget that.

The rainstorm came on fast and heavy but didn't last long. By the time he got to the train station it was over and he was soaked. His jeans clung to his legs as he trudged across the concourse. Rain dripped from his hair and trickled down his neck. He stopped and looked at the departures board. Nothing until morning. The concourse was as desolate as he felt. He left by the main entrance and walked along Academy Street to the bus station.

An ambulance had parked outside a pub, back doors open. A small crowd watched from a safe distance as two paramedics tried to get a shrieking woman with blood streaming down her face into the back of it.

I want him to fucking well come with me.

A fat, ugly lunk swayed in the street behind the ambulance.

Behave yerself pishflaps and get into the fucking ambulance.

I want you to come with me, you big bastard.

A couple emerged from a pub further down the street and glanced towards the commotion. Boyle's heart lurched. Jenny, on her date with the mystery man.

They'll no let me on, you silly cunt.

Jenny didn't notice him, her attention on the street cabaret. Boyle mistrusted the skinny dude she was with on sight. He was standing too tight in, crowding her, fancying his chances. He said something, his grinning mouth way closer to her ear than it had any right or need to be. Jenny subtly pulled back from him. Boyle smirked. The skinny dude didn't know it yet, but he was already history.

They turned their backs on the entertainment and walked along the street, away from Boyle. Cool, fresh air blew through the gap between them. Tomorrow she'd be starting a new life, well away from this creep as well as the one her mother was shacking up with. Good luck sweetheart.

A police car screeched to a halt in front of Boyle. A cop he vaguely recognised got out and treated him to a double take. Maybe it was his beat up face that caught the cop's attention or maybe he recognised him but couldn't place him. Either way he took a good look. Boyle gave no indication that he knew the cop and kept on walking. The cop looked like he was about to say something but was distracted by Juliet and her Romeo.

But I love you.

I love you as well, my wee pishflaps.

I don't wanna go without you.

Get in the bastarding ambulance, you silly cunting woman.

Who was it said romance was dead?

The bus station was twice as bleak as the train station. All the overnight rides had long since left town and it was a long time till morning. There wasn't even a pigeon in sight, though Boyle did catch a dark movement, which may or may not have been a rat. He shuddered. He didn't like rats. Having no place else to go, he drifted into Harry's All Nite Café.

He ordered a cup of tea. The woman behind the counter served him without taking a second look. Sights worse than Boyle's face passed through the café on a daily basis.

"There you go, love."

She slid his tea towards him. She was thin, with a worn face and clamped-in cheeks. A purple clasp pulled her hair back revealing a good inch of dark roots against the blonde. She looked like she lived on cigarettes and diesel fumes. He decided he liked her without knowing or caring why.

He more or less had his pick of seats. He chose a booth at the back and, having nothing better to do with his time, took a good long look at his fellow patrons.

A man with greasy black hair was shovelling an all-night breakfast into his mouth, his face two inches above the plate like he was scared someone would steal his food before he got it down his throat.

A young couple at a window table giggled as they fed each other pieces of tray bake.

Three teenage boys ate burgers and chips, laughing as

they punched each other on the arm.

An old jakey sat in the corner near the toilets, eating sugar. Boyle recognised him.

Dodo Stink was a Friday night regular at the cells when the weather was cold. He'd sit in the street causing an obstruction until he was arrested, knowing full well he'd have to be kept in jail till the courts opened on Monday morning. Until then he could enjoy the luxury of a bunk and three squares a day. He stank and he was a bloody nuisance, but Boyle liked him. Seemed that Boyle's cup was fairly running over with love for his fellow man. He finished his tea and ordered two more. One for himself, and one for Dodo. The old wino threw him a suspicious look but accepted the tea.

People piled into the café in noisy bursts as the pubs closed down. There was a brisk trade in bacon rolls, all-night breakfasts and Harry's curry special. The curry was a toxic shade of yellow and had sultanas in it. Seats were in short supply but one look at Boyle was enough to deter anyone asking if the seat beside him was taken.

The hubbub flowed, the hubbub ebbed. The only detritus left on the strandline was Boyle. Seemed that even Dodo Stink had someplace else to be. Boyle nursed his tea like an old jakey pro, making it last. The café would fill up again when the clubs came out. After that would come the long stretch till it was properly morning and he could catch the next bus out of Dodge. Only six hours to go. Three hundred and sixty minutes. Twenty one thousand, six hundred seconds. Tick-tock.

Someone had left a newspaper folded up on one of the seats. Boyle fetched it and had a flick through. On page five there was a photograph of a car being pulled from a loch. The driver, found dead at the wheel, had been identified as forty five year old James Jardine. The car had been reported stolen in Elgin.

Boyle sat back and let out a soundless whistle. So, Jimmy Jardine was dead. Bad news for Jimmy, good news for Boyle. His dealings with the taciturn Jimmy had been minimal and strictly on a need-to-know basis, but with him dead there was nothing to link Boyle to the carry-on in the village, and even less to link that to the heist. The only person left alive who could link Boyle to any of it was Stella. There wasn't anything he could do or wanted to do about that. The body count wasn't going to get any higher.

He continued flicking through the paper, eyes growing heavy, type blurring.

Chapter 40

Sunday

"Well, if it isn't Charlie-fucking-no-mates."

Boyle's head jerked up as Polo slid into the seat opposite him. His mind was fuzzy from the doze he'd fallen into.

"Fuck you, Polo." He straightened himself up. "I was enjoying that."

"Fuck you too, Boyle. How's the tea?"

Boyle looked at his half empty mug, thinking about the cop who had clocked him and that it was no co-incidence that Polo was here now. Realising that this was the beginning of the end for him.

"Cold," he replied.

Polo called to the woman behind the counter. "Two teas, please." He turned back to Boyle, grinning. "Did you hear that - *two teas please*. I'm a poet and I don't even know it. What happened to your coupon?"

"I walked into a door."

"Must have been a big bastard of a door."

"Yeah, with pale blue eyes and size ten boots."

"I think I know the door to which you refer. Want to

make a complaint?"

Boyle gazed at Polo's slab of a face and thought about it for a moment.

"No, but there's something you could mention to SID."

"Oh aye, and what would that be?"

"It would have to be from an anonymous intelligence source..."

"Goes without saying."

They stopped talking as the teas arrived.

"There you go, gentlemen."

The woman from the counter put the fresh teas on the table and took Boyle's old one away. He watched her go. She'd let him doze, undisturbed. There was no sway to her skinny hips, but he still liked her.

"Well?" Polo looked expectantly at Boyle.

"Danny King is fucking around with Rohypnol."

Polo pursed his lips and sucked in some air. "How do you know?"

"How do you think he managed to do this?" Boyle pointed to his face.

"He spiked your drink?" Polo tutted. His mouth was set in a grim line. "That's dirty. Very fucking dirty. I don't like that at all. I wonder what else the dirty cunt's been up to."

"It's not called the date rape drug for nothing, and when it comes to a guy like King..." Boyle left the suggestion hanging.

"I can see him doing it alright. Dirty bastard."

"So you'll submit it to SID?" Boyle asked, referring to the Scottish Intelligence Database.

"I'll submit it alright. And don't worry, I'll say it came from an anonymous source. I can't see it hanging around on SID for long. Something like that will be booted straight upstairs. It'll disappear from the system pronto. But you can be fucking well assured that the rubber heelers from Complaints and Discipline will be all over

Danny King like fleas on a rat. If he's doing something he shouldn't be, they'll find out."

"Good."

"No problem."

"Fine."

They sat in silence for a while. Boyle wondering when Polo was going to get started on him. Polo sipping at his tea like he had all the time in the world. Hats off to Polo, for once it was Boyle who cracked first.

"Danny King's a bastard."

"I know, but we'll get him."

"How was Glasgow?"

"Dirty big fucker of a place, but interesting. There are eight million stories in the Naked City, and this is only one of them."

"What?"

"*The Naked City*. An old American TV show. You never watch it?"

"Sounds vaguely familiar."

"Never mind." Polo flapped his hand as if shooing the idea away. "I found out a lot about our mutual friend Macallister when I was down there."

"*Mutual* friend?"

Boyle knew it was coming, but it didn't stop his scalp prickling all the same.

"Yeah, a real coincidence. Turns out that the thief stabbed by baker boy in Dornoch was your best buddy from school."

Polo stared at Boyle, waiting for him to fill in the blanks.

"*Sammy* Macallister?"

Boyle knew then it was as good as over, but he was going to play the wide-eyed and innocent game to the end.

"That's right, *Sammy* Macallister. I found out all about you saving his life. Seems you were quite the local hero."

"It was a long time ago."

"Yeah, but the past has a way of sneaking up behind

and biting you on the arse, don't you think?" Polo ploughed on before Boyle could answer. "So here's the set up. Wee Charlie, that's you, and your pal, wee Sammy, are playing down by the frozen canal even though you've been told a million times not to go there. Wee Sammy decides to try a spot of ice skating, only the ice is thin and can't take his weight. He crashes through and you grab a hold of his arm. How am I doing so far?"

"Close, but Sammy never made a decision in his puff."

"Don't tell me you pushed the wee fucker in?" Polo grinned.

"Not quite. But I dared him to do it, which for us pretty much amounted to the same thing."

"So the poor bastard's only in there because of you, but now you've got his arm and you're looking into his face and he's looking into yours. And his eyes are the size of big fucking dinner plates and full of fear and he's roaring and greetin' because he thinks he's going to die. How am I doing now?"

Polo was laughing like a bastard. Enjoying himself.

"It's just like you were there." Boyle played along, delaying the inevitable.

"What about you, Charlie? Were you crying as well, a big line of green snot running from your nose into your mouth?"

Boyle shrugged. "Maybe. I don't remember."

"I bet your arm was sore though, wasn't it?"

Boyle nodded. He remembered that alright. His arm feeling like it was going to be torn from its socket. Terror slashed across Sammy's face, knowing his pal was losing his grip.

"I bet it was burning like fuck from holding on, but you didn't let go, not even when help came."

Boyle shook his head. "That's not how it was. I was losing it, could feel him slipping away."

"Don't spoil a good story, Charlie. When they hauled Sammy out of the canal they had to prise your frozen fingers off his arm. That's how it was, wasn't it? Fucking marvellous. I mean, it might have been your fault the stupid wee bastard was in the canal in the first place, but you saved his life. Just thinking about it fair warms the cockles of my cold, miserable heart."

"He'd have done the same for me."

"Yeah, maybe. Thick as thieves you two."

"Meaning?" Boyle's mind working overtime again. How much fact, how much conjecture? What did Polo actually have on him?

"Meaning nothing in particular. You know some people say saving a life makes you responsible for it. Did you feel responsible for Sammy?"

"Me, responsible for Sammy Macallister? Now I know you're taking the piss."

"All the same, you'd think you'd keep in touch with someone after a thing like that."

Boyle shrugged. "Same as everybody else after school - he went his way, I went mine."

"Funny how his way ended up in this neck of the woods."

"It's a small world."

"Didn't happen to know he was in town did you?"

"There were a lot of kids at my school. They could all be living up here and I wouldn't know a thing about it. I didn't keep in touch with anyone."

"That's right, how could I forget - you're Charlie fucking no-mates."

"Fuck you, Polo."

"Fuck you too, Boyle. What's the bag for?" Polo asked, like he'd just noticed the duffel bag. "Going somewhere?"

"I was thinking about it."

"Maybe me and you should take a trip together."

"What have you got in mind?" Boyle asked.

"The station," Polo replied. Maybe he had something after all.

"Fine by me." Keeping it casual. What else was he going to do, cry into his tea? Make a run for it?

"Okay, Boyle, let's go."

Chapter 41

Polo sat in the back of the unmarked car beside Boyle. Watching him, making sure he didn't try to do anything silly, like trying to escape when the car stopped at a junction. Or, more thrillingly, dive out when the car was moving.

He needn't have worried. The name was Boyle, not Bourne. Besides which, Boyle was feeling very bloody knackered. He wondered if Jason Bourne ever felt like he just couldn't be arsed any more.

The driver was Ian Campbell, the young cocky cop desperate to get into SCD. He reminded Boyle of himself back in the day.

"Alright, Ian?" Boyle said.

"Okay, Charlie," Campbell replied. "What happened to you?"

"I walked into a door."

Campbell didn't say anything after that but every now and again he glanced at Boyle in the rear view mirror, maybe figuring him as a lesson on how not to do it. Fair play to him.

Polo sat with the duffel bag on his knee. Boyle assumed there was at least one unmarked car following them but he couldn't be bothered to look.

They stopped at a red light and watched as a stream of clubbers traipsed across the road. The females, no matter size or shape, teetered in spectacularly high heels, wearing little more than fake tans and tattoos. The males, wearing more in the way of clothes, looked like drunken twonks.

"It's a different fucking world out there." Polo said.

"Throwing fucking shapes and listening to shite. What the fuck was wrong with Northern Soul?"

"You're getting old, Polo, that's all."

Boyle noticed how the streetlights and shadows emphasised the lines and creases of Polo's face. They weren't kids any more. In keeping with his earlier feelings towards his fellow humans, Boyle felt a small surge of affection for Polo. If anyone had to collar him, Boyle was glad it was him.

"Aye, and don't I fucking know it," Polo said.

"Did you get back in time to take Maggie out?"

"No, fucking missed it thanks to your pal Sammy and his carry on. But I'm going to make it up to her. I've got a night booked in the Roc Pool."

"Nice one."

"Yeah, cost me a fucking fortune but I reckon she's worth it for putting up with the job all these years. Fucking marriage killer this job."

"You're a lucky man, Polo."

"I know it, Boyle. I fucking well know it. I've bought her something special, going to give it to her when we're at the hotel."

"What's that then?"

"A diamond ring, Boyle. A big fuck-off job. Cost me another fucking fortune but she's never had one before and I wanted to get her something special. You like diamonds, Boyle?"

Clever Polo, Boyle thought.

"Can't say I'm fussed one way or another," he replied. And he meant it.

"It's funny the way some people get about them."

The car was moving again. Polo pretended to stare past Boyle, out of the window as he spoke, watching the people strutting and stumbling on the pavement, but all the time he was checking out Boyle's reactions. Looking for giveaway flickers and tics.

"Like fucking Gollum in Lord of the bastarding Rings," Polo continued, "they get that gleam in their eye. They'll steal them, murder for them, risk everything for them and all for a shiny wee bit of glassy stone. Fucking mental if you ask me."

Boyle grinned. Even as a doomed man, he couldn't help but enjoy Polo when he was in his stride.

The room was stark. No window. One door. A table bolted to the floor and wall. Three chairs. Recording equipment on the table. A camera on the wall. Boyle had been in this one, and others like it, many times over the years. But never on this side of the table.

"Are you arresting me, Polo?" he asked.

"Don't be so fucking stupid. Sit the fuck down. We're just having a wee chat - you're helping me with my fucking enquiries is all."

Fine with Boyle if that was the way Polo wanted to play it. He pulled out a chair and sat. This simple act could be his last as a free man for a long time to come.

Campbell stood at the door behind him. Polo had pulled a chair to the table end so that there was nothing between him and Boyle's body language but stale air. Good luck to him with that. Boyle had already resigned himself to his fate and consequently was feeling very relaxed, thanks very much.

It didn't matter what Polo knew, or thought he knew. As soon as he opened the bag and found the jewellery he would have everything he needed.

It wouldn't matter whether they knew about Boyle's connection with Frank's death or not. His involvement with the diamond heist would be enough. They'd want to make a big shiny example of him. He'd be put away for years. By the time he got out he'd be looking like Uncle Albert for real. No point in getting weepy about it. He'd known what the score was all along. There had always been a chance of the whole thing going tits up.

He toyed with the idea of telling Polo the whole story. Would almost be worth it just to see the look on his face. But that would mean giving Stella up, and he wasn't about to do that.

"Tea?" Polo asked, playing nice cop.

"Why not," Boyle replied, playing nice suspect.

"A tea for Sergeant Boyle, if you don't mind, Constable, and one for myself."

Boyle heard the door opening and closing behind him. Polo lifted the duffel bag onto the table. They stared at it while the tea was fetched.

The tea finally came.

They sipped.

"How is it, Boyle?" Polo asked. Meaning the tea, but also not meaning the tea.

"Fine," Boyle replied. Meaning the tea, even though it wasn't. It had barely been glanced at by a tea bag. There was too much milk in it. And he didn't take sugar.

"Good. We aim to please."

Boyle wondered how long Polo was going to keep the charade going.

They continued to sip at their tea. Polo finally finished his with an exaggerated smack of the lips.

"Ah, that was good."

He put the mug down and turned the neck of the duffel bag towards himself.

Boyle's insides tightened a couple of notches. Finally, they were getting down to it. Polo loosened the drawstring and opened it up. He peered inside, raised his eyebrows then stuck his hand into the guts of the bag. It came out clutching Boyle's passport. He flicked through

258

it then sat it on the table.

"Going far were you?"

Boyle thought about sun on his back and sand between his toes. What the hell. The sun would have burned his pasty Scottish skin red and the sand would have got on his nerves after a while.

"Who knows?" he said.

"Hmm, like that is it?"

Polo slowly removed the contents from the bag and lined them up neatly on the table. Toothbrush and toothpaste. Two pairs of socks. Two pairs of pants. One rolled-up sweatshirt. When he'd taken everything out, he turned the bag upside down and gave it a theatrical shake.

"You travel light," he said.

"Is there any other way?"

"Some people carry a lot of baggage."

"Not this guy."

"Evidently not."

Polo ran his gaze over the pathetic display. He prodded the sweatshirt, glanced at Boyle, then prodded it again. He cleared a space in front of himself and filled it with the sweatshirt.

Boyle's scalp prickled as Polo unrolled it. This was it. It was all over now. Too late, Boyle realised how badly he didn't want to go to prison.

Everyone focussed on the sweatshirt. Polo. Boyle. He could feel Campbell staring at it over his shoulder as Polo carefully unrolled its length. Something bulged inside, but the contents were covered by the folded-over sides and sleeves of the garment.

Polo glanced at Boyle then slowly lifted away one sleeve. Boyle caught his breath, but the contents were still covered by the other sleeve.

With a final, triumphant look at Boyle, Polo pulled it aside and the contents were revealed. Campbell let out the merest of gasps. Polo's eyes widened. Boyle stared, slack-jawed.

Three items lay exposed on the marl grey. One bottle of factor 50 sun lotion. One can of insect repellent. One copy of Raymond Chandler's *Farewell My Lovely*.

Realisation crept up on Boyle and he began to laugh.

Chapter 42

Once he started laughing, Boyle couldn't stop. Polo stared at him, not in the least bit amused.

"What's so fucking funny?"

"Nothing."

"Stop fucking well laughing then."

He picked up the copy of *Farewell My Lovely* and flicked through it. "What's this all about?" he demanded.

"A private eye called Philip Marlowe," Boyle said between snorts. "There was a film with Robert Mitchum as Marlowe."

Looking thoroughly sickened, Polo tossed the book on the table.

"Don't be such a smart arse. I don't know what the fuck is going on, but I fucking well know that you're involved in *something*, Boyle. It was all over your face when I opened that bag. You were as fucking well surprised as I was when I unrolled that sweatshirt."

"I'd like to help, Polo, but I really don't know what you're talking about."

"Aye right, and my name's Mickey fucking Mouse. Tell me Boyle - if we search that flat of yours are we going to find anything?"

"Not a thing," Boyle said truthfully.

"Jesus, Boyle. I don't know what the fuck you're into here, but I know you're into *something*. I can fucking well smell it on you."

"I hate to disappoint you like this." Boyle couldn't stop grinning.

"Sure you do. It's written all over your ugly face."

"Can I go now?"

"As you very well know, you were free to go any damn time you pleased."

"Cheers."

Boyle scraped back his chair and stood up. Polo paced up and down, frowning and rubbing at the back of his head. He kept looking at the contents of Boyle's bag as if he was missing something.

"Can I take my stuff?" Boyle asked.

"It's yours, isn't it? Why should I bastarding care? Fucking well take it."

Boyle picked up the bag and shoved his stuff back inside, including the sun lotion, insect repellent, and the book.

"Right, that's me," he said when he was done.

"Aye, right, right." Polo rubbed at the back of his head again, wondering how he'd managed to fuck up so badly. He looked round at Boyle. "We'll come along and take a look at your flat anyway."

"Be my guest, but you should know, I moved out already."

"What? When the fuck did that happen?"

"Today. I mean yesterday."

"Well, where are you living now?"

"No fixed abode."

"Oh Jesus fucking Christ, Boyle. You get better and better by the minute. You should sell tickets. You really fucking should. Is there any point in me asking you not to leave town?"

"None whatsoever."

"Fucking marvellous. What about the job?"

Boyle shook his head. "Posted my resignation yesterday. It'll be on Saunder's desk by Monday, Tuesday at the latest. In fact, you may as well have this."

Boyle took his warrant card out of his pocket and tossed it on the table.

Polo looked at it, then back at Boyle.

"What about your notice?"

"I don't think they'll hold me to it, do you?"

"Suppose not. The fuckers upstairs will be glad to see the back of you."

"That's what I thought."

"Where you going?"

Boyle shrugged. "Dunno. Guess I'll get on the first bus out of here and see where it takes me."

"Fucking hobo."

"Guess so." Boyle slung the bag over his shoulder and paused. "Polo?"

"You still here?"

"You won't forget to tell SID will you?"

Polo held Boyle's gaze.

"No, I won't forget."

"Good."

"You're a funny bastard, Boyle," Polo muttered. "A law unto your fucking self."

Boyle grinned and turned to Campbell. "Thanks for the tea," he said.

"Welcome," Campbell said automatically. Staring at Boyle like he had a pair of horns growing out of his head.

And then he was gone, Polo watching the door swing shut behind him. Knowing he'd been had and there wasn't a damned thing he could do about it.

Chapter 43

Tired, yet feeling strangely happy, Boyle scuffed along the street. He'd felt a bit sorry for Polo back there, though not sorry enough to blurt the story. Poor Polo. He'd managed to put most of it together just to see it crumble to dust. Without the diamonds it was all just so much talk. They had nothing on him. Nothing. Not for the heist, Macallister, or Frank.

He wasn't even in the picture for Frank and they hadn't figured out yet that Macallister had been murdered. Maybe they never would. He was in the clear. Still, best not to hang around too long. You never knew when nothing might turn into something. Or when something might turn into nothing. Like a sweatshirt full of diamonds turning into beach essentials.

Smoke and mirrors.

He had to laugh. He wondered how long she'd been planning it. Right from when he'd told her about the haul of jewellery?

He didn't like to think so, because if that was the case then she'd taken him for a mug right from the start. He liked to think she'd had some sort of feelings for him, that it hadn't all been about her ripping him off.

Maybe she'd never planned it at all. Maybe it just happened, the way things sometimes do. The sight of the sparklies could have set her off - given her that Gollum gleam Polo had been on about. She saw them and had to have them. *My precious*. Yeah, that was it. A moment of insanity. He preferred this version of events. Stella came out of it less cold, less calculating. It made him less of a mug. Gave him the chance to preserve some of sense of dignity. Let's face it, he had fuck all else. Not quite true. He had his freedom.

Not so long ago he could all but taste the stench of rotten feet and foul body odours of his fellow prisoners as the cell door clanged shut on him.

It was murder in the cells at the weekend. The stink just built and built. And being locked up for the weekend would only be the start of it. But now, thanks to Stella ripping him off, here he was, walking the streets and breathing the night air - a free man. And funnily enough, the street he was walking down happened to be the one she lived on.

Boyle wasn't sure exactly what it was had brought him here. Certainly not any thoughts of finding Stella's loving arms laying wide open for him. More likely he had a desire to tie up loose ends. To make sure it had gone down the way he figured it.

He'd rolled the diamonds back up in the sweatshirt himself. The bag had been left downstairs. Could be she'd slipped down and removed them when he was dozing, but then she'd have been chancing on him not waking up.

No, more likely she'd done the switcheroo when she'd been making coffee for the Commander and his pet Sergeant. *No it's all right, thank you, I'll manage.*

No wonder the lady didn't want help. And they'd have been only too glad to let her get on with it. Anything other than risk having to make small talk in such ghastly circumstances. Or, even worse, deal with tears and sobbing.

It wasn't a casual substitution either. She hadn't grabbed the nearest thing to hand - she'd put a bit of thought into it. More than a bit. Oh how she must have laughed as she rolled up the sun lotion and insect repellent, not to mention his book for the beach. Chandler's *Farewell My Lovely* had been the final poetic sting.

She was a bitch, but she was a classy bitch.

She couldn't have hidden the diamonds in the kitchen or he'd have found them, so where did she put them? Boyle pondered this as he approached Frank's house.

It was as he expected it to be. Shrouded in shadow and locked up tight. He walked around and tried the back door anyway. It was locked. No surprises there.

He went around the front and just for the hell of it, tried knocking. There was no answer. Of course she could have been upstairs in bed, in a deep slumber. Could have taken one or two of those tablets, the possession of which had been so useful of late, but he didn't think so. The house had that hollow, empty feel. She was gone.

He turned and walked back to the street, looking at Frank's roses as he did so. A flutter of battered petals lay on the ground, slaughtered by the rainstorm.

Boyle knew she'd told the truth about Frank. Which truth he wasn't so sure about. Maybe it was all true. Maybe he had been a monster. And maybe he had threatened to kill himself if she left him. And maybe she was terrified of him. There was more than one truth in any situation and who the hell was he to judge?

He wondered how long she'd waited after he'd left before leaving the house. She'd have given him plenty of time to get out of the way, might even have waited until the rainstorm was over, although she'd have been twitching to get going.

He wondered if she noticed the roses on her way out,

or was she too pre-occupied with her plans, too pleased with herself for managing everything so beautifully to be bothered with small details like empty roses.

He could picture her, walking smartly down the drive. Valise in one hand and that capacious black handbag she carried everywhere in the other.

He cracked up. It was so beautifully funny you had to laugh. She hadn't had to find any hidey hole for the diamonds. She'd simply slipped them into that cavernous bag of hers and carted it off to the morgue.

So why had she bothered coming back? Why not just leave?

He walked along the street. There was a space where the fancy hire car had been. Maybe she'd driven by him in the rain. Her all cosy and warm in the Merc, him all wet and cold outside. If she had, then it was no more than he deserved.

She'd tested him. That's why she'd come back. She'd given him a final chance and he'd failed.

He kept on walking, heading east, towards the A9. He guessed she did get packed when she went upstairs to change. She had always planned on going away. Just not with him.

She'd touched him that one last time. Her hand on his wrist. *No, you keep the diamonds, Charlie. Make a future for yourself. A good future. And don't forget your daughter.*

The crack about Jenny had been a beautiful distracter, designed to stop him opening up the bag and discovering that the diamonds weren't there. She had played him like a violin.

He wondered where she was going. If she really did have a sister. And if he'd ever really known her at all. He had loved her, he knew that much. He loved her still, though what his love meant or what it was worth he couldn't say.

She'd been making a deal with him when she said she wouldn't say anything to the police. She wouldn't if he didn't. Seemed like they were still inextricably entwined, each the master of the other's fate. Maybe he should give her up. Murder is murder after all. And maybe she should give him up, because murder was still murder. But he knew he wouldn't and he didn't think she would either.

Funny how he'd got away with everything and ended up with nothing. But as far as Boyle was concerned, it had never been about the diamonds. It was always about Stella. He'd told himself that all along. It was one version of the truth.

He didn't think he'd bother heading to the bus station after all. Polo may well have come up with a reason to detain him by now, maybe thought of a vital question he had to ask. The bus station was where he'd told Polo he was heading. Best to give it a wide berth. The train station too.

Boyle walked over the bridge crossing the dual carriageway then down to a slip road on the southbound side of the A9. He stood at the side of the road, raising his thumb as a vehicle approached. A Ford Galaxy whizzed by him without slowing. The second car he thumbed pulled over. It was an old, beat-up Volvo. Boyle jogged up to it, opened the door and leaned in. There was a sweet, minty smell in the car. The driver was an old guy with a jowly face and grey wispy hair. There was a humbug sized lump in his cheek.

"Thanks for stopping," Boyle said.

"Where you going, pal?" The sweet clacked against the old guy's teeth as he spoke.

"South," Boyle said. "As far as you can take me."

"Hop aboard," the old guy said.

Boyle got in. The old guy didn't remark on Boyle's face so Boyle didn't say anything about walking into doors. The car pulled away, heading south. The sky had cleared and was beginning to lighten in the east.

"Going to be a beautiful day," the old guy said.

"I guess it is at that," Boyle replied.

He settled into his seat, enjoying the sweet warmth of the car. Beyond south, he had no idea of where he was going or what he was going to do when he got there.

Maybe he had ended up with nothing but his freedom, but sometimes freedom was all a man needed.

THE END

If you have enjoyed reading Boyle's Law, please consider leaving a short review on Amazon. It would be appreciated.

Acknowledgements

For their support, encouragement and feedback, my sincere thanks go to Phil Jones, Liz Reid, Stephen Keeler, Irene Brandt, Doris Watt, and Pete Urpeth at Emergents. Thanks also to Kenny Paton for his valuable advice. And finally, special thanks to cover models, Catherine Glennie and Mark Poe.

About the Author

L.G. Thomson was born in Glasgow and grew up in modernist New Town experiment, Cumbernauld. Since graduating from art school in Dundee, she has worked in a variety of places throughout Scotland, including museums, remote islands, a large police station, a small shed, and a medium-sized croft. She has won a national writing competition and was short-listed for the Dundee Book Prize. She took a break from writing to raise her daughters, home-educating them for several years. She now lives in Ullapool, on the north west coast of Scotland, where she writes Thrillers With Attitude.

www.thrillerswithattitude.co.uk

OUT NOW - EACH NEW MORN

A rogue prion disease has wiped out most of the world's population. Some survivors have been infected by a secondary disease. Aggressive and erratic, they become known as Screamers. They are not the only enemy. Society has broken down. Violent mobs rule the streets. Gangs of raiders swarm through the countryside. Pests and parasites thrive and the worst winter in decades is about to descend. Who will survive Each New Morn?

Available now in paperback and from
Amazon's online Kindle Store.

Coming soon - EROSION

Ten people are stranded on a remote Scottish island. From the start there are undercurrents of tension within the group. A woman suspects her husband of infidelity and plans her revenge. Elsewhere, jealousy, lust and anger raise the temperature. It's not long before ten become nine. The battle for survival has begun.

www.thrillerswithattitude.co.uk

Made in the USA
Charleston, SC
10 September 2014